TOUCHED BY MADNESS

NICOLE LECLERCQ

ACKNOWLEDGEMENTS

A special thanks to Claire Chilton for editing this book and for her patience when I asked her thousands of questions.

I would also like to thank Philippa Pride and Linda Kirkemo. Without them, this book would never have been written.

Thanks to Jennifer Ellis for being the first to read and correct several drafts of my novel.

Thanks to Eileen Gormley, Caroline McCall, Pat Hauldren and Elaine Kennedy for helping me become a better writer.

First published in the United States by Ragz Books
2013

This edition published by Ragz Books 2019

Published in the United States by Ragz Books

Illustrated by Claire Chilton

Cover Art by Claire Chilton

Library of Congress Control Number: 2013932546

Print Version: 2

ISBN 13: 978-1-938988-12-7
ISBN 10: 1-938988-12-4

TOUCHED BY MADNESS

NICOLE LECLERCQ

www.ragz-books.com

ONE

Dane Lynch stood in muggy darkness of the Devereaux Church with the smell of dust, sweat and blood strong in his nostrils. It was eerily quiet, but his vampiric hearing could easily pick up the mumbling of the policemen outside the old building. Inside the church, there wasn't a sound, neither the rustling of clothes, nor a hint of movement behind the thick wooden door.

Dane and the policemen were too late. Even if Dane hadn't smelled the blood, he would have sensed the discharge of power that hung heavy in the air. He realized that the ritual killing inside the church must have been a success. The silence told him that Oliver Merenda, the voodoo priest whom he'd suspected had performed the ritual, had already fled the scene.

For a few seconds, Dane closed his eyes and sighed. Why had Merenda chosen his territory to raise hell? While most voodoo priests focused on healing and prayer, Merenda practiced darker magic. Dane wondered if he should be confronting

Merenda without back-up from the other vampires in his clan, but he couldn't trust any of them—tonight proved it.

Merenda had been receiving help from Altman, Dane's second-in-command. Dane knew that if Altman had somehow miraculously managed to survive Merenda's plans, he would have to punish him in such a public way that no other vampire would ever dare enter into an alliance with the enemy.

Wheezing sounds from the other room caught his attention, surprising him. He shut out the conversations of the policemen outside and realized someone's heart was pounding so hard that he could hear its frantic rhythm through the solid oak door. The banging grated on his already raw nerves. He inhaled sharply when he heard voices on the other side of the door.

"What the hell? Where is he! I'll kill that lying jerk!" a man yelled.

"I-I can't move," a woman said.

"Ann? Where is Dad?" a girl asked.

"Shut up! Let me think!" Dane recognized Altman.

"Oh, my God!"

"That's me!"

"So much blood..."

Still, Dane could hear only one person breathing.

Merenda?

Dane tensed as he opened the door, preparing for a fight. He expected to at least find Merenda waiting for him when he swung the door wide, but was surprised to find no one there and nothing stopping him from entering the room.

The voices increased in volume as he stepped across the threshold. He warily scanned the chapel for movement. The candlelight cast dancing shadows on the five bodies that were lying on the floor in a circle with swords sticking out of their chests. Blood splattered the statue of Jesus hanging on the far wall, and the figure of Christ glared accusingly at Dane.

The pentagram drawn on the floor was dark red. The five-pointed star could have been created with paint, but after taking a deep breath, he dismissed that thought as the coppery taint of blood wafted past his nostrils. He inspected everything, determined to find Merenda. But apart from the bodies on the floor, the room was abandoned. Confused, he glanced down. People were talking, but he couldn't see any lips moving.

He swallowed, and his eyes honed in on his second-in-command. A sword pierced Altman's heart, yet his voice lingered.

He walked over to Altman to see if the red-headed corpse continued to be one of the undead, but there was no 'un' about it—Altman was dead. The spark in his gray eyes was extinguished. Only an empty stare remained.

Dane examined the other bodies. The woman was an attractive thirty-something with short blond hair. He recognized her as Ann Holland, Merenda's lover and a witch.

TOUCHED BY MADNESS

Hope Acres' chief of police had told Dane that he believed she had been the one to warn the police about Merenda's plans. Had Merenda found out and punished her for that betrayal?

The sword had sliced open Ann's dress from neck to waist. The blade still penetrated her body with her hand resting near the hilt of the weapon. The hands of the other victims were in a similar position.

A mass suicide?

A man in his early twenties was dressed in black and lying on the other side of the circle. He had a strange smile on his face and a blank stare.

Dane really didn't want to examine the last two corpses because they were children. As soon as he inhaled the older girl's scent, he pictured a large cat marked with black spots in a rosette pattern.

Leopard.

The girl had a dark complexion and looked about sixteen years old. The younger girl couldn't have been older than seven. She had wispy blond hair and a much lighter complexion than the first girl. He approached the little child, realizing the voices became louder the closer he got to her.

He crouched next to her, staring at the long sword protruding from her tiny chest. His gaze travelled up to her face. Her golden eyes were open and fixed on the other corpses. The blond curls falling across her brow made her appear angelic. She didn't blink, but he could tell by the quick and shallow way her chest moved up and down that she was fighting to stay alive.

4

He caught a glimpse of silver and frowned at the chain around the girl's neck. He reached up slowly, brushing aside her hair, before pulling at the necklace. A black dagger-shaped crystal appeared. *For protection?* When his fingers touched the amulet, he narrowed his eyes. Oddly, the pendant felt warm. He rubbed his thumb over the pointy part of the crystal and hissed, releasing it when it cut his flesh.

He heard the voices again and realized they were coming from her. Something must have gone wrong with the ritual. He examined her impaled chest. The sword was buried inside her, but the blade must have missed her heart.

The young girl looked like Merenda's lover. He had heard that Merenda had children.

Did Merenda try to murder his own daughter? Or daughters?

When he studied the older girl, he noticed that she resembled Merenda. There was no hope left for her, but the younger child was a fighter. For the second time since he had been turned, he experienced compassion for a human. Other than the affection he had felt for his sister, he felt none for humans and regarded dealing with them as a necessary evil.

He stroked the golden curls of the little girl, and as he touched her, the voices stopped. The child's gaze fell upon him. He froze for a moment under the scrutiny of her innocent stare.

"Hello, Goldilocks. I'm here to help you."

To his great surprise, when he removed his fingers from her hair the voices returned.

She whimpered, and her eyes filled up with tears.

When he put his hand on the girl's forehead again, the voices disappeared. In spite of the loss of blood the child's fingers tried to encircle his thick wrist like a handcuff, as if she needed to hold on to him, to hold on to the quiet. For the first time since his death, someone wanted him—she did not reject him.

He recalled how his sister Jane had preferred death to accepting his help. He had allowed her to make that decision. This time however, he refused to relinquish his control over life and death.

The girl looked so fragile. Anger welled at the back of his throat when he glanced at the puddle of blood surrounding her body.

How could Merenda have done this to his own children?

Since Merenda wasn't there, Dane's anger had nowhere to go, so he became fiercely protective over the little girl instead.

Acting upon instinct, he plunged his elongated fangs into his own wrist, biting and tearing it open. He held the open wound in front of the child's mouth and urged her to drink. With the added strength of his blood, he knew her chances of survival would increase.

The girl tried to turn away, but with his left hand, he restrained her and forced her deep golden eyes to meet his. As he did so, his mind tuned itself to hers, taking command.

You will drink.

He was aware that a bond would be created between the two of them, but that couldn't be avoided. Her lips touched his wrist, and she eventually swallowed. His life force ran down her throat and spilled over her chin. He felt the power in her grow as she continued to gulp down his blood.

An alluring smell teased his nose. He glanced down at the wound in the girl's chest. The rich scent of her blood called out to him—it distracted him. Removing his wrist, he leaned over her.

He didn't hear the policemen barging into the room until a voice filtered through his hungered haze.

"What the hell are you doing?" a policeman yelled as he ran toward Dane. The cop grabbed him and attempted to pull him off the girl.

Dane jerked up his head and stared at the officer with feral possessiveness. His demons leaped, raged and burst free.

How dare this pitiful human interfere?

Never had Dane experienced such terrible fury. It rushed over him, claimed him, became him. He grabbed the policeman by the throat and threw him against the wall.

He then located the chief of police and smiled, but he knew that there was no amusement in the white flash of teeth, only the promise of savagery.

Chief Lepareur's indrawn breath was audible.

TOUCHED BY MADNESS

In spite of the obvious danger, the chief walked up to him with a watchful gaze. "*Arrête,* Dane. She needs to go to the hospital," Lepareur quietly said.

"We shouldn't have told him, Chief," the cop Dane had thrown against the wall said while glaring at him.

Lepareur's cool gaze swept over the policeman just once, but it was enough of a command.

The policeman's hands clenched into fists, but he remained silent.

"You're not gonna be hurtin' that girl," Lepareur said in the same quiet voice.

A ribbon of sanity fluttered through Dane's mind and caught his attention. He *was* hurting her. He closed his eyes. The anger receded, leaving a feeling of lethargy and numbness in its wake.

The child's slender frame trembled while her heart was laboring with a slow beat. Her lungs were fighting for air, as her body struggled to survive.

Dane took her pale, limp hand in his strong calloused palm and gently squeezed it. She was so small. It brought about feelings he had never before experienced.

In the end, he removed his hands. The girl sobbed in protest. He stepped aside and allowed the paramedics to take her.

Before they lifted her in the ambulance, Dane touched her one last time, and a strange tenderness stole over him.

"Be strong, Goldilocks," he said. "I will come for you."

Dawn streaked the sky as Dane impatiently paced up and down his basement. A day had passed since the Devereaux massacre. He wearily glanced around the room, worried by the intensity of his emotions. It was a new feeling, one he wished he didn't have.

Why does this child affect me so much?

Earlier that night he had visited the hospital, but Merenda's daughter had already disappeared. He had instructed one of his vampires to locate her, but the sun was climbing in the sky and time was running out.

He clenched his fists in frustration. Even his most devoted employee, Vincenzo had let him down. He had still not returned with news of the girl.

Dane found it impossible to relax as images of the previous night replayed in his mind. It made no sense. He was always in control of his emotions. How could he suddenly form an attachment to a stranger, particularly a child?

He couldn't suppress the sense of urgency. She needed him to take away the voices. He didn't want them tormenting her. He also worried about Merenda.

What if Merenda is looking for her, so he can finish the job?

"Never," Dane said. *I'd die before I let Merenda hurt her again.*

A hesitant knock interrupted his thoughts, and he stiffened.

Vincenzo opened the door. "May I come in?"

Dane suppressed a sigh. "Hurry up."

The black-haired vampire kept his eyes fixed on the floor as he entered the room.

"I-I c-couldn't find her," he stammered.

Dane's head snapped up. He took a step toward the quailing vampire, but his own reflection in the mirror behind Vincenzo froze him in his tracks. His white teeth had snapped together in a show of aggression. His incisors were sharp and lethal-looking as he glared at himself, and black fury darkened his gaze.

What's wrong with me?

Vincenzo gaped at him with his mouth open wide. "A-a-are you all right?"

Dane stared at his reflection. The stranger staring at him in the mirror was barely recognizable. He was not himself. The encounter with the child had awakened something in him that should have remained dormant, but he could never admit such a weakness to Vincenzo.

"Forget it." His tone was final.

"F-forget what? Do you want me to stop looking for her?"

"Yes," he said. "Get out."

Vincenzo bowed twice before leaving the room.

Dane continued to stare at the door after it had been closed. He considered calling out and making Vincenzo continue his search, but he realized he could not afford it.

The girl was fortunate Vincenzo had failed. She should remain hidden from him.

"It's for the best," he said quietly.

For both of us.

TWO

Twenty years later.

A Marilyn Manson song blared in Erin Holland's ear, waking her up. She tried to jump out of bed to switch off the radio alarm, but the tight handcuffs wrapped around her wrists yanked her back down. She flinched.

Great, just what I need. The neighbors are going to go ballistic over all this noise.

She stared at the handcuffs, feeling hopeful. It had been a precautionary tactic to stop her body from being taken over while she slept. It was the final solution to any nighttime adventures her body was taking without her conscious mind being aware of them.

Did it work?

She wasn't sure, but one thing she knew was that she needed to silence the blaring alarm. She slid the cuffs along the rail of her headboard and reached for the key on the bedside table. She stopped when she noticed the key wasn't there.

Where the hell is it?

The noise from the alarm was starting to drive

her insane. With her heart pounding, she tried to pull out the plug of the alarm clock with her foot, but she was unable to reach it. She couldn't remember turning up the volume of the radio alarm, and after a few moments of struggling, it struck her that the missing key and loud alarm could only mean one thing—someone else must have done it.

Leila.

"Thank you very much, Leila," she muttered.

Maniacal laughter in her head confirmed her suspicions. She should have known better. Whenever she aimed to outsmart Leila, it resulted in the ghost of her beloved half-sister seeking retaliation.

Why had she thought the handcuffs would interfere with Leila taking over her body? Erin hoped that turning up the volume was the only thing that Leila had done during the night, but then her gaze fell on the T-shirt on the floor. Her cotton underwear was casually dumped next to the garment she used as a nightgown.

She sighed, feeling exhausted as she glanced down at her naked body.

Why does Leila always have to make things worse?

"Very mature," Erin grumbled while she searched for the keys to the handcuffs, but she quickly realized that Leila must have hidden them.

"I hate my life. Okay, Leila, you've had your fun. Ha ha. Where are they?"

No response.

Great.

All her life, Erin had wanted to be free of the four ghosts haunting her, and now that she needed them, they chose to give her the silent treatment.

Mr. Jenkins, a grumpy elderly man who lived next door, banged on the wall.

She quickly rolled out of bed, swallowing a curse when she stepped on the notebook that she used as her spell book. Her weight had caused a couple of pages to tear, but right now her number one priority was turning off the noise.

She gripped the headboard of the bed and dragged the heavy bed frame with her as she moved toward the alarm. She had finally reached the radio when there was a knock at her door. She turned off the noise, praying that whoever it was would just leave, but the pounding continued.

She refused to panic because she never panicked. She needed to come across as a normal, sane human being. She couldn't afford to draw anyone's attention to the supernatural elements in her life.

She considered staying quiet, but rejected that idea. Whoever was outside continued beating on the door, as if they knew she was inside the apartment. They probably realized that the radio couldn't have turned itself off.

She glanced at the pile of clothes, which were strewn across the wooden floor of her small, brightly-colored apartment. Nothing should be able to disappear in such a tiny room, but she had created such a mess that she could probably hide an elephant in here. She frowned and scanned the apartment, searching for the key to the handcuffs. It could be lying underneath the plastic bags on the table, or maybe she should try the pile of bills next to the phone?

Once more, her gaze fell upon the open notebook on the floor. It had been one of her first purchases after she had arrived in Hope Acres. She had written down a location spell in it about four weeks ago, but she felt too agitated right now to remember the spell.

If I can just reach the book before someone beats down my front door.

She moved her hand toward the notebook, but she was cuffed to the center of the headboard, and there wasn't enough slack to reach it.

"The key is hidden underneath the cat," Erin heard the ghost of her mother say.

Hopeful, she inspected the room for her stray cat, but she couldn't see the cat anywhere. The animal had probably run off, although she found it hard to picture the fat cat moving very fast. Then she noticed the orange stuffed cat on the chair that had been standing next to the bed. She smiled with relief.

"Thanks, Mom," she whispered as she shoved the bed toward the cuddly toy. She cringed at the harsh grating noise the bed made as it scraped across the floor.

"Erin, are you all right?" a male voice asked from the other side of the door.

"Fine!" she shouted, realizing who it was.

15

TOUCHED BY MADNESS

Victor lived in the apartment above. She had been fantasizing about the hunky guy ever since he had moved into the building. Not that she would ever act on those fantasies. She didn't care for his personality. She had never seen him go out to work. Also, whenever she saw Victor walking up the stairs, he had a different girl with him, but that didn't stop him from ogling Erin. He had the shoulders of a surfer and wavy brown hair. His puppy-dog eyes didn't fool her. He had a raw sex appeal. An untamed aura clung to him like an animal—like her.

She did her best to suppress her animalistic nature. The main reason for fighting her attraction to Victor was that she didn't wish to perform for a crowd, even if three out of the four ghosts tied to her wanted her to have a more exciting life.

Her mother was the only one who didn't object to her behaving like a nun. Leila hated it. Her half-sister had been a were-leopard while alive. Apparently, the species suffered from hormonal cycles where they could think of nothing but procreation, but for were-leopards 'cycle' meant every single day...

Leila had been making comments about Victor for a while now. It dawned on her that Leila had intended this awkward situation to happen.

When Erin had finally reached the cat, she kicked the orange creature onto the floor with her foot. The key shone innocently in the morning light.

"Erin, I'm coming in," Victor said, sounding determined.

"No! Go away," she shouted as she struggled with her chained hands to pick up the small key.

Thank God I locked the door! Or did I?

"Leila?" she whispered.

The doorknob turned.

"Hello, surfer boy." Leila sounded as if she were gloating.

There was a terrifying click, and the door opened.

Erin cursed as she rapidly turned her naked back to the man entering the room. She closed her eyes, hoping that if she pretended not to be here, maybe Victor would pretend not to see her and leave.

"Erin?" he rasped.

She felt so mortified that she believed she was having an out-of-body experience.

"I'm er, okay," she croaked. "Could you please come back later?"

"Party pooper!" Leila complained.

Erin could smell Victor's skin. He always used coconut sunscreen, and she loved the smell. It made her think of tropical beaches and vacations in the sun.

She wished she didn't have the raging hormones and the keen sense of smell of a leopard. Her body throbbed with need, responding to Victor's presence. She heard the door close, and she prayed it meant that Victor had shut the door as he'd left the room. She was reluctant to open her eyes and turn around.

What if he's still here?

17

His scent lingered in the room. Keeping her back to the door, she opened her eyes and tried to grab the keys again.

The moment Victor entered the small apartment, his attention, as if drawn by a magnet, focused on his sweet neighbor from downstairs. His eyes drank in the slender form of the naked woman standing before him. Her back was turned, and her blond hair covered it in silken waves.

She was trying to grab something in the cluttered room. He knew she probably thought that he would do the decent thing and leave her alone, but she was out of luck because he wasn't a gentleman, and it seemed she wasn't as innocent as he had initially thought either.

When an employee of Jonathan Stratton had approached Victor to watch Erin, he had thought it would be another boring surveillance job for an extremely wealthy client. However, he found his downstairs neighbor anything but boring.

Victor's gaze moved to the handcuffs, and he saw her struggling with a small key.

Okay, enough surveillance, time to get closer to my neighbor.

"Holy shit," Victor uttered.

Erin spun her head around and felt her cheeks flame with embarrassment. He moved like a striking rattlesnake. Reaching out, he caught her arm and swung her around before hauling her up against his body in a single movement that stunned her with its swiftness.

He wrapped his left arm around her waist, anchoring her naked back to his front, making her shiver. His other hand caught her bound wrists, holding her still. His fingers seemed to want to linger, to stroke. She tried to pull forward, twisting in an effort to escape him, but he merely tightened his grip.

She closed her eyes and struggled to remain calm as this stranger held her close to him.

She wasn't afraid of him, yet the excitement that was racing along her body felt very similar to fear. Her heart reacted immediately to his touch, shifting into double time. Her own unwilling, but powerful attraction to him made her uneasy. In her mind, she cursed Leila as well as her own body for betraying her.

"Don't pull away from me," Victor ordered, his deep voice stroking her senses like dark velvet. She sensed rather than heard Leila cheering in her head.

"Let's bite him," Erin heard Altman say.

Great.

Of course, being a vampire ghost, Altman must have had several biting fantasies over the past twenty years. Now that Leila's needs were finally being met, the other voices would start making demands too.

19

TOUCHED BY MADNESS

Erin stared at Victor's large hand on her bare stomach. She couldn't help but wonder what it would feel like if he moved his hand a bit lower. She was so intrigued by his hand that she didn't realize until the handcuffs came off that he had been working on releasing her.

"That wasn't so hard, was it?" he whispered softly against her ear as he let her go.

She couldn't answer.

"No, but something else is. Hard, that is." Leila laughed.

"Leila, will you please stop it?"

Thank God for her mom.

Victor walked back to the door. He turned to watch as she grabbed a blanket to cover herself.

"Ain't no use, honey. I have a photographic memory."

"Well, there's no point in making it any easier for you, is there?" Erin mumbled. With her body completely covered, she turned to Victor. "Look, could you please forget this happened?"

He smiled before shaking his head.

"Nope. Sorry, babe. This is just too much fun."

"Fine!" She gritted her teeth. "Do you mind leaving my apartment, then? You're trespassing."

His laughter sounded like barking.

She was not amused.

"What are you going to do if I don't, call the police? Care to explain to them what you were doing tied up like that?" he asked.

Fed up with her annoying upstairs neighbor, she knew Altman would agree if she retaliated. She closed her eyes and channeled her energy into her voice. When she opened her eyes, she focused her gaze on a curious Victor. With Altman's help, she used his vampiric power to try to control Victor with her words.

"You will leave this room and never enter this apartment again. If you mention this incident to anyone, you will suffer from extreme headaches. Just looking at me will make you feel as though knives are being pushed through your eyeballs."

She heard Leila shrieking in protest. Erin usually disagreed with Altman's technique, but she couldn't regret putting a thrall on Victor.

The first time she had used this form of hypnosis on someone, she had been horrified by what she had done. After she had survived her father's ritual killing, the ghosts of his other victims, as well as their powers had become a part of her. Altman never blamed her for getting his vampiric powers. In fact, he enjoyed it when she brainwashed humans. Sometimes he did it for her.

She usually managed to fight him, but when her adoptive parents had put her in the asylum, she had been too doped-up to resist him. Sometimes she had been grateful for his interference. She shivered as she remembered the one time she had been more than grateful to Altman.

She stared at Victor again, wondering why he hadn't left the apartment yet. Had she lost the gift?

Victor did seem to be affected by her voice. His pupils appeared larger, and his right hand made a fist while his left hand grabbed the door handle. His knuckles whitened.

Is he able to resist the compulsion to leave?

She stared at him with fascination, feeling slightly worried. For the first time, someone was trying to fight her thrall. Victor growled, and his face began to change.

"What the—?" Erin widened her eyes as she tried to take a step back. The bed behind her prevented her from retreating, and she fell back onto it.

She rolled off the bed and moved to the window. Victor's face was shifting. Instead of a mouth and nose, she saw a muzzle begin to form.

"Oh, shit. We've tried to thrall a werewolf!" Altman sounded alarmed.

"Is that bad?" she asked as she tried to pick up her underwear.

Victor's gaze was glued on her, and he continued to growl.

"Never mind. I think I know the answer to that." Erin slowly put on her underwear underneath the blanket. Then she moved toward her trousers.

"There's no time for modesty. Erin, run!" Altman cried out.

Victor looked as though he was ready to pounce on her at any time.

Erin suddenly didn't care much about modesty either. She jumped through the open window beside her bed and onto the stairs of the fire escape, turning just in time to see Victor running after her.

She quickly shoved the window shut from the outside and held it down with all her strength. Luckily, Victor's hands had transformed into paws so he couldn't open the window. He began barking angrily at her, trying to push his transformed body through the glass pane.

"Shush, nice doggy," she mumbled while leaning her back against the window.

Unfortunately, Victor refused to act like a nice dog. He continued to make a lot of noise while pounding on the glass.

"Maybe I should turn into a leopard myself, so I can fight him?" she suggested.

"You must be careful. You don't want to draw anyone's attention. You must appear to be normal," her mother advised.

"You're standing outside in your underwear, trying to keep a werewolf from attacking you. I wouldn't call that normal," Altman argued.

"Well, thank you very much for your input, Altman. Couldn't you at least have told me that I can't keep werewolves..." She hesitated, searching for the right word. "Enthralled."

She shivered as her bare legs touched the cold metal of the fire escape. She began to worry she might be there all morning. Turning her head, she stared at the werewolf through the glass. His large fangs were dripping with saliva, and his thick brown fur was standing up where his hackles were raised.

He pounded against the window inside her apartment, raking his claws over the glass.

She let out a deep sigh. Why couldn't she be an ordinary girl surrounded by real human beings?

She spotted something orange moving out of the corner of her eye and watched as her lazy cat walked toward her. Originally a stray, the feline had wandered into her apartment when she moved in and had chosen to stay.

"Some familiar you are! Aren't you supposed to protect me?" The animal purred and sat down as Erin stroked her. The overweight cat peered through the window at the werewolf and hissed at it before turning away from the sight of the violent beast with a flick of its tail. Without wasting another moment on Erin, the cat calmly walked down the fire escape.

The growling and pounding eventually stopped.

"Ah, he has overexerted himself. Not much stamina. He'll never do," Leila, the lusty-leopard said.

Erin flinched as everyone in her head shouted at Leila. She turned around to peer through the window into her apartment. Victor had turned human again, and he was lying on the floor beside the window with his eyes closed. He was also quite naked. His clothes had been shredded when he had transformed.

"His body is still impressive," Leila couldn't help but notice.

"Great! Now, how am I supposed to go to work?" Erin complained.

She hesitated for a second before opening the window. Carefully, she entered the room without letting her feet touch Victor's body.

Quietly, without letting Victor out of her sight, she put on her security guard uniform and her shoes. She tied up her curly blond hair in a ponytail and suppressed her need for the toilet.

I'll have to go at work, instead.

Fortunately, the bike ride to the hospital only took her about fifteen minutes, so it wouldn't be too long a wait.

She glanced at her notebook, which was on the floor next to Victor. She didn't want her upstairs neighbor to find her spells, especially not the section on black magic that she had written in order to appease Gideon.

Gideon had been a warlock while alive. Her father had lured him to his evil ritual with promises of power, but then he had betrayed the young warlock. Ending up with his spirit tied to a little girl had not made Gideon a friendly ghost. He had been silent so far today, but he was still trapped in her mind and regularly spilled his dark secrets into it.

Quickly, she picked up the notebook, dropped it in a plastic bag, took an apple from the fruit bowl and opened the door. She took one last, longing peek at Victor.

"Too bad you're an asshole and a werewolf."

She left the apartment and softly shut the door. She was tempted to lock it, but she didn't really want to find Victor in her apartment when she got back from work.

TOUCHED BY MADNESS

Hopefully, he will have left by then.

Although the sun was not yet at its full strength, the air felt thick and hot against her skin as Erin rode her bike to work. The fragrance of magnolias drifted through the cypress trees, which were adorned with Spanish moss.

She glanced down at her watch and flinched when she saw that she was already twenty minutes late. Luckily, Hope Acres had few inhabitants, so she didn't have to worry about traffic in the small town.

She paid little attention to the Devereaux Church as she approached it, but sensed its looming presence. She passed it as fast as she could. As she crossed the bridge, an SUV honked when it overtook her. She ignored the car and peeked down at her watch instead. She was nearly thirty minutes late. Fortunately, the familiar sight of the large hospital building came into view from behind the trees.

When she arrived at the hospital, Erin didn't waste any time putting a double lock on her bike.

Who would want to steal the rusty old thing anyway?

She ran into the gray building and nearly collided with the automatic doors that opened far too slowly. As soon as she entered the hospital, she was hit by a mixed smell of different disinfectants and air fresheners.

After a short visit to the bathroom, she raced around the information desk to her office and burst into the small room. Her co-worker, Frank, grinned at her as she entered the small security office.

She glanced around to ensure no one else was here to report her tardiness. The room was lined with security monitors and home to the CCTV data storage machines for the hospital.

"Good afternoon, ma'am," Frank said.

Erin glanced at the digital clock on the wall. It flashed nine-thirty a.m.

"Yes, sorry about that," she said.

"Don't worry about it, *ma soeur.*" He winked at her.

Frank was one of the few men she felt comfortable with. He was an enormous man with ebony skin covering well-defined muscles. He looked fierce, yet he was as aggressive as a kitten. He was happily married to Janice—a tiny nursery-school teacher, who was pregnant.

"Nikko called." Frank stared at the monitors as if avoiding eye contact.

She sighed. "Swell. What does he want now?"

"He wants you to call him back as soon as possible."

"Let's hope he has finally decided to have me fired," she joked. "I'd so be out of here if bloody Nikko hadn't made me sign that stupid contract!"

Frank shook his head.

"I don't get why they keep you tied down to this damn place. My contract says I can leave the company within one month if I want. I can't believe you must pay them two years' pay if you leave in two years. They didn't get me any trainin'. I didn't get a physical. And they didn't make me do no weird personality tests either. I only had one job interview before they hired me."

"Obviously they learned from their mistakes." She laughed. She waved at Frank as he left the room to do his rounds. But when she picked up the phone, she couldn't help but wonder at Securistate's motives.

I don't believe they're making me stay here because of the investment they put into my training—no matter what Nikko says.

She frowned, concerned that this job at the hospital was nothing more than a cover for something more ominous. There was a constant nagging feeling in the back of her mind that it was all just a setup. Most days, she wrote it off as paranoia, but today the irrational fear of being lulled into some kind of trap seemed stronger than usual. She feared that if she let her guard down for one second, then when she least expected it Doctor Quirkhart would reappear in her life and rip her away from her safe little world. Every day, she swallowed the fear of him re-appearing and locking her in the psych ward of the hospital, so he could continue with his creepy tests. The only basis for her fears were the lackluster explanations from Nikko about her contract and the coincidences surrounding her position in the hospital. This was the place she nearly died in, after all.

No wonder I'm always late.

She shook herself out of it and forced herself to suppress all thoughts of the doctor as she dialed Nikko's number.

"I told Frank you had to call me back as soon as possible," Nikko snapped.

Irritated, Erin heaved a sigh. "He did. I just arrived."

"You are this close—this close—to getting fired," he threatened. "And don't think that that would be the end of it, honey. We would sue you for all that you are worth, and then some!"

"Sue me just for being thirty minutes late?" she asked incredulously.

"No, chère. We will sue you for all the clients you have cost us."

A sense of foreboding overcame her.

"So far we have received five complaints against you."

"If I do such a poor job, why don't you fire me then?" she challenged.

"No, honey. We won't let you off the hook that easily. And don't even think about leaving. I'm not making idle threats about suing your ass."

"Why bother? You know I have no money." She should have gotten used to his hostility by now, but somehow it still managed to confuse her. Why did he hate her so much?

"I want you to know your place. I want you to know that we own you."

"You own me, whatever for?" She wanted to roar with rage and struggled to get her emotions under control.

29

"Jesus! Are you growling? You're more animal than human, aren't you? You know, we've been watching you. You're one of those freaks, aren't you?"

She stiffened.

Have they been following me? Do they know about my little escapades into the woods? Have they checked my hospital records, or worse, got in touch with Doctor Quirkhart? Oh God, please don't let them contact Doctor Quirky!

"Well, you'd better suppress your freakiness. I have a famous client who needs a female bodyguard who can blend in. This Saturday evening you will go to Star Knight's villa, and you're going to do an excellent job of representing us. You should also do something about your appearance. As a Securistate representative, you should wear some makeup. Change your shoes. High heels would be nice."

Furious, she clenched her fist. When she noticed that the fingers on her right hand had changed into claws, she rapidly hid them under her legs in case Frank came back.

"I can't wear high heels," she yelled. "I'm a security guard. What should I do if some guy attacks Ms. Knight and runs away? Take off my shoes and run after him barefoot?"

"You will run after him naked if we tell you to," her manager said before hanging up. She cursed as she slammed down the phone.

"Erin, are you okay?" Frank asked.

She rolled her eyes. "Just Nikko being Nikko. I have to work for Star Knight this Saturday."

"You're lucky to be gettin' this gig," Frank said. "I could sure use that extra money."

"I hate celebrity parties. They always try to do something outrageous in order to get in the tabloids. If I have to be present at another orgy, I might end up hurting someone," she admitted with a laugh.

When Frank didn't join in, she sighed. "Nikko knows that. He's only being a bully."

"Maybe you should talk to his boss," Frank suggested.

"Sure. If you can give me his name and telephone number, I'll give him a call right away."

"I don't know Jonathan Stratton's telephone number, but I'm sure I can find out. I always wanted to be a detective."

"*The* Jonathan Stratton?" she asked. "The tycoon?"

"I don't know how much money he has, but I think he owns half of Las Vegas."

"Why would someone like him own a small security company in a tiny town in Louisiana?"

"I don't know. It doesn't matter. You could try gettin' in touch with him."

She shook her head. "I'm sure he has better things to do than talk to a disgruntled employee."

"You don't have to directly talk to Stratton if you're afraid. You could talk to someone workin' for him," Frank teased.

"Afraid to speak up, me?" She chuckled as she left the room.

TOUCHED BY MADNESS

Heading for the stairs on her way to do her rounds around the hospital, she told herself to focus on the bright side of her job. She knew she'd been treated in this hospital after her ordeal twenty years ago. She wanted to find the hospital records, yet was terrified at the same time.

Did they know about the voices? Did they think I was crazy?

She sighed as she walked through the endless bleak corridors. The answers were here. She was sure of it.

When she reached the fourth-floor, she headed down the main corridor, quickly passing by several unoccupied wards. The hollow echo of her footsteps resonated loudly through the empty hallway. She stopped at the psychiatric ward and paused to stare through the window. The corridor was deserted. Her hand moved toward her electronic card, which would unlock the door. She knew she wasn't supposed to use it, but all the answers could lie behind this door.

Should I or shouldn't I? What if I get caught? I can't exactly tell them I want to break into their archives. They'd probably take my card away from me.

"*Go on,*" Leila said. "*What are you waiting for?*"

"I might get caught," Erin whispered. "Maybe there aren't even any records about what happened twenty years ago."

"*And maybe you're afraid to find those records because you don't want to read what they say. Come on, Erin. It's either this or looking up the person responsible for the mess we're in...*" Altman said.

As usual, a wave of nausea crashed through Erin as she thought about her father.

Her gloomy thoughts were interrupted when she saw one of the orderlies walk down the hall. He spotted her before she could move away from the window. The orderly froze.

She waved at him, giving him what she hoped was an innocent smile.

His surprised expression transformed into a glare.

I need to plan this better or I'll never get in there.

With a sigh, she turned on her heel and walked toward the elevator. She still needed to finish her rounds.

Breaking into the archives will have to wait another day.

She rushed to complete her rounds on the other floors. When she reached the basement, she slipped into the morgue and took a seat in one of the aluminum chairs behind the autopsy table.

Lying underneath the green sheet of the examination table in front of her was a corpse.

She stared at it, feeling curious. She glanced at the bare foot of the corpse, which was sticking out from under the sheet. A nametag hung loosely from the big toe.

"*Go on. Lift the sheet.*" Leila was always eager to get her in trouble.

"*Yes, finally a little action.*" Gideon sounded relieved.

"Hello, irritating warlock. It's been a while. You've been so quiet lately, I had hoped you had successfully used one of your dark magic spells to leave me," Erin said.

"No such luck," Gideon complained.

Erin felt pretty unlucky too, most of the time. Again, her gaze locked onto the feet of the corpse next to her.

There are always people who are worse off.

Suddenly she spotted a slight movement of the left foot of the body.

She jumped out of her chair. Goosebumps covered her arms.

Is that a spasm or am I imagining things? Why not? I'm already hearing the voices of the dead. It wouldn't be that far-fetched if I started seeing things as well.

She walked toward the door and lifted her hands, but couldn't feel a draft. She did feel a bit of a chill, but that was understandable—a morgue should be cold.

"Bodies sometimes have gas," Altman tried to reassure her.

"Sure." She sounded unconvinced.

"You should take a peek," Gideon said.

Determined, Erin straightened her back as she returned to the autopsy table. She lifted the sheet to uncover the man's face. His eyes were closed, and his mouth was sewn shut with bloody twine. He didn't appear to be breathing.

"Yuck! He looks dead to me," she said.

"Vincenzo!" Altman cried out.

"Friend of yours?" Gideon taunted.

Erin made a move to cover up the body, and then Altman protested, *"No, you must examine the chest."*

Erin pulled down the sheet.

"Yummy," Leila drawled. *"That's a nice broad chest. See Erin, a real man doesn't shave."*

"Eww, Leila! Corpses are not sexy," Erin protested.

"Maybe he's not dead," Leila replied.

"He's still alive," Altman said.

"See, it's okay. I can enjoy it now." Leila giggled, and Erin rolled her eyes.

"If he's a vampire, I would not agree," Gideon said.

"Well, he is a vampire, and the only way to kill vampires is through sunlight, fire, a beheading or by impaling them through the heart. Therefore, he can't be dead," Altman patiently explained.

"Do you want me to get Vincenzo to a doctor?" Erin hesitated. He appeared to be as dead as a doornail. She didn't want to draw anyone's attention by alleging that a dead man was alive.

"You must show me the whole body," Altman said.

Thankful for small miracles when Leila remained silent, Erin removed the entire sheet.

The naked corpse seemed to be in excellent condition—no wounds, no scars, nothing to account for his death. However, the string sewn through Vincenzo's lips made him appear disfigured, and she felt uncomfortable when she glanced at it.

TOUCHED BY MADNESS

The killer probably didn't like what his victim was saying.

"Remove the string," Altman told her.

She picked up a knife from the pathologist's trolley. With a steady hand, she moved the knife toward the mouth of the inert vampire. As the knife touched the twine, a sharp shock shot through her hand, causing her to drop the knife, and it clattered as it fell to the floor. She raised her hands without touching the body, holding them over Vincenzo. It seemed as though there was an invisible energy field surrounding the corpse. Sensing magic, she took a step back and studied Vincenzo.

"Witchcraft." Altman sounded disgusted. *"To make sure other witches won't touch him."*

"No." Erin's mother was quick to defend her own kind. *"Witches are good, honey."*

"Well, this doesn't feel good, and I can sense that someone used a spell. Altman is right," Erin said. "But, how can we undo this?"

She widened her eyes when she saw something move underneath his skin on his chest. Startled, she jumped backward.

What is that?

It seemed to be about the size of a mouse. Then it moved again before it disappeared.

"Oh goody, a dema," Gideon cheered. *"That is so great! I have never seen one in action before."*

"Sorry for sounding ignorant, but what the hell is a dema?" Erin asked.

"Well, I'm not going to tell you." Gideon laughed.

She decided to ignore Gideon and picked up the knife.

"Or should I start with the spell?" her voice wavered.

"No, if a paralysis spell was used to put that creature inside the vampire, then he would probably get very agitated if he were to wake up with that thing inside him. I'll work on the spell," her mother said.

"You really think a witch could break a paralysis spell? How? By lighting a candle or making up a couple of rhymes?" Gideon mocked them.

"You pretend to be such a strong, powerful warlock, but I've never seen you perform any black magic. You're all talk, Gideon," her mother argued.

Erin wished they would all talk less while she cut open the string binding his mouth. Trying to ignore the burning sensation each time she touched him, she pried open his mouth with her fingers.

"Okay, you can come out now," she joked as she gazed into the gaping mouth of the vampire. His white canine teeth gleamed under the harsh light of the morgue. They were elongated into sharp and deadly points, and the gums were slightly raised above them.

"Werewolves and vampires." She shook her head and sighed. "Why didn't I stay in England?" She stepped back and stared at the corpse.

"I don't see that dema thing anymore. How am I supposed to remove it? I can't cut out something that I can't see."

She approached the corpse once more.

TOUCHED BY MADNESS

"I'm sorry, but if it's a kind of parasite, then you might use yourself as bait," Altman suggested. *"It might be feeding on the vampire, but it would probably prefer live flesh."*

"How am I supposed to hold my flesh in front of this dema?"

She didn't receive an answer.

With a daunting realization, it became clear to her that the best way to lure the creature out was by sticking her fingers into the vampire's mouth, hoping he wouldn't suddenly awaken and snap his sharp teeth on her soft flesh.

She groaned as she raised her hand over the vampire's face. She pushed her index finger into the vampire's mouth and experienced tiny jolts of pain as she touched him, but she refused to remove her hand. While relying on the paralysis spell to keep the vampire immobilized, she tried meditation to take her mind off the constant sharp shocks emitting from the bewitched body.

She focused on breathing in and breathing out, waiting for the dema to take a bite and hoping that it wouldn't have teeth. If it did have teeth, she hoped that they wouldn't be too sharp.

She was about to withdraw her hand from the vampire's mouth when something cold and slimy slithered past her fingers.

Her first impulse was to snatch her hand away, but she managed to suppress that feeling. When the creature finally did bite her, she experienced such relief that she felt no pain. Careful not to detach the dema from her hand and have it go back into the corpse, she held her fingers steady as she removed her hand from Vincenzo's mouth.

A large worm-like creature dangled from her fingers and she shuddered in revulsion. The bite wasn't comfortable, but the pain was not as sharp as she had feared it would be. A couple of drops of her blood had fallen into the vampire's mouth. Luckily, he didn't react to it.

She quickly tore the dema from her fingers, crying out when it took a bit of skin from her index finger with it. She cursed loudly and dropped the dema onto the polished floor. It started to slither away, so she swiftly slammed her foot on it, feeling its body pop beneath her heel. She ground her heel on it to ensure it was squashed under her shoe.

"And now I need to find tools to wake you up," she said. "I'll be right back."

In the tiny kitchen of the pediatric ward, Erin was excited to discover some matches and a small birthday-cake candle that was shaped like a four.

She also found some cinnamon, a fern, two glasses and an empty jar. She grabbed a plastic waste bag from the dispenser on the wall and put the items inside it to prevent drawing any attention to herself. Next stop was the emergency room where she deftly scooped up a bag of blood and added it to the other items. When she returned to the morgue her mother said, "*I don't really have a spell yet.*"

"That's all right, Mom. I'll think of something," Erin whispered.

She remembered that she needed a green ribbon, but settled for some scrubs instead. She locked the door, took a pair of scissors and cut a long piece from the bottom of the green shirt. The piece could pass for a ribbon. When it came to witchcraft, one always had to improvise.

She prayed that no one would try to enter the room while she attempted to undo the spell. She took one of the glasses and filled it with water, deciding that acting quickly would reduce the chances of getting caught.

"*I taught you well,*" her mother proudly stated.

Erin grinned. Whenever Doctor Quirkhart hadn't drugged her too much at the asylum, her mother had tried to teach her spells. She thought of her notebook lying in the office.

"My notebook could come in handy," she muttered. "I know there is a healing spell in there somewhere."

"*You shouldn't try a lame healing spell to break a curse. You would need at least a blood sacrifice. I don't believe this. I'm stuck with a bunch of amateurs!*" Gideon complained.

Erin ignored him while she cast a circle around Vincenzo and herself. On one side of the circle, she put the glass of water. On the other side, she lit the candle, which she placed in the second glass, symbolizing fire.

She placed the fern in the circle because it represented earth. She used the lucky feather, which she always carried with her, in the circle to represent air. For her, the feather also represented freedom. She believed that someday she would be free of the voices.

Next, she used the scissors to cut a lock of Vincenzo's black hair, cursing when she felt the shock again. Fortunately, after she cut the hair, the stinging stopped.

She sprinkled the cinnamon over the ribbon, the glass jar, the lock of hair and Vincenzo's body before sitting cross-legged in the middle of the circle.

She felt a bit self-conscious and slowly exhaled to connect with her powers. She closed her eyes and began chanting the spell.

"Herb for healing, herb to start feeling, herb for pain to stop, herb to wake up, herb to get well, herb to break this paralysis spell. I call on thee, spirits of water, earth, fire and air to aid me in this healing."

"Charmed had better rhymes than that," Gideon said.

She didn't respond. She sensed the energy in the air, raising the tiny blond hairs on her arms, indicating that something was about to happen. Her breath escaped in a little rush, and her body felt drained.

Without opening her eyes, she repeated the spell again. The palm of her hand began to burn when the lock of hair in it quickly heated up.

She felt small electrical charges flash through her body, and her eyes snapped open. Astonished, she saw not only the lock of hair light up in a glow, but Vincenzo's entire body.

With a sense of awe, she picked up the jar and bound the ribbon around it three times. While she did this, she chanted. "Thrice I bind thee, and so with nine calls you will heal."

Next, she put Vincenzo's hair into the jar, locked it and shook it nine times. The glow increased, lighting up the whole morgue. Power and magic seared through her body and shimmered in the air around her.

"Power of healing, I command you. Heal Vincenzo from all sickness," she repeated, her voice slightly shaking.

After the spell was cast, she thanked the elements. With unsteady hands, she took down the circle. Meanwhile, the glow dimmed, and the only light in the morgue came from the tiny birthday cake candle. Silence reigned.

She slowly stood up on shaky legs and took deep breaths, trying to stop her knees from shaking while she walked toward the vampire. She stared at his face, but he still wasn't moving. Without any hesitation, she touched his brow, feeling relieved that she no longer received any shocks from him.

"Maybe you could give him that blood," Altman proposed. That suggestion must have appealed to the vampire for he immediately opened his eyes.

"Altman?" Vincenzo croaked.

Erin enjoyed a moment of triumph when she heard the vampire speak. It had worked. She couldn't wait to write the spell down.

It took a while for her to register what Vincenzo had said. With a mixture of elation and confusion, she retreated from the vampire, stunned for a moment.

"Do you hear him too?"

"W-what?" Vincenzo frowned. He briefly sat up, then his head wobbled, and he fell on his back. He glanced around, wearing a puzzled expression.

"You're in the morgue," she explained. "Do you remember what happened?"

He remained quiet while staring at her.

A shiver of apprehension shot straight down her spine. For a moment, something touched her mind. She felt the struggle for entrance and recognized it because she had tried doing it herself that morning with Victor.

"You will come to me," Vincenzo said.

"Uh oh, I do believe someone is hungry," Altman said.

"Sorry. I understand that you must feed a-after your nap, but I didn't wake you in order to get bitten, thank you very much. Here you go," she said as she handed him the bag of blood from the emergency room. "And now," she said as she stepped back once more, "I must return to my post before anyone wonders where I am."

Vincenzo shook his head, confused, staring at the bag of blood. He dropped it in disgust.

What am I doing in the morgue? Am I hallucinating?

He could have sworn he had just heard Altman's voice, but that wasn't possible.

And who is this young woman? How can she resist me? Has someone stolen my power?

The woman had reached the doorway by the time he tried getting up again. He didn't succeed in standing, but he did manage to pick up the glass jar to examine the lock of hair inside.

Witchcraft. Did she just put a spell on me?

"You should put that somewhere safe," she said. "Well, it was nice knowing you. Bye." The woman—witch unlocked the door and stepped out into the hallway.

"Wait!" Vincenzo yelled out, but the witch continued walking away from the morgue.

"Please," he whispered. The sound of echoing footsteps ceased, and he realized she must have stopped walking away.

He heard a soft voice. *"Oh Erin, you are such a sucker."* Then the witch reappeared in the doorway.

"What?" The witch folded her arms.

Why is she acting angry? I'm the victim here.

"Will you come back?"

When she pulled a face, he pleaded, "Please, you can't just leave me here!"

"How the mighty have fallen," he heard a familiar voice say with disgust.

"Altman?" Vincenzo asked once more, as he searched around the room.

How can this be?

He knew that Altman was dead.

Is Altman haunting me? Did the spell somehow make me hear ghosts?

"Why do I keep hearing Altman?" Vincenzo asked. "He's been gone for ages. Ever since..."

That night at the Devereaux Church. He silently completed the sentence.

"Oh, my God!" he cried feeling a grin spread across his face. "You're the one!"

He examined the nametag on her uniform. "Yes, Holland. That's it."

When he started to laugh, the witch gave him a hostile look. Even though not many people could intimidate a vampire of over two hundred years, he felt uncomfortable beneath her glare, so uncomfortable that he did something out of character.

"I'm sorry," he apologized. He'd wanted to tell her more, to explain to her the irony of it all, to explain to her that when the situation with her father had arisen, he had been ordered to find her. When he hadn't been able to, he'd known that he would probably have been better off dead.

Over the years, Dane had become renowned for breaking down vampires who disobeyed him. Fortunately, in this instance, Dane had miraculously changed his mind, and Vincenzo had broken off his search.

But if Dane hadn't ... And to find her now...

TOUCHED BY MADNESS

Vincenzo had come to resent her over the years. Because of her, he had not been able to prove to Dane what he was capable of. Dane had stopped giving him orders. But now, he had finally found a way to ingratiate himself with Dane again.

She frowned at him. "Look. I have to go back to work. Just forget you ever laid eyes on me okay?"

He nodded as the security guard ran from the morgue, leaving her fresh fragrance behind her. He took a sip of blood from the bag and shuddered in revulsion. It tasted awful. He forced it down anyway.

Vincenzo's internal clock told him that the sun wouldn't set for another four hours. He planned to conserve his strength during those hours because, as soon as darkness fell, he was going to return to Dane.

I can't wait to tell Dane that I found his enemy's daughter.

THREE

Dane Lynch lay awake in his bed, staring at the ceiling of the basement. He didn't need a watch to inform him that the sun hadn't set yet. For the past three months, he had been having trouble sleeping. He felt restless. To him, life had become a boring chain of endless nights that were filled with conflict.

He shifted his gaze to the computer on his desk. The idea of checking the status of the shopping mall he was building on the outskirts of New Orleans seemed a tempting option, rather than lying in bed frustrated. But he had other concerns that needed to be dealt with.

First, there was Karma, another master vampire who had recently arrived in his small town. Karma only seemed to be here to deliberately provoke him. However, vampire politics had been a part of Dane's afterlife ever since he had been turned at thirty-five. After two hundred and forty-three years, he should have gotten used to it by now. Instead, he suffered from weariness whenever he encountered Karma.

TOUCHED BY MADNESS

His second problem was that his vampires had been going missing. Dane had been the master vampire of Hope Acres for over twenty years, and recently there had been signs that his rule was under threat.

Over the past seven weeks, three vampires had disappeared and everyone expected him to do something about it. The first two disappearances had not been very surprising. Jerry was a recently turned vampire, who only wanted to enjoy himself. Dane had felt no surprise when he left. Although Jerry had not dared to openly declare himself against him, he knew that it was in Jerry's nature to rebel against the rules he had set up. Since Dane hadn't been the one to sire him, he didn't feel responsible enough to force Jerry to stay.

But then Rafferty had left. He had been with Dane for nearly fifty years. Rafferty hadn't informed him of any decision to leave, but he understood that Rafferty longed to spread his wings. The older vampire had leadership potential. He knew that Rafferty would one day become a master vampire himself. Strangely enough, he hadn't felt anything when Rafferty left without telling him.

Rafferty had been his most loyal supporter after he had killed his predecessor, the ancient Gregorio and gained the title of master vampire of Hope Acres.

Dane's role had been chosen for him. He had been forced to take Gregorio's place as master vampire of Hope Acres, and Rafferty had been a good friend during dangerous times. But he didn't understand why Rafferty would leave without a word. It seemed out of character.

Why this numbness, have I tired of being Hope Acres' master vampire?

Tired didn't even begin to describe his drained state. He knew that he should have gone after Rafferty to at least question him, and possibly torture him. It would stop the others from leaving. But he had chosen to let him leave without making him pay for disrupting the order.

He frowned up at the ceiling. Now Vincenzo had disappeared.

It just doesn't make any sense.

Vincenzo was a submissive who merely wanted to please everyone. He would never go against anyone with authority. He was terrified of Dane and his punishments.

Gregorio had sired Vincenzo and had taken a lot of pleasure in breaking him. When Dane had killed Gregorio he had accepted the responsibility of Vincenzo, much like a human would accept the care of an abused dog. Vincenzo would never have left of his own volition.

Dane had asked his second-in-command, Brock to investigate, but so far he had found out nothing.

He rolled out of bed and stood up. He put on his faded jeans and a T-shirt before running his fingers through his messy dark hair to try and smooth it.

He peered down at his crumpled T-shirt and thought about the wardrobe of Jonathan Stratton, the Las Vegas master vampire. Stratton wore only Armani suits. Dane smiled, he didn't believe in flaunting his wealth by wearing expensive attire. He wore comfortable clothes, and he didn't care what others thought.

He briefly considered asking Stratton for help with the disappearances, but immediately rejected that thought.

Whenever Jonathan Stratton assisted someone he usually demanded something in return, and the price was always too steep. Because Stratton still tried to convince humans that he was a normal and wealthy human being, he kept his contacts with the vampire community outside his territory to a minimum. Another reason for Stratton to distrust vampires outside his territory was the wealth of Vegas. Most master vampires envied Stratton, and he had been challenged several times. Stratton had used underhanded tactics to get Las Vegas, and his competitors would not hesitate to do the same.

No, working with Stratton on this would only complicate matters.

Dane left his bedroom and was accosted by Hazel, another vampire he had inherited from Gregorio.

"Excuse me Master, I really would like to talk to you," she humbly said, peering down at her designer shoes.

"What is it, Hazel?" He found it difficult to be polite to her. She had been acting up for the past three months, almost as if she wanted him to punish her. He'd been making excuses because Gregorio had turned her just before Dane had killed him. Being so young, she'd had a hard time learning how to be a vampire without the help of her sire. But he was tiring of her adolescent behavior.

"It's Eve and Maura. They took two customers from the bar to our living room, and they fed there, right in front of me! They did it on purpose," she whined.

He walked up to Hazel and smelled her breath.

"Well, apparently you managed to restrain yourself, so there's no harm done." He turned to leave, but she grabbed his arm.

He froze and turned to her, letting his annoyance show as his eyes swept her from head to toe. She instantly released his arm.

"Please," she begged.

"You chose to be around temptation," he coldly informed her. "It's only been eight weeks. Are you sure you wouldn't prefer to be locked up for a year instead?"

"Please, change your punishment. It's unbearable."

"Already?" He laughed without mirth. "You know, Hazel, I really had you pegged as someone stronger. I mean, someone weak wouldn't dare to ignore an order made by a master vampire, right?"

"I'm sorry," she wailed.

"Well, I'm disappointed. You're giving up so easily. So do you want me to lock you up, or do you want me to ask one of the others to do the honors, Eve, perhaps? Or would you rather have me take out your fangs?"

Hazel's fangs would grow back as she was a vampire, so he would have to remove them more than once. "Without anesthetic," he murmured.

"You're evil," she snapped.

"You should not forget that."

Her jaw tightened in anger before she turned and walked away with her head held high. It appeared she would not give in so easily, after all.

He heaved another sigh.

God's teeth, but I'm tired.

"You should be careful." He heard Brock's voice behind him before he turned to face the muscular black vampire.

"What is this? First, I'm told I'm too soft on her, and now you're telling me I have to be careful. Make up your mind, Brock."

"No, I agree with your punishment. I am just afraid that she's still trying to undermine your position," Brock explained.

"Have you found evidence that she is working with Karma against me?" Dane asked.

"Nothing concrete, I'm afraid. Do you want me to follow her?"

"No. With the new shopping center and Vincenzo's disappearance, you have enough on your plate. Right now, I want you to focus on finding out what happened to Vincenzo. Something tells me he isn't going to be the last vampire of Hope Acres to disappear," Dane predicted.

Brock nodded briefly and took two steps when a familiar voice called out Dane's name. Brock's eyes met Dane's in recognition, before they both rushed to the entrance.

They found Vincenzo standing barefoot in the hallway. Dane frowned when he took in Vincenzo's messy appearance.

"Are you wearing hospital clothes?" Dane's voice sounded very soft and gentle.

"Y-yes!" Vincenzo stammered. "I got attacked! We are all under attack!" he cried.

"Calm down," Dane said coolly. "What happened?"

"I-I-I'm not sure. I found a note from you, saying I had to go to town to get Karma some cats, and then I felt something sharp on my back, like ... like a dart. And then it got dark! That is until I woke up in the hospital. That's all I remember. P-p-p-p please! I would never leave you, sir!" Vincenzo said meekly, and he fell to his knees.

Dane stared at the terrified vampire before him, unmoved by his performance. He shot a glance at Brock. Nothing needed to be said. They both knew Vincenzo was telling the truth.

"No, wait! I-I-I also have some great news," Vincenzo said.

Dane noticed beads of sweat appear on Vincenzo's upper lip as he rushed out his words. He frowned. It was hard to see anything positive in this situation.

"I think I found that girl you wanted me to find, but then didn't. Well technically, she's not really a girl anymore. She's more like a w-woman. You remember, right? She was the blond girl who had

Altman in her head and survived that massacre twenty years ago?"

Merenda's daughter. Unconsciously, he started walking toward Vincenzo as relief flooded him.

She made it. She survived.

When he noticed Brock eyeing him curiously, he froze. He realized that his behavior was out of character, and ice formed in his stomach. Even if it had been twenty years since he had laid eyes on her, she still influenced his behavior. With his position under fire, he could not afford this. He could not afford her. She was a complication he didn't need right now.

"Are you sure?" Dane tried to be realistic.

It is Vincenzo after all. He makes mistakes all the time.

"Y-y-yes, Master. At least, I-I-I think so," Vincenzo said. "No, I'm sure. The nametag said Holland. That was her last name. I remember, I heard Altman's voice. I also heard other voices. It was weird."

"Where is she?" He was getting impatient with Vincenzo.

"At the hospital. I think she did something to make me regain consciousness." He showed Dane the jar with his lock of hair. "I don't know if she's still there. She wore a uniform like a security guard. She might work there, or maybe she was just visiting someone, a patient. Maybe she left." Vincenzo was obviously trying to cover every possibility and his own ass in the process.

With his patience wearing thin, Dane turned to Brock.

"Brock, find out if the hospital has a female security guard and uncover anything else you can about her. If she doesn't work for them, get me the security tapes. I want to see if she visited anyone, and if she did, who it was."

Rubbing the back of his neck in a gesture that underlined his frustration, Dane frowned as Brock nodded and left, taking Vincenzo with him.

I should not have asked Brock to find out more about her. I need to call him back in here.

Alarmed by his indecision, Dane cursed. He always knew what to do in every situation.

Intellectually, he knew he was probably overreacting. Seeing Merenda's daughter after twenty years was not likely to have any effect on him at all. He hoped the meeting would leave him cold, but he could not help thinking that his initial response to her had been a warning.

She should have stayed hidden. Knowing she lived nearby, would occupy his mind even though he should be thinking about other matters. Worse, he could not risk running into her and have her complicate matters for him. Therefore, she forced him to be proactive. She was a liability.

Liabilities had to be annihilated.

FOUR

E rin was only ten minutes late when she appeared in the open French doors of Star's villa. The perfume of gardenia hung heavy in the air. In the distance, she heard the harsh song of the common grackle.

The party hadn't started yet, but a pale-skinned elderly assistant walked up to her with a frown on her face.

"I was told that you would blend in," the woman complained as she took in Erin's appearance.

"As an employee of Securistate, I have to wear a uniform. Why, did you expect me to wear a cocktail dress?"

"You insolent girl! You were hired to blend in. You should not have come in through the general entrance. Members of staff are supposed to arrive through the back entrance. Well, aren't you going to apologize?"

Erin could think of a couple of things to say instead of apologizing, things that would probably be reported back to Nikko, so she decided to go for a shrug instead.

The other woman shook her head and gestured that Erin should follow her as she headed toward the kitchen.

The actress's villa impressed Erin. The plantation house's old-world architecture had been blended with a modern style. The back of the house had a peaceful view of the Mississippi river. The stables appeared to have once been the slave quarters and had been converted for Ms. Knight's thoroughbreds.

In spite of the lovely setting, she wished she could be anywhere else, preferably at home in her own bed. Last night she had decided not to use handcuffs anymore since they only encouraged Leila to take over her body. It was as if by restraining her own body, she had deliberately challenged Leila. She didn't wake up that morning to loud music, and at first, she had been very grateful for that. However, she was certain she had locked the door the night before, but it hadn't been locked this morning.

Did I visit Victor last night?

The thought sent a shiver of worry down her spine. How long could she live like this, unaware of what her body was doing while she slept?

To make matters worse, instead of avoiding her, her werewolf neighbor had been waiting outside her door this morning. He had flashed a knowing smirk, and she'd been unable to stop thinking about it since then.

What does he know? What did I do?

TOUCHED BY MADNESS

It was like being in the mental hospital all over again. Once, the nurse had told her that she had stabbed a pencil through one of doctor Quirky's testicles. However, because of all the drugs, she remembered little of the event. What she did remember, she wished to forget.

If something happened, do I want to know?

She sighed, spotting the other bodyguard she had to work with. Talk about not blending in. His jacket hung open with his gun in plain sight. He might as well be wearing a uniform.

"James, this is Erin from Securistate. She will be following your orders tonight," the personal assistant said before cold-shouldering Erin as she walked away.

James smiled apologetically. "I suppose she's already commented on your choice of clothes. It's just that people tend to get nervous when they see us in uniform. They worry that the presence of security means there's a risk. Never mind, I can get you a nice dress. If you want to fix your hair, Star has a curling iron and gel you can use. I'll make sure you fit right in."

"I don't see you hiding your gun," Erin objected.

"Oh, right," he said uncomfortably. He quickly closed his jacket.

She decided not to increase his discomfort by commenting on the bulge the gun made in his jacket.

After he took her upstairs and gave her new clothes, she studied the dress. Unfortunately, the green gown that he gave her was a bit too revealing for her taste. In spite of the convenient large split between the legs where she hid her gun, she preferred a dress without such a deep cleavage. When she bent over, her nipples showed.

I won't be blending in wearing this!

The fact that Leila and Gideon made no derogatory comments while she stood in front of the mirror, made Erin worry again over what had happened the previous night.

She cursed when she stepped into the stilettos. They fitted like a glove, but she'd never been tempted to wear high heels. She felt as clumsy as Bambi on ice and was bound to fall flat on her face.

She refused to do anything with her hair. She already had to endure wearing a dress and uncomfortable shoes.

She had expected that when James saw her he would tell her to change into something else. Instead, he said, "perfect."

She decided to let it go. She knew tonight was going to be an ordeal anyway. She just had to grit her teeth and get through it. She hoped that Star Knight didn't act like one of those celebrities who used these parties for publicity purposes by encouraging their guests to behave badly.

She had laughed about it when she talked to Frank, but orgies were not uncommon at this kind of event. Even worse, orgies with otherworldly creatures like vampires and werewolves were popular because they created more publicity. She feared what might happen if a large group high on drugs and alcohol noticed her otherness.

She didn't know if Star had ever organized any kinky soirees, because Erin had never been interested in reading gossip magazines. She enjoyed movies, but had not seen the B-list actress in any good ones lately.

What if Star believes there is no such thing as bad publicity?

"Where would you like to be during the party?" James asked, interrupting her thoughts.

She wanted to tell him that she'd like to be at home, but she decided on a more professional answer.

"I prefer monitoring the exit."

Relief flooded through her when he let her stand by the back door while he placed himself next to the entrance.

She scanned the garden and the water. She could not detect any boats. If someone tried to swim to the house, he or she would have to have super-strength to survive the notorious currents of the Mississippi, but she wouldn't underestimate the determination of stalkers.

She turned back to observe the entrance. Night had fallen, and the first guests had arrived. She heaved a sigh of relief when she spotted the other women. Her dress would not draw that much attention, after all. It was positively demure in comparison to some of the other women's attire. Another upside to these all-too-revealing clothes was that no weapons could be hidden, so most of the female guests could be disregarded as a possible threat.

She watched James talking to the men while casually checking them for weapons.

The personal assistant who had introduced her to James earlier was now greeting the guests. She seemed a lot friendlier with the partygoers than the staff.

Star hadn't come down to face the crowd yet, but Erin assumed that she was waiting for all her visitors to arrive so she could make a grand entrance.

Trusting James's skills as a security guard, she turned around to face the backyard again. She relaxed in the warm evening air, enjoying the sound of authentic Cajun music behind her.

A couple walked past her to go outside. They were holding hands. The woman giggled as they moved toward the stables.

"No comments from you, Leila? Nothing about how that could have been me?" Erin muttered.

"I don't want to be too predictable," Leila said.

A nervous feeling fluttered in her stomach as she glanced around to see if anyone noticed her talking to herself. Fortunately, the visitors acted more interested in the host than in a crazy security guard.

Star walked down the marble stairs in a white transparent dress. Everyone stared at the actress while Erin observed the crowd. As big entrances went, Erin found this one a bit disappointing, but the other guests seemed mesmerized.

"Is that something you'd like me to wear, Leila?" Erin asked.

TOUCHED BY MADNESS

Erin heard a man behind her clear his throat. She flinched as she turned around to face the person who must have heard her last comment.

Great job of blending in! Of course, it has to be James standing behind me.

"Are you all right? I wanted to ask you if you needed a break to have something to eat..."

She tried to give him her best 'I'm not a lunatic smile' before thanking him and rushing toward the kitchen.

Yes, I definitely need a break!

As soon as Brock had informed Dane that Merenda's daughter would be working at Star Knight's party that evening, he had called Star to request an invitation. If she had been surprised by his request, she hadn't shown it. She appeared pleased that the master vampire of Hope Acres had finally deemed her worthy of a visit after turning down several of her invitations in the past.

As he left his car in front of the plantation house, all of his senses were fully alert. The party was in full swing. The loud music called out to him with the beat of the drums heating his blood.

People stared at him as he entered the building, and some of them stopped talking.

He tried to sense her as he walked into the lounge, but looking around, he realized he couldn't see anyone resembling her. He frowned.

I'd better not have come out here for nothing.

He tried not to let his annoyance show as Star walked up to him with her arms spread. It was obvious that she intended to hug him, but one look at the expression on his face must have deterred her because she lowered her arms and breathed a kiss past his left cheek instead.

Good.

He had little patience for routine pleasantries.

"Hello Mr. Lynch, I'm honored to welcome you to my humble soiree!"

"Thank you for having me," he replied politely.

"I hope this means you will visit us more often?" she asked with an eager smile.

He ignored her and observed the people around him, trying to detect a female security guard.

An irritated cough interrupted his search. He frowned and turned to face Star, who was apparently waiting for an answer of some kind. Unfortunately for her, he was too old to worry about something as trivial as etiquette.

"I don't wish to take up all your time. Perhaps you'd wish to entertain some of the other guests?"

She spun around and walked away from him, but not before he saw the crushed expression in her eyes. Disgusted with her neediness and with himself for attracting attention he didn't seek, he walked toward the garden and away from the crowd.

When he spotted the girl he was looking for, she had almost reached the border of the Mississippi river. She stood next to some Chinese lanterns, staring out over the water with her back to the house. Her blond hair was tied back in a ponytail, and he couldn't see her face from this angle. He might not have recognized her had it not been for his gut feeling, informing him that she was the little girl he had given his blood to all those years ago.

Goldilocks.

She didn't dress like a security guard, nor did she seem particularly alert to danger. Shaking his head as he took in the backless dress and the frivolous heeled sandals, he concluded that he did not need to kill her. Wearing such provocative outfits, she would soon draw the attention of some psychopath who would finish her off for him.

Of course, if necessary, he would destroy her. He stared intently at her and realized that it would be best for both of them if he discovered that she had no effect on him at all. If he murdered her to stop anyone from using her against him, it may bring about the one thing he wished to avoid. It'd send out a signal to his enemies that he had a weakness they could exploit.

I do not have failings.

His thoughts involuntarily moved to his sister. Jane had been his Achilles' heel. She had been about the same age as Erin was now when she had died. Instinctively, he knew that it would probably be for the best if he turned around and left, but he told himself he couldn't.

He had to know if this Erin Holland had any power over him, even if he was mostly convinced he would be immune to her. He let his eyes flicker over her slim body. His gaze lingered on the slight curve of her hips.

Damn it, she still affects me.

His body went rigid with frustration.

Her mesmerizing scent seemed to travel across the lawn and seeped into his skin as if trying to mark him. He clenched his fists in an attempt to deny the sudden urges she invoked in him, but a quiet moan escaped his lips. With a feeling of self-loathing, he shook his head.

His face felt as if it had turned to stone, and his eyes burned as he watched her. The fact that his every sense responded to her as though plugged into high-voltage electricity profoundly disturbed him. He exhaled, and she quickly turned around to face him, her golden eyes wide and alert to danger. She dropped the apple she had been eating and scanned the area.

So she does have the right instincts for a guard, after all. Can she sense what I want to do to her?

Erin faced the man whose silent approach had startled her. A chill ran through her body, which felt as if it reached her soul and turned it to ice.

"Holy crap, Dane Lynch," Altman swore.

Despite the fact that she did not watch the local news, she didn't need to ask him for any identification. The man in front of her was quite a celebrity in Hope Acres. No, not man—vampire, a vampire people talked about fearfully in whispered tones.

Dane Lynch had a reputation for making people disappear. Having read that fire was his favorite method of disposal, she felt concerned by his presence at the party.

Is he here to incinerate someone?

The expression in his eyes sent jolts of fear shooting down her spine. Sensing he did not have much experience of being denied, she shuddered when his gaze locked onto her.

Her instincts were screaming at her to find a wooden stick, do a little stabbing and get the hell out, but she forced herself not to trigger this predator.

"Am I making you nervous?"

His soft voice drew her nerves taut. The sound caused a nervous flutter in her stomach and goosebumps to pop up on her arms. His voice overpowered her senses, ensuring he'd get the response he wanted. That response was more alarming than the fear.

She felt as if her skin was on fire, and the master vampire was igniting the flames. His masculine scent was intoxicating, and she was drawn to him.

She mentally kicked herself.

What the hell am I thinking?

Irritated, she blamed her leopard hormones.

One day, I'd just like one day without raging cat hormones!

She cautiously inspected him through long lashes. He looked positively sinful. He was tall and muscular with inky-black hair, and his eyes were piercing blue.

Besieged with unfamiliar emotions, she felt a sharp tingle of delight snake up her spine. A part of her wanted his frightening attention.

He elevated an impatient brow, making her conscious of the fact that she hadn't answered his question.

She defiantly glared at him. His rude question did not warrant a reply.

Time stood still as they stared at each other. It was a cool standoff that turned her blood to ice. She forced herself to meet his devilish eyes, unwilling to give in.

"You should be nervous. You should also be careful, Goldilocks," he warned. "You will live a very short life if you challenge me like that."

In spite of the spike of fear that seemed to run through her veins, she refused to submit. But with his predatory eyes glued to hers, she felt captured, swallowed by the dark depths of his pupils as if they were connected to her, controlling her.

Connected to a notorious monster?

She shook her head to break the spell. She had been so caught up in his gaze that she'd forgotten what she was doing. She blinked at him, trying to bring him back into focus. Shaking a little, she began to move toward the safety of the house.

"Yes, run. I want you to."

She hesitated.

TOUCHED BY MADNESS

Some security guard I am if I let myself be chased away by one of the guests. Unless he wasn't invited...?

"Did you get an invitation to this party?"

"Yes, I did—unlike you."

Without thinking, she spread the split in her dress and pointed at the gun strapped to her right thigh. "I'm working here."

Only after she had concealed the weapon once more did she realize she had been showing the Hope Acres' master vampire her undies. She heard someone snorting in her head and inwardly winced. She felt a fevered blush seep up her neck to her face.

"You are impulsive. Impulsive behavior can get you killed," he said.

"Are you threatening me?"

"Do you feel threatened?"

She did, but she refused to acknowledge that. Fortunately, he did not seem to expect an answer.

"I want you to leave Hope Acres." It was nothing less than an order. His warning tone was as sharp as a blade.

"Ah, bloody hell," Altman said.

"Why?" Erin rasped.

"He knows," Altman said.

Knows what?

"That you're Merenda's daughter."

Not wanting to enter into a discussion with Altman in front of Dane Lynch, she ignored the voice and waited for Dane to speak.

"You are my enemy's daughter," Dane said, confirming Altman's suspicions. "Oliver Merenda killed my second-in-command twenty years ago.

The coward ran before I could confront him. Having you here is the closest I'll ever get to revenge. Stay here and I'll consider you fair game."

"Fair game? I'm not responsible for what my father did. That's not fair."

He laughed, startling her. "Life is fair? Didn't your father kill your mother and sister before trying to kill you? You should have learnt by now that life just isn't fair, Goldilocks."

"He can have his revenge on me anytime, anyway he likes," Leila said. *"This guy is absolutely delicious."*

"Shut up," Altman said.

"You're such a party pooper, Altman," Leila whined.

"Don't you think we've had enough parties lately?" Altman commented.

"We should be working together. We all want the same thing, don't we?" Erin's mother said.

Erin appreciated Altman's and her mom's support. It would be nice if everyone was that selfless. She scrutinized the man beside her and put him in the same category as Gideon or Leila.

Or worse.

The chill in his blue eyes was nerve-wracking. Something she saw in their rich depths made her heart kick into a suffocating rhythm. She wanted to lower her blond lashes in concealment, compelled by a sudden instinct for self-preservation, but she stubbornly refused to cower.

"You will go home and pack your bags tonight." His instruction was so absolute, she knew he expected instant obedience.

TOUCHED BY MADNESS

Alarm bells rang in her head. She could sense the lazy menace in him as clearly as she felt her own deeply intrigued response. A response she suppressed immediately. His name was terrifying enough to make her want to forget about doing her job and run, but she wouldn't. At all costs, she must avoid triggering a response in this dangerous creature, but she refused to act like prey.

Annoyed and with her jaw clenched, she turned to face him. "I'm not entirely powerless, you know," she retorted.

Her only warning of an attack was a slight headache. Her next conscious thought was that her left hand was pointing her own gun at her chest. She hadn't even been aware that she had taken the weapon out of the holster.

"Or would a bullet through your mouth be more efficient?" he asked.

She opened her mouth to put the barrel inside. The cold iron on her tongue caused her eyes to water, and the metallic taste made her gag.

"Or directly to the brain?" he continued.

She desperately tried to block him, but he played with her body as though she were nothing more than his puppet. As he had instructed, she took the gun out of her mouth and put it against her temple. Surprised, she noticed that her hand didn't shake.

Did Dane control that, too?

She attempted to make eye contact in order to plead with him to end this cruel game, but it had no effect on him.

"You see, this is just no fun. You're making this too easy, Goldilocks. If you stay, I'll have to think of something more creative."

He let go of his hold on her mind. She let out a breath of relief. She didn't care that he must have heard it. Ignoring him, she hurried back to Star Knight's house.

So what if he thinks I'm a coward.

She forced herself to calm down as she reached the back door.

"Goodnight," she mumbled, aware of the trembling in her voice and worried he would also notice it.

He grinned as if he read her mind. "Just so you know. I like my meat bloody."

Shaking from head to toe, she hurried through the doorway. She wished she could close the glass door behind her. She needed a cold drink to relieve that dryness in her mouth.

James walked up to her and aggressively grabbed her arm. "Where have you been? You were away for nearly forty minutes!"

She noticed the guests eyeing them with curiosity.

"Do you mind? You don't want to create a scene, do you?" she muttered while she nodded at his grip on her arm.

"Let. Her. Go," a soft voice said behind them. The tone was calm, but each word was loaded with threat. The sound made the hairs at the back of her neck rise up and gave her goosebumps all over her body.

"Mr. Lynch!" James gasped, quickly releasing her and stepping away from her. "I-I'm sorry. It's j-just," James stammered.

Erin patted James on his arm to reassure him. She peered up to see Dane furiously staring at her hand on the bodyguard's arm. She immediately removed it, trying to ignore Dane as she spoke to James.

"I'm sorry, James. I was in the garden—"

"With me," Dane interrupted.

She set her jaw and tried to suppress her anger. Now he'd made it sound as if she had been intimate with him while she should have been working.

"Working! I wanted to see if there was anything suspicious on the river. There wasn't. I didn't realize I had been away for so long. If there is anyone who should apologize here, it's me."

There. See, I can be humble. Nikko would be so proud.

"Oh, that's fine. I just wondered where you were." James shot her a warm smile, and then peered at Dane as if he was trying to appease the flare of anger in his eyes.

"Do you want me to watch the main entrance?" she offered. She only wanted to go home and hide from the inquisitive stares. She tried to pay no heed to Dane, but saw his brow furrow into a frown out of the corner of her eye.

"Ah, there you are, the elusive Mr. Lynch! I was worried you had already left us." Star walked up toward them beaming a bright smile.

Erin tried to suppress a grin when she noticed how Dane unsuccessfully attempted to chase away the actress with an aggravated glare.

He must have noticed Erin's mischievous delight, because his brief glance at her promised retaliation.

She swallowed as a nervous knot twisted in her stomach. With difficulty, she focused her attention on James, who was telling her something work-related.

"...and if you watch the entrance until midnight, we'll switch positions afterward."

"Sure," she said, and she walked toward the front door. She watched James descend the stairs to the basement.

Why is he going down there?

She worried if she would end up having to witness another orgy after all or, even worse, find herself caught up in the middle of one. The stirring of her leopard whenever it took a peek at Dane was unexpected. Fortunately, Dane's disturbing behavior had successfully cooled off her cat.

She caught Dane staring at her and sighed.

How can I get rid of the voices if I let him chase me away from Hope Acres?

"So Altman, you wanted Vincenzo to introduce me into the supernatural community? Brilliant idea," she whispered.

"Oh, come on, Erin. This guy is really tasty," Leila said.

"That man is our enemy."

"I saw the way he leered at you. I'm sure you could convince him to forget his homicidal tendencies..."

"I'm not sure it would be a good idea to ever get near him again," she disagreed.

"I think you should test that theory, get up close and personal with him now," Leila mumbled.

Erin was about to ask the others what their next move should be when a familiar voice behind her interrupted.

"They say it's one of the first signs of madness, you know."

"What?" she snapped as she spun around to find Victor standing behind her.

"Talking to yourself. Hello there neighbor, what a coincidence seeing you here." Victor smirked.

"What? I'm talking into an earpiece. What the hell are you doing here? Are you stalking me?"

"I was invited. I'm very popular. Didn't you know that Star is interested in anything that isn't human? Witches and vampires are present at every party. She especially likes doggies."

She frowned at him. "I've always been more of a cat person myself."

"Oh me too, I just love the pussies." Victor laughed.

She surveyed the room to see if she needed to be anywhere else. Unfortunately, nobody was misbehaving.

"Do you mind talking to someone else, someone who is interested? I have to work."

Victor continued to laugh while he ogled her cleavage.

She peered down and was relieved her nipples weren't showing.

"Yes, I can see that. I suppose I could leave you, so you can continue talking to yourself or whoever you're talking to. It's probably more interesting than talking to me, right?" He brushed a finger across her earlobe, and she realized that both her ears were highly visible with her hair tied up in a ponytail.

Crap! He knows I just lied about the earpiece.

As he walked away, she tried not to panic.

He probably just thinks I'm crazy.

He couldn't know about the voices.

He doesn't know anything.

"I don't believe in coincidences," Altman said.

Erin agreed with him. However, to appear sane, she chose to remain silent.

While she watched the guests from the entrance, the party continued without any interruptions. She had not seen Dane for quite some time, not that she had been looking for him, of course. She noticed some giggling adults going down to the basement and hoped that whatever was happening down there would not require any interference from her. She had just decided to find James when a howl from the basement caught her attention.

It has to be Victor.

Anxious, she gazed outside. The full moon mocked her.

TOUCHED BY MADNESS

What the hell is a werewolf doing at a party with humans during the full moon, anyway?

She didn't care if she upset the guests. She removed the gun from between her legs before walking to the door of the cellar.

Several people screamed and fought to get out of the basement in a hurry. They didn't appear to care if they hurt others on the stairs while they escaped.

She refused to waste her breath urging them to stay calm. Her goal was to enter the basement and eliminate the threat.

She smelled the blood first. Disgusted, she sensed Altman's interest. She gagged as the stench of sweat and urine hit her next. When she reached the bottom of the stairs, she heard someone, or rather something, whining as if in excruciating pain.

She stood in the open doorway of the cellar, beside an industrial-looking metal door. Weapon raised, she slowly entered the room, then froze in horror. Obviously, Star Knight's darker side turned out to be S&M-oriented.

Goosebumps broke out over Erin's body. The room contained flickering torches, candles and leather masks—things that made her uneasy. A basket made of straw holding whips and canes stood next to an examination table that was equipped with restraints.

Her eyes widened when she noticed the struggling werewolf strapped to the table.

She had a flashback of herself lying on top of one of those tables with Doctor Quirkhart hovering over her.

Nervously, she tightened her grip on her gun. Feeling a wave of sickness rise in her throat, she swallowed hard and tried to clear her mind. She focused on the problem in front of her.

What the hell is this?

She watched the naked brown werewolf pulling on the chains with all its strength. It was a mess and appeared to have peed on itself. Next to the table and watching him, were two young women in long white gowns. One was a blonde and the other had short black hair.

Erin assumed these were the witches Victor had mentioned because they were wearing occult amulets. The black-haired girl wore doctor's gloves and smelt as if she had bathed in disinfectant. They were both acting terrified, although the blonde also appeared to be excited.

Erin glanced at the male werewolf, and she spotted the two silver rings that had been pierced through its nipples.

Shit! Maybe, after the werewolf calms down I should let it tie up the blonde.

She stared at the growling creature and doubted it would ever be calm.

James and Victor stood in the corner of the room, observing her.

She was tempted to shoot them, but fought to swallow her anger instead. She noticed Victor's dilated pupils.

TOUCHED BY MADNESS

Is he about to shift?

Appalled, Erin wondered if the full moon affected Victor or if he reacted this way because the situation excited him.

She walked up to the creature, which growled at her. The wolf's despairing eyes met hers, but she could see no understanding in them.

"Don't untie him," the woman with the short black hair shrieked at her.

"What the hell were you thinking?" Erin yelled back.

"We are cleansing his body. He wanted us to rid him of the infection!" The blonde sounded proud.

"You can't make a werewolf human by sticking silver in his body. Idiots!" Erin remembered a similar situation where Doctor Quirkhart had tried to make her human. She quickly suppressed the painful memory. She touched the silver ring on the creature's left nipple. The werewolf howled, tears gliding down its cheeks.

"I have to remove the rings. Do you understand me?" she said softly. The werewolf ungratefully snapped at her.

"I'm *so* not cut out to be a superhero," she mumbled, realizing that this was the second time in two days she'd been confronted with a creature that would rather stick its teeth in her instead of letting her help.

"I don't think it can understand anything, Erin." James sounded amused.

"Can't any of you help me out here?" It took an act of will for her to curb her temper. She put the gun on the floor. Victor walked toward the table to hold down the werewolf's legs.

Her hands were steady as she tried to remove the ring, but because the werewolf kept moving around so much, she tore it off its body.

The werewolf cried in agony. The nipple was torn and bleeding. The dark blood covered her fingers. She wanted to apologize. She hoped that it had super healing powers, like her. Deep inside, she experienced the urge to lift the fingers to her mouth to lick them clean. She shook her head, hoping that no one there could read her disturbed mind.

She continued to hold its body down on the table while she used her other hand to remove the other silver ring. Too focused on not hurting the creature, she did not see that the wolf had succeeded in releasing its left paw.

It pushed against her neck and pulled her face toward its mouth.

She shouted and struggled, trying to keep her face from its eager muzzle. Then it attempted to bite her arms. She hissed in pain when the wolf managed to release its other paw and scratch her on her left leg.

Shit!

She climbed on top of the werewolf and managed to grab both paws, pushing them down on the table.

The werewolf tried to throw her off its body by violently kicking its legs.

When did it free its legs? She glanced behind her, shocked to see Victor standing next to James again.

"What the fuck, Victor? What are you doing?"

Acting helpless, Victor raised his hands. "Hey, I don't want to get bitten."

"Asshole! Other than causing a minor sting, a bite won't affect you, but it'll harm me." She panted while continuing to push the werewolf down on the table.

"I can't hold him much longer! James, use my gun!" she shouted.

"I'm not gonna shoot a guest at my boss's party! I'd get fired!" James protested.

"You need to change! You can't defend yourself against a werewolf if you stay in human form!" Leila told Erin.

Erin gazed up at the people in the room. She decided against it.

The werewolf took advantage of her distraction by throwing its body against hers in order to kick her off the table. The back of her head slammed against the floor, and her breath exploded out of her. She let go of the creature's paws.

"Stop that," the dark-haired girl reprimanded the creature as it lay down on top of Erin, breathing heavily in her face. Saliva fell from its tongue onto her lips.

Nauseated, she stopped caring about exposing herself, and her survival instincts kicked in. Underneath the werewolf's body, she felt her hands lengthen as well as her teeth.

Let's see who's biting whom.

"Erin, no! You don't want to expose yourself!" Altman protested.

"Nor does she want to get bitten," Gideon retorted, joining in on the discussion.

As if the creature could sense the cat trying to emerge, it growled while it smelled her. Then it whined.

"A spell anyone?" she whispered as a wet nose touched her neck. She noticed that the girl with the black hair avoided eye-contact.

"Come on, Pauline," the blonde said, leaving the room. "Let's go see Selena." The other woman followed her without sparing Erin a glance.

As Erin fought for breath, her chest heaved, and the wolf's gaze wandered downward. He moved down to sniff her breasts.

Oh, God.

She didn't know what was worse, to get bitten or to be molested by a wolf.

Meanwhile, her hands had become sharp claws. Slowly, as if she wanted to stroke it, she moved the paws up its body toward a vulnerable soft spot. The creature's mouth opened. A rough tongue licked the flesh of her collarbone.

She closed her eyes and considered whining herself. At any minute, she expected its teeth to close over her windpipe and crush it.

Why isn't anyone helping me?

Her paws had reached its heart. She knew she had to be relentless. If she showed any doubt, if it realized what she intended to do, it was going to bite her throat even before she had scratched it. She closed her eyes and inhaled a sharp breath.

Before she could apply pressure on the heart, the head of the werewolf exploded. A shower of blood and flesh particles splattered onto her face.

She opened her eyes to see Dane standing in the doorway, holding her gun. Grateful, but confused, she tried to smile at him. Some blood slid from her cheeks into her mouth. She quickly spat it out and pushed the headless body off her before standing up.

Feeling sticky and tainted, she peeked down and flinched when she noticed her torn dress. She was definitely exposing herself, but hiding her breasts didn't seem so important anymore. Maybe it was because she was covered in blood and wolf-flesh. She couldn't imagine the view was very appealing anyway.

This is what Carrie must have felt like at her graduation party.

All she had to do now was start killing everyone.

She glanced at Victor, feeling murderous.

He's first.

She cursed when she noticed Victor's claws. Fortunately, her own hands appeared to be human again.

James was staring at her with an awestruck expression on his face.

She walked across the room to James and slapped him across the face as hard as she could.

"W-what?"

"Snap out of it! Look at Victor. Don't you see what's happening to him?"

The wolf in question was already growling and reaching out for her.

She quickly stepped aside and caught Victor on the jaw with a fist that carried the full force of her upper body strength.

Victor staggered back against the wall and slid slowly to the floor with his eyes glazed, although unfortunately still conscious.

She brushed past him and took her gun from Dane before walking up the stairs. Tired of fighting, she hoped James would deal with Victor.

"I'm going home. Goddamn celebrity parties!"

She put her right hand on the wall as she walked up the stairs. She saw that her hand left behind a red smudge as she let out a long, deep breath.

Nikko will not be happy.

As she entered the hallway, a woman screamed when she noticed her.

Erin suppressed a smile. She was always willing to provide entertainment.

Star walked up to her and opened her mouth, probably to yell at her. Something in Erin's gaze, however, changed Star's mind.

"I just want my uniform, and then I'll be on my way."

Star nodded as Erin walked away to fetch the clothes she'd left in the bedroom.

TOUCHED BY MADNESS

As she stood in front of the mirror, Erin wondered if she could just leave the way she looked now, but she was afraid of getting arrested.

She was in the bathroom when someone knocked on the bedroom door.

"What do you want?"

No answer.

She was reluctant to open the door, but curiosity got the better of her, and she cracked it open.

There stood Dane Lynch in his black jeans and T-shirt.

Her first instinct was to slam the door shut in his face, so she did. Unfortunately, the door had no lock. She immediately regretted it when he effortlessly walked into the room and scowled at her.

Swallowing uneasily, she noticed his furious stare. He looked as if he wanted to attack her. She took a deep breath and moved backward.

"Turn into a leopard," Leila urged.

"You shouldn't have done that," he said. "Take care. You don't want to make me any more pissed off than I already am."

She wasn't sure what to say. Tonight had been confusing enough, but trying to deal with Dane right now was too much for her exhausted mind. Instead, she examined her bloody body.

"Okay. Well, I need a shower," she muttered and turned toward the bathroom. Before she could reach it, he blocked her path, crowding her against the wall and cutting off her escape.

Avoiding eye contact, she focused on his chest. For a few seconds neither of them said anything.

What does he have to be so angry about? I'm the one with dog guts on my face.

"Thank you for—for what you did in the basement," she stammered, hoping it would appease him, and he'd go away.

When he didn't move and remained silent, she glanced up at him. The impact of his heated gaze hit her like a physical blow.

He leaned over her like a predator taunting its prey. She felt his mouth brush her earlobe, and his breath tickled her skin.

"You know, when I'd imagined you covered in blood, I had pictured it to be your own, not a werewolf's," he whispered.

His comment evoked such rage in her that she managed to push him away from her. "Had you not interfered in the basement, I'm sure that your wish would have been granted!" She cocked her head. "I thought you wanted me dead, so why did you shoot that werewolf?"

A shadow passed over his face, and then it was gone, replaced by a cold smile. "I finally have Merenda's daughter in my territory. The only one to hurt you will be me."

"I thought you wanted me to leave," she said. "If I do, you won't be able to have your revenge."

"If you do? Are you still thinking about staying? Do you want me to hurt you, then?" His firm hand grabbed her wrist, sending a jolt of confounded awareness through her.

"Why are you warning me if hurting me is what you want? Why don't you just take your revenge?" she asked.

"Don't tempt me," he said. "It's a question of timing. Right now, I have enough to occupy my nights, and you are not a priority. However, if you decide to stay you will force me to reassess my priorities."

He released her, and she rushed to the bathroom, shutting the door and hoping the lock would keep him out.

Trembling, she tore off her dress then turned on the shower. She couldn't help but think of Dane.

"You can't let him chase you away," Altman said.

Silently, she agreed.

Still hovering in the bedroom, Dane heard Altman's comment. He shook his head slightly in disbelief. Altman had witnessed his punishments and knew what he was capable of.

Has he forgotten? Does my old second-in-command need a reminder of what I can do?

It irritated him, yet he smiled a dangerous smirk.

"I will punish you, then, Goldilocks," he said in a low, rough voice. "And if you don't want to get hurt, you'd better run and run fast because I'm going to start chasing."

FIVE

Erin flinched at the anger and impatience in her father's voice.

"Come on, ma petite. Don't let me down. Not again."

She tried to tell him she was sorry she was bad, but somehow, her mouth wasn't working properly. Nothing was. Her hands were trembling so badly she kept dropping the heavy sword.

Her mom and Leila were standing in the circle with her, as were two strangers. She liked the man with the red hair. He had winked at her earlier that night. Now they were all frozen, pointing swords at themselves and waiting for her.

She didn't like this game, but she was used to Daddy playing games she didn't like. She also knew what would happen if she didn't play along. The image of her father being upset with her sent a chill down her spine. Fighting her rising nausea, she lifted the sword once more.

She gazed at her father and met his golden-eyed impassive stare.

"You all have to do it at the same time for the magic to work. You want the magic to work for Daddy, don't you, ma petite?"

She wanted her father to be happy, but this was so hard. When she tried to point the sword at her chest, she swayed slightly before finding her balance.

"Now," her father said, and everyone around her fell as one being, a slow-motion pirouette orchestrated by a cruel conductor and staged with the elegance of a ballet.

Just like the others, Erin had pushed the sword down, but a part of her must have been a bad girl because the magic didn't work for Daddy. The sword wouldn't stay inside her, and with a din, it fell on the cold, stone floor of the church.

She staggered backward in agony. Her breath was coming in painful, hard gusts. Next, she dropped to her knees and pressed her hand to her chest. Her palm came away stained with blood.

She looked up to find her father walking toward her. Scrambling on all fours, she tried to get away. But then, she finally realized that it didn't matter if she was a good girl or not, Daddy was going to hurt her anyway, just like the others. Silent tears rolled down her cheeks, but she fought her tall, muscular father with every ounce of strength she possessed. Kicking at him when she could draw her legs up, beating at him until her fists were bruised and aching.

A horrific thought crossed her mind as she glanced at her fallen mother. There was no one left to protect her anymore. The blood seeping out of her chest weakened her. She reached out to scratch his face and long claws extended from her paw.

Her father's eyes widened in shock, and he grabbed her wrist and stared at the paw. "A leopard's paw, you bitch! You stole my power!"

Her father grabbed the bloody sword lying next to her and lifted it. His eyes were hard, glaring down at her with hatred and triumph.

"I will get it back. You will give it back to me, you hear!"

She spotted a dark silhouette out of the corner of her eye. A man was watching them, observing. She felt an odd sense of recognition. His hair was short and as black as the midnight sky. His deep blue eyes found hers. But while she silently pleaded with him, his eyes remained hard with determination and devoid of emotion.

"I will show you how to do it right!" her father said, his mouth set in a cruel line. Then he was stabbing her in the chest.

There should have been pain, but all she could feel was blissful numbness. She thought it was weird that there were no stains on her father's immaculate shirt, but a puddle of thick, sticky blood was pooling around her body.

Finally, she noticed the man walking toward them. Was her mind playing tricks on her? Why did she feel as if she knew him? Was he going to try to rescue her? It was too late, and she wanted to tell him so, but she was getting so tired. She had to close her eyes.

TOUCHED BY MADNESS

Cool lips touched her ear. With difficulty, she forced her eyes to open. Her father, her mother, everyone had disappeared. Like a rag doll, she was lying in a heap on the floor. The man was lying next to her. His breath tickled her neck as he whispered. "I finally get to see you covered in your own blood, very tasty." The man, who had seemed vaguely familiar, became horrifyingly familiar.

Her stomach lurched, and her skin crawled as she felt the scrape of teeth. "Stay here, and next time, I will bite you for real," Dane Lynch promised.

Erin abruptly awoke with her hand pressed against her neck. Her skin burned, and dread filled the pit of her stomach. Without hesitation, she left the bed, drowsily bumping her knee against the pantry as she ran toward the bathroom. She cursed, but didn't give herself time to rub the sore spot. She limped to the bathroom, switched on the lights and took her hand away from her neck. There wasn't a mark on her. She moved closer to the mirror and rubbed the spot, but apart from a tiny mole, her neck was unblemished.

"Doctor Quirky was right after all. I am crazy!" she mumbled.

"Erin, what's wrong? Did you have a nightmare? Was it about Doctor Quirkhart again?"

"A nightmare? Yes, Mom, but not about the asylum."

"Not the asylum?" Altman sounded doubtful.

Erin decided not to respond, but to switch off the lights and go back to bed. As she lay down, she noticed that she had left the curtains open. She groaned as she got up to close the yellow drapes.

She peered outside. As usual, the street was deserted. She rarely saw people outside at night. Occasionally, people went out in packs, afraid of the things skulking in the canals.

Or in the shadows...

The glow from the lamppost next to the gray building prevented her from seeing the small stars in the clear night sky, but she could still see the bright moon.

On top of the lamppost across the street, a giant bird flapped its wings, drawing her attention. The large bird was dark brown with a white head and upper neck.

She had heard that bald eagles were common in this area, but she had not imagined the creatures would be so large. She stared at it, and it stared right back.

She leaned on the windowsill and watched as the animal spread its enormous wings and launched itself off the lamppost. It flew skyward, and she drank in the beauty of the bird in flight, climbing higher and higher until it disappeared in the darkness.

She closed her eyes and put her head against the cold window for a moment. When she opened her eyes and examined the alarm clock, she saw it was only four-thirty in the morning. She sighed knowing she would be wide-awake for the rest of the night. She decided she needed a distraction and left her apartment.

TOUCHED BY MADNESS

The forest next to the bayou was large and easy to get lost in. Cottonmouths and other predators made the forest dangerous for the inhabitants of Hope Acres. Not many people dared to venture there.

She hid her bike behind a tree and stopped to inspect her surroundings. Her superior hearing and sharp eyesight detected no humans nearby. She suppressed the need to shift and waited. A few minutes passed and the only things she heard were the wind blowing through leaves, snakes slithering through bushes, chirping grasshoppers and birds singing peacefully. These sounds soothed her, and a sense of peace settled over her. She quickly undressed after a final look around. Unfortunately, because of Nikko's threat, Erin didn't feel as carefree as usual, but she could not wait. Her muscles jerked as her skin flowed into leopard form. The transformation was less painful because she wasn't resisting it. In fact, she was looking forward to running through the forest in animal form.

The area was her playground, her hidden kingdom. She became a lithe, orange-tinged shape with rosette patterns decorating her sleek body. She was one with the night as the wind ruffled her fur, and the sounds and scents of the early morning tantalized her senses.

She hated that as a leopard she would eat just about any animal. Dogs or birds, nothing was safe from her. Later, she would experience embarrassment when she remembered the rodents she had eaten. But for now, she ran free.

The sun moved slowly across the sky as Dane hurried home. Luckily, as he had aged as a vampire, the rays from the sun hurt less. He could even appreciate the beautiful colors the sun left behind as it rose in the sky.

When he arrived at the house, he was relieved not to find any human demonstrators awaiting his return. He landed in front of the gate and scanned the street. It was deserted. He changed to his human form.

He didn't need to ring the bell for the gate to open. Maura took her job very seriously, and she wouldn't take her eyes off the security monitors for anything unless it was work-related.

He nodded to the camera as he entered the garden.

The garden path had been swept up. The hedges were cut without any leaves sticking out. No dead flowers. Even the water in the pond was clean.

Hazel was responsible for the garden, and he wished he had an excuse to send her away, but it couldn't be because of her work. He should have sent her away after she had sired Jerry, but at the time, a one-year starvation had seemed like the right punishment. It would send out a clear signal to the other vampires. Of course, if she fed, he could use that as a reason to get rid of her.

Much like its surroundings, the building was splendid. The house was built of old, weathered wood that blended into the tall trees surrounding it. Still, he didn't think it felt like home.

He smiled, thinking of Erin as he walked into the building. Perhaps if he had someone like her waiting for him at the house, it would feel as though he belonged there. As soon as that thought had emerged, he cursed.

"Dane?"

He turned to see an exhausted Maura standing in the doorway.

"I would like to retire. Do you need anything?" she asked.

He shook his head and watched her go up the stairs to Eve, her lover.

He felt someone else watching him and turned to face Hazel with a sigh. Apparently, she didn't feel like fighting him, because she avoided his annoyed gaze and slipped into the shadows.

He needed to go to bed. Without sparing Hazel another glance, he opened the door to the basement and walked down the stairs. With all his enemies, he couldn't afford to rest upstairs because all the rooms there had windows.

In spite of the dark location, he had made sure that the basement didn't remind him of a tomb. The room was almost as wide as the foundation of the mansion. Instead of having several chambers in the basement, he had settled for one large room and a small bathroom on the right. The bedroom had all the comforts of the twenty-first century combined with an old-fashioned, four-poster bed and a classical Monet Water Lilies painting.

He took off his clothes, dropped them on the floor and stepped into bed. He climbed into bed naked, feeling drained, yet he found it hard to fall asleep. He kept thinking about Erin.

She was far more impressive than he had imagined her to be. Instead of secretly climbing out of the window after their confrontation at Star's, she had walked down the stairs with her head held high.

Everyone in the room had been staring at her, and conversations had stopped.

She had refused to avoid his gaze, and his admiration had grown as she had walked toward the hostess and held out her hand to her.

A bit clumsily, Star had shaken her employee's hand.

Erin had turned to glance at the werewolf she had called Victor and her colleague, who had cowered in the corner. She had shaken her head in disgust. Then, after giving a small bow to a captivated audience, she had left the building through the front entrance.

Much to his frustration, Dane had struggled to restrain himself from applauding.

Before he had decided to leave the party to follow Erin home, he had noticed that Star hadn't seemed as entertained as he had been, and Victor had appeared apprehensive or even slightly guilty.

Why the guilt? Had he deliberately set up Erin's attack? Does Erin have enemies other than me?

Brock would have to investigate Victor. If Victor was trying to do anything bad to Erin, Dane would deal with it. The only person hurting her would be him.

His first priority had been to find out where Erin lived. Her response to their encounter that evening made him realize she was not going to be chased away so easily, and he wanted to make sure that he got the message across. Luckily, she rode a bike and it had been easy for him to catch up with her in his eagle form.

Altman must not have sensed his presence.

She lived in a neighborhood that was just an inch above qualifying as a slum. Underneath the layer of cement, the foundation of the block was visible.

When she had stopped in front of the crumbling building that she presumably called home, he'd felt mixed feelings. On the one hand, he couldn't wait to have another confrontation with her. On the other hand, he was worried at how eager he was to have that confrontation.

He had gotten annoyed sitting outside her window in his eagle form, watching her turn on the lights and take off her clothes without remembering to close the curtains.

She must have been exhausted. Without brushing her teeth, she had crawled into bed and had turned off the lights.

Deep within the body of the bird, he had smiled. Entering the dreams of humans was relatively simple.

He broke off his train of thought. If he kept thinking about her and the dream they had shared, he would not be able to rest at all. He needed rest so he could have a clear head to face the problems of his vampires disappearing, and to investigate the weird behavior of the werewolf at Star's party.

He knew he should contact Crispin, the alpha werewolf of the Hope Acres pack, before going after one of his werewolves. Hell, he should get in touch with Crispin anyway to tell him about the werewolf whose brains he had blown out. However, he didn't care about politics, and if anyone tried to attack Erin, he would deal with it himself.

His last thought before he went to sleep was that no one was allowed to go after Erin—no one but him.

Hazel was convinced that everyone was asleep. They had to be because she couldn't take it anymore. She needed to call Selena, but Hazel could not afford to have anyone overhear the conversation. With vampires having such acute hearing, it was likely she would be overheard.

She took the Mercedes with the tinted windows, put on her sunglasses and covered her head with a shawl. She knew that she ran the risk of being discovered, but the hunger was intense, and she couldn't suppress the urge to feed for another day.

Luckily, there was no traffic in Hope Acres at seven o'clock on Sunday morning. She jumped all the lights and nearly drove the car into the bayou. After a twenty-minute ride down the woodland trail, she drove onto a small path that led her to a tiny cabin.

She stopped the car. When she opened the door, a beeping sound informed her that she had forgotten to turn the lights off. She cursed, but turned them off before running to the hut.

Smoke came off her body as she impatiently pounded on the door. She swallowed another curse as Eartha opened the door. Eartha was a pale blond witch with a big hatred of vampires. She smiled as if she enjoyed Hazel's discomfort.

"Let me in, Eartha. I need to see Selena."

Eartha continued to block the entrance. "Really? I seem to recall Selena telling you not to come back here. I think she said that she would get in touch with you if necessary."

"Let me in, psycho bitch!"

"Did she call you? Did she invite you over? She didn't tell me. Hmm, is something burning?" Eartha taunted.

"Eartha, stop playing with her, and let her in," a deep sultry voice said from inside the cabin.

"Fine. Hazel, please come in."

Hazel roughly pushed Eartha aside as she entered the cottage.

Selena stood in front of the window. She was just closing the drapes as Hazel walked into the lounge. She was wearing a red nightgown, but didn't look disheveled. No matter what situation Hazel found Selena in, the beautiful black woman always managed to impress her.

Hazel knew that Selena was at least fifty years old, but she did not seem a day over thirty. The witch seemed obsessed with keeping her looks, even if it meant occasionally ingesting vampire blood, but she refused to become a vampire herself. One of the other witches had implied that Selena intended to be a mother someday. Selena a mother—now that was a horrifying thought.

Hazel realized that Selena was waiting for her to explain her visit.

"I'm sorry if I woke you, but I really needed to see you."

"I'm not happy," Selena said, turning to face her. In spite of the anger in her voice, Selena's face showed no expression whatsoever. "I thought we had an agreement. You can't risk exposing us all by coming here. You need to stay cool."

"I thought all vampires were cool." Eartha snickered.

"I'm sorry. I just can't stand it anymore. No more games! We need to get rid of Dane right now!" Hazel shrieked.

"I suppose we could cast a spell on Hazel to suppress the hunger," Eartha said. "I'd love to put a spell on her."

"No, we can't," Selena said. "Dane Lynch would sense that. He'd get suspicious and investigate."

"I don't want your spells, anyway. It's not just the hunger. I can't stand seeing his face anymore! His smugness disgusts me. And he should be made to realize that he's not that strong."

"How can he be smug with all the vampires disappearing? Doesn't anyone blame him?" Eartha asked.

"No, they don't care. Only Karma asked questions."

"How is Karma doing?"

Hazel shrugged. "He's weak. I thought he would have challenged Dane right after Jerry vanished, but he's still waiting. I don't know what he's waiting for—to grow some balls, probably."

"Very charming," Eartha muttered.

"Well, I'm sorry to have offended you, you psycho bitch!" Hazel yelled.

"Hazel," Selena intoned calmly.

She avoided Selena's gaze and mumbled an apology.

"If Karma doesn't get rid of Dane, we will find another way."

"There is something else. Vincenzo is back." She peeked at Selena, but as always, Selena's face showed nothing.

"How can you just stand there? I'm telling you Vincenzo came back! What the hell happened? Why didn't you burn him like Jerry and Rafferty?"

"Vincenzo should have been a message," Selena replied. "Dane was supposed to have found

Vincenzo's body, but without being able to help him. Dane should have been powerless against our magic."

"I guess Dane's not so powerless after all... What are we going to do? What if Vincenzo remembers?"

"Stop your shrieking, you're giving me a headache," Eartha complained.

Selena raised her hand to silence Eartha.

"The vampire is right to be concerned. Have you seen Vincenzo since his return? Has he pointed any fingers yet?"

"I don't know. Shouldn't we stop him before he starts talking?"

Selena shook her head. "That may be just what they're expecting us to do. There might be more security. We will discuss this in detail after you leave, Hazel."

"But—"

"No, we don't want you to draw any attention. If you stay away, they will know that it's you."

"Well, you'd better do something fast," Hazel threatened, "because Dane is getting suspicious anyway, and I'm not going down alone!"

Eartha was about to strike Hazel when Selena grabbed her wrist.

"Don't bother letting me out. I know my way." Hazel covered herself with the scarf and ran outside.

"You're letting that—that *thing* try to intimidate us?" Eartha asked incredulously.

"No, I'm not. She's become a liability. We need to get rid of her. She'll be the next vampire to disappear."

"Won't *he* mind?" Eartha asked.

Selena frowned. "Are you questioning me?"

"No, no." Eartha smiled. "I'm glad."

"I want you to find out how Vincenzo managed to rise again. If there is another witch in Hope Acres, we need to know who that person is. No one will stand in our way," Selena stated before she left the room to return to bed.

Eartha, however, always got up early. Even if she had wanted to, she couldn't lie down. She was too eager to start plotting Hazel's demise.

"Did I hear right? Are we going to kill Hazel?" a soft voice inquired behind Eartha.

Eartha turned to face the last witch who had joined their coven. Like Eartha, Aislin was in her late twenties and pale. But where Eartha's hair was like that of a Scandinavian blonde, Aislin's hair was as black as a starless night. Her hair seemed to reflect her mood. Aislin was always suffering from a bad-hair day. She also suffered from psychic visions.

"I don't mind killing Hazel, but I know of someone who will object," Aislin warned.

"Someone," Eartha derided. "I don't know how you can call that thing a someone! Really Aislin, you have the worst taste in men!"

Aislin refused to let Eartha rile her. "You shouldn't speak so loud. That *thing* might be able to hear you." She kept her voice even and carefully modulated.

Eartha laughed. "Don't fret so. And don't worry about your great love getting upset about our plans for Hazel. We'll let Pauline tell him when it's done. I'm tired of the way that neat freak keeps getting on our nerves."

As Eartha sneered, Aislin frowned at Eartha. Then she shrugged and walked to her bedroom.

The radio alarm woke Erin with a religious song, and she climbed out of her bed feeling exhausted. She quickly turned off the music then took a shower in the dark, hoping that the others would give her some privacy. Luckily, they stayed quiet for once.

Without looking at herself in the mirror, she dried off her body and got dressed in her uniform. Instead of tying her hair back the way she always did, she decided it was time for a change and let it fall loosely down her back instead. She grabbed an apple for breakfast and left the apartment in a hurry.

For the first time since her return to Hope Acres, she managed to arrive on time at the hospital. When she walked into the small security office, she was surprised to find it empty. She inspected her watch and saw that she was only a few minutes early. She had expected conscientious Frank to have arrived by now.

She made a cup of tea and sat down, intending to glance briefly at the screens before doing her rounds. However, the person she saw entering the hospital made her jump up, spilling the hot tea on her trousers.

She cursed and was about to leave the office to put some cold water on her legs when the phone rang.

"Good morning, Erin." Nikko sounded cheerful.

Why does he act so happy?

"What's good about it?"

"Frank's wife is in labor right now, but don't you worry. We managed to find a replacement."

She froze and found it hard to focus on Nikko's words. With a sense of foreboding, she stared at the monitor where a few seconds earlier she had noticed Victor walk into the hospital.

"Who is it?" she asked.

Nikko continued, however, as if she hadn't spoken.

"...expect you to welcome him, show him the ropes..."

"Who is it?" she repeated.

A reply was not necessary. Victor entered the office with a huge, wicked grin on his handsome face.

"Hey neighbor, fancy seeing you here!"

"Hello coward, still afraid of getting bitten?" she grumbled.

She heard Nikko start to complain and hung up on him. Victor's smile had also faded from his face.

Good.

"You don't have to worry about the party. No hard feelings," Victor told her.

She stared at him, confused.

"I'm sorry, but I don't speak Chinese. No hard feelings?"

He cringed, and she smiled as she remembered hitting his jaw. Unfortunately, no bruises were showing as a reminder.

"Why are you here?" she asked. "I thought you considered working beneath you."

He studied her briefly before winking at her. "You inspired me."

"How long are you staying here?"

He shrugged.

She opened a drawer, took out a walky-talky and placed it on the table.

"I suppose you don't need me to explain how this works." Relieved when he shook his head, she walked to the door and pointed to the chairs in front of the monitors.

"Please have a seat. If you see any action on the screens, tell me. Don't even think about handling it yourself."

"Aye, aye, Captain!"

She was about to leave when she hesitated. Standing in the doorway, she turned to face him. "Have you told them?" she asked.

TOUCHED BY MADNESS

When he did not answer her, she clarified, "About you being a werewolf? I can't imagine a security firm hiring a werewolf to guard a hospital."

She thought about the S&M basement at the party, and the excited look he'd had on his face when he looked at the blood.

When he remained silent, she turned around.

"And you? Have you told them?" he asked her.

Shock slammed into her like a tidal wave. She inhaled sharply, her knees instantly feeling weak. She spun around to face him, and the bottom dropped out of her stomach when she saw his knowing gaze. She reached out and gripped the door while her own pulse roared in her ears.

How much does he know?

Forcing a serene smile, she pushed her body into motion. She managed to unlock her fingers from the doorframe and slowly moved toward the hallway. Outwardly, she tried to appear calm, deciding to focus on her rounds. Hopefully the routine of her work would relax her shattered nerves.

Victor's just playing with me. He doesn't know anything. Nobody knows anything. Nobody apart from Doctor Quirkhart, and he's still in England.

I'm safe.

"Are you going to do a round?" Victor's voice was silky smooth, and his face was expressionless.

She gritted her teeth to hold back the exclamation of pure frustration she wanted to hurl at the gloating monster sitting behind the desk. She would not complain and give him the satisfaction of knowing he was getting to her.

She was about to leave the office when the phone rang.

He immediately picked up the receiver. "This is Victor Nichols. Yes, she's here."

She sighed, expecting it to be Nikko. Reluctantly, she walked up to Victor to listen to whatever Nikko was going to complain about now.

"Hey chère, it's Frank. I'm finally a daddy! We called her Daphne, mother and daughter are doin' fine."

"Congratulations," she said. She tried to think of something to say, but her mind went blank.

"We wanted the hospital in Hope Acres, but we were visitin' Janice's mother in New Orleans when the water broke. She's four weeks early, so they'll keep Daphne in the hospital for a while. It doesn't matter. You okay? Who's that guy pickin' up the phone? My replacement?"

She noticed Victor eavesdropping on their conversation and turned her back on him.

"Yes," she answered.

"He's listenin', ain't he?"

"That's right," she said.

"I hope he ain't too good," Frank joked.

She turned around to face Victor. "Not at all."

Victor glared at her.

She heard Frank laugh. "Good. We're expectin' you to visit. Oh, Janice is callin' me, gotta go. Bye."

TOUCHED BY MADNESS

After she hung up, Erin avoided Victor's inquisitive gaze as she left the office and locked herself in the bathroom.

She had mixed feelings about Frank becoming a father and was relieved that he had hung up before she'd unintentionally revealed how she truly felt. She struggled to pull off enthusiasm about Daphne.

She couldn't tell him she wasn't interested in seeing his child. That would hurt his feelings, and he would want an explanation. She put a hand on her stomach and closed her eyes, picturing Doctor Quirkhart. An icy wave crept down her spine, and she opened her eyes.

She heard someone entering the bathroom and realized she couldn't stay in here. She didn't want to face Victor either and decided to do her rounds. Anything was better than being stuck in a small room with a werewolf whose sole purpose in life seemed to be finding ways to annoy her. The only upside of the messy situation was that she was cured of her attraction to Victor. She had not felt even a spark when he had touched her hand earlier.

While she did her rounds, Victor found excuses to talk to her; someone refusing to pay for his dessert in the cafeteria, a couple of nurses kissing, an old woman falling down and why had she been tied to the bed?

Erin had felt a swift rush of panic when he had asked her that question. Luckily, he had not hounded her for an answer.

He also made other comments of a personal nature. He particularly liked her new hairstyle. He believed she should wear her hair down more often. In order to prove that she did not wish to draw his attention, she tied her hair in a bun.

When the tirade of comments from him became unbearable, she went outside to catch her breath.

Hurricane season had started early this year, and it rained nearly every day in Hope Acres. The rain might have reminded her of the weather in England had it not been for the heat. The wind was sharp, whipping her clothes and trying to undo her bun, blowing the tresses it had released against her cheeks.

She stared at her watch. Only twenty more minutes until she could go home. She hugged herself.

How am I going to get through the next couple of days with Victor? Perhaps I can chase him away. And what am I going to do about Nikko? It's as if everybody is out to get me.

When Dane spotted her, a poignant loneliness radiated from Erin, causing him unconsciously to quicken his steps. Before he could reach her, she entered the hospital again. He clenched his fists as she eluded him once more. This unfamiliar emotion grated on his nerves.

He was impatient to see her. He knew rationally that he should not have left the mansion before nightfall. It would draw the attention of his enemies. Acting out of character now would be like waving a red flag at them.

He had spent most of the afternoon awake fighting his gut instinct, which was bawling him out for leaving Erin free to run around Hope Acres when he should have forced her to leave immediately.

When he entered the hospital, he did not need to ask the way. He could find her with his eyes closed by merely using his nose. She used no perfume. The sweet scent of her was more potent and alluring than any expensive perfume could ever be. Her natural scent acted like a powerful drug, an aphrodisiac that his body reacted to.

As he walked toward the room where he sensed her presence, he faltered. She was not alone.

He closed his eyes and inhaled.

Lupine. Male.

He bit back an instinctive snarl. Anger turned his vision black. For a split second, he felt his fangs lengthen in anticipation of the wounds he would inflict on any man who dared to come near her. He opened his eyes and took another deep breath. He had to stay calm and steady. He would force her to leave, and no one would ever know how she affected him.

He entered the office to see Victor hovering over Erin with his hand on her shoulder. Luckily for Erin, Dane saw that she was not amused.

"Take. Your. Hand. Off. Her." He bit out each word from between clenched teeth. His voice was rough and devoid of all civility. He glared at Victor, almost snarling.

Victor quickly removed his hand and took a step backward, bumping against the desk.

"Dane Lynch? W-what are you doing here?" Erin stammered. She froze when she recalled his threat and the dream she had the previous night. He refused to answer her and kept his eyes glued to the werewolf. The two men eyed each other for a long, strained moment, sizing each other up. Dane fixed an intent, hair-raising stare on Victor, as if he was making it perfectly clear that Erin was off-limits to thewerewolf.

She cleared her throat in an attempt to clear the tense atmosphere in the room. She did not really understand what was going on, but it made her feel very uncomfortable.

She didn't like Victor, but she felt she had to defend him from the lethal-looking vampire. She did not want to think about the reason why she felt she had to protect a werewolf from a vampire. There was something inside of Dane, a dangerous and watchful presence that exuded danger. It caused her heart to beat hard in her chest. She placed herself in front of the werewolf while she raised her chin and squarely met Dane's eyes.

"Erin, maybe you shouldn't get involved," Altman warned.

TOUCHED BY MADNESS

"You should get involved. Look at him! That man is sin walking," Leila encouraged Erin. She was probably picturing a scenario where Dane would spank Erin in punishment.

Erin quickly suppressed that disturbing thought. She folded her arms in rebellion and refused to move. She was a security guard after all. It was about time she started acting like one.

"Mr. Lynch, what are you doing in our office?" She was proud that her voice didn't tremble.

"Call me Dane. We have unfinished business, so get rid of the dog."

She frowned as she studied Victor.

How does he know what my new colleague is? Or did Victor betray himself at Star Knight's party?

"Now wait a minute—" Victor began.

"Shoo," Dane growled.

Without wasting another second on Victor, Dane concentrated on Erin, the only person who mattered to him.

Victor muttered something rude under his breath as he left the room. A comment Dane heard, thanks to his superior senses.

"See you tomorrow," Erin said.

Dane studied her as she unlocked her arms. He wanted to applaud her for remaining cool under what he knew must be his ravenous gaze. He also wanted to kill her for defying him.

"Have I entered a staring contest?"

He laughed. "No, but if you had, I would definitely win. I'm sure it's easier for me to stare at you than the other way around."

She frowned. "If you're here about me leaving, then I would like to say that I'm definitely thinking about it."

He remained silent.

"You know, I have a job. I can't just leave. Even if I wanted to, which I do, they won't let me. It's in my contract. I'd get sued."

"If I were you, I'd be more concerned about how to stay alive than mere legalities. We'll talk about it, but not here," he said as he noticed the security camera inside the room.

When she looked down and refused to respond, he said, "We either talk out there or in your apartment. You decide."

She clenched her fists, but nodded.

"All right. My shift has just ended. If you don't mind waiting for the next shift, I can join you in a few minutes."

He smiled with triumph. "Don't worry, Goldilocks. I'm not going anywhere."

The phone was picked up immediately.

"Yes."

"Mr. Stratton, this is Victor Nichols. I—I was given your number."

TOUCHED BY MADNESS

The silence that followed his statement made Victor squirm. He heard a deep sigh.

"You were given strict instructions to call this number only if you had anything urgent to report," Jonathan Stratton reprimanded the werewolf.

"Well, er, I had my first day working with Erin."

"Congratulations," Stratton muttered sarcastically. "We arranged that job for you, so please don't waste my time telling me what we did."

"I'm sorry." Victor hesitated briefly before continuing, "I—I just wanted to tell you that she doesn't like me. She doesn't seem to like anyone. She's too independent. Although... Maybe she does like someone... The master vampire of Hope Acres visited her today."

"Are you telling me that Dane Lynch went to see her?" That did get Stratton's attention.

"Well, yes, but what she sees in a dead guy, I have no idea."

"Don't worry about Dane. I will deal with him." Stratton sounded irritated. "As for Erin's independence..." Victor frowned when he heard the tycoon chuckle. "I have something planned that will have her screaming for help. All you need to do is be near her when the time comes."

Before Victor could reply, a laughing Stratton hung up on him. Victor sighed as he heard the disconnected signal. He wondered what the joke was about. Then he shrugged as he put the cell phone in his pocket. He didn't care that his boss was a jerk. He paid him well for very little work.

He watched Erin and Dane leave the hospital together and cursed when he noticed that the vampire had spotted him. He waved at Dane, but the vampire refused to acknowledge him.

The werewolf got in his car and drove away frustrated, because he could not follow them without risking exposure.

He briefly wondered what Stratton had planned for Erin and what she had done to earn his wrath. Victor then promised himself never to do anything that could enrage Stratton. He seemed quite a vengeful adversary.

SIX

Erin watched as Victor drove off in his small brown Volkswagen. The car was very different from the sleek dark blue Mercedes that Dane stood next to. The sight of Dane sent a chill through her, which she quickly suppressed.

He unlocked the doors and walked to the passenger's side, opening the door for her.

"I'm not going anywhere with you. If you have something to discuss, we will do so here." She was proud that, in spite of the fear he invoked, she was able to stand up to him.

"Besides," she continued, "I refuse to leave my bike."

"Give me the key, and I will put it in the back of the car. It will fit if I put the back seat down." He held out his hand and waited patiently. That she could refuse did not appear to occur to him.

"No, dear, don't go with him. Don't let him hurt you," her mother warned.

"Oh, my God, I can't believe I'm stuck with such boring people. Live a little!" Leila snarled inside her, making her desires plain. Erin's leopard wanted to

play. It wanted to play wild and dangerous games with a horrible man who wished to harm her.

"Why don't you want to get into my car? Are you afraid?" His mocking tone disgusted her.

"I thought you wanted me afraid. It's why you threatened me last night with your little gun routine, isn't it?" Her voice was cold and remote as she turned around to get her bike.

He grabbed her wrists, and she drew in a deep breath, her hands clenching into fists. She wished his rough handling did not arouse her, but her body seemed to have a will of its own. The masculine scent of him filled her nose and her head. She had to stop reacting like a cat in heat.

She hoped he wasn't aware of the fact that she wanted to jump him every time he moved a muscle. He probably already realized it because she saw his mouth twitch a little.

While her wrists were trapped in his tight grip, she felt his thumbs stroke the underside of them. Her nipples tightened in response, a reaction that shot all the way to her loins. She saw him staring at her breasts and tried to pull her arms back in an attempt to cover them.

He did not relinquish his hold and drew her against him, bending over to whisper softly in her ear. "This is what you get for not leaving."

She started to struggle as she felt his warm breath on her neck and the effect it was having on her libido.

He slowly released her from his grip, but she still stumbled in her haste to retreat from him. He moved as if he wanted to assist her, but she raised her hands in protest. "Stop it, mister, no more touching. I'm going home."

She walked toward the lamppost that her bike was tied to. She bent to unlock the chain, frowning as her mind filled with doubts.

If Dane was so adamant about not wanting her in *his* town, then why did he keep seeking her out? His forceful behavior seemed to have an effect on his body too. Leila might be right. Instead of letting him intimidate her, maybe she should try to reason with him and see if she could change his mind.

Her pulse raced, and there was a lump in her throat. She swallowed with difficulty as she turned to face him. "What did you want to talk about?"

"Get in the car," he ordered. He opened the trunk of his car and pushed down the seats in the back. After lifting the bike out of her hands and placing it in the Mercedes, he slammed the trunk shut and moved to the driver's door. He shot a glance back at her that left no room for argument before he took his seat behind the steering wheel.

"Stop stalling. He might be able to help us," Gideon said.

"If he doesn't kill us first," Altman added.

Reluctantly, Erin climbed into the passenger seat beside Dane and slammed the door shut.

He was staring straight ahead, but his mouth quivered. Did he find her amusing? She couldn't find any humor in the situation.

"Fine!" she said. "What is it that you need to discuss?"

She peered at him as he started the car and drove slowly out of the small parking lot. His knuckles whitened as his hands tightened on the steering wheel.

"Seeing you at work and hearing your excuses again, I realize that my message may not have come across the way I intended," he said. "I did not mean *leave tomorrow*. I meant *leave today*. Just so we're both clear on my meaning, I'd like you to repeat it."

His dark gaze didn't blink once as it bore into her eyes. A shiver of apprehension raced down her spine.

"Er, leave today?" she said.

"Now that didn't sound very convincing, did it?" He held up his hand, effectively silencing her before she could speak. "I think you will have to reassure me. You know what happens if you don't," he uttered in a soft warning tone, which was as mesmerizing as his eyes. Although his voice was calm and reasonable, the darker more threatening tone in it seemed all the more deadly.

His blue eyes glowed with an intense hunger that robbed her of her breath when he briefly locked onto the pulse beating in her neck before looking back at the road ahead.

Her throat suddenly felt very dry. "You—you will hurt me?"

"Good. I'm glad that there are no more misunderstandings." He smiled a smile tinged with a good deal of satisfaction, which infuriated her. She tried to put a lid on her anger but failed.

"You know, I think there are," she said.

He squeezed his eyes shut. "There you go, acting all impulsive again."

"Well, I guess you'll just have to exact your revenge on me," she said.

"Erin, what the hell are you doing?" Altman said. *"Stop goading him!"*

Anger flushed Dane's face. "Fine, I've just made you my first priority."

She felt the blood drain from her face, and fear welled in her stomach at the promise of retaliation that shimmered in his eyes. She gasped and covered her neck with her hands.

"Stop the car. I want out, right now!"

He started laughing. "My poor deluded girl, if I wanted to bite you, there are far more interesting places than your neck to sink my teeth into."

"Ugh! You're disgusting," she snapped as her hand went to open the door.

He pressed the button on the dashboard, which automatically locked the car doors.

"That's the pot calling the kettle black, isn't it? You're not exactly human, are you?"

She gave up struggling with the locked door and said nothing. He was right, and if she wanted to be human again, she needed help. She doubted, however, that Dane was the type of man who felt inclined to assist people.

Dane pulled over to the side of the road, turned the engine off and pondered his options. He could kill her or have her kill herself, and be done with it. It was the easy solution. However, as he watched Erin sitting in silence beside him, he felt a deep connection to her that drew him to her like a magnet. He instinctively knew that he would regret the loss of her.

Another option was that he could turn her into a vampire. This solution appealed to him. Her response to the idea of him biting her had triggered a reaction in him that was difficult to subdue. It could also be seen as fitting revenge. He could use Merenda's daughter to regain the vampire her father had taken from him. However, he was aware that making her a vampire would only intensify his already troublesome feelings for her. That was something he was not willing to risk.

The only solution he could think of now was to make sure she got whatever it was she had come to Hope Acres for. The sooner she got it, the sooner she would leave.

"Why are you here? Is it about the voices?" Dane asked.

"V-voices?" she stammered, trying not to show how nervous she was. Did he think she was schizophrenic too?

TOUCHED BY MADNESS

She wondered briefly if anyone had ever made her feel as confused and edgy as he did. There was something in his eyes that made every warning sense shriek at her. It felt dangerous being around him. She was not accustomed to fearing much of anything, but she instinctively recognized the threat he posed to her.

She gave herself a little shake and slowly straightened her shoulders. He already knew too many of her secrets. She refused to let him affect her anymore.

"I know about the voices." His statement caused a shiver to slip down her spine.

Her first impulse was to deny it. She thought about the fourth-floor at the hospital and trembled. Goosebumps appeared on her skin, and she hugged herself, feeling uncomfortable.

"Please don't worry. You're no crazier than I am. In fact, I think that you're remarkably sane for someone who is burdened with these voices."

"What makes you think that I hear voices? Just because I talk to myself doesn't mean—" she bluffed, but ended with a gasp, because he was reaching toward her face. "What—?"

She didn't finish. He didn't bother to answer. His hand had already gotten what it was after, the tight bun at the nape of her neck. He tugged at it once and dislodged the clip that held it, sending her hair unraveling down her back.

She was so surprised that she forgot to protest as he grasped the mane of hair and brought it forward to hang over her right breast. He dropped the band on her lap.

"Better," he muttered as his eyes slowly drank in each of her features, before moving to the long length of curly blond hair that fell to her waist.

Her cheeks burned with embarrassment, which changed to annoyance when Leila started cheering in her head. She wondered what was worse, having Dane want her dead or having him want her sexually?

"I know people. I might be able to help you," he murmured.

"Finally, we're getting somewhere," Gideon said.

Erin wished she could smack Gideon.

Dane gave her a wry glance. "You're afraid to let me help, aren't you?"

"Yes." The single word of agreement was dragged from her.

"I want you to leave Hope Acres. If I help you get what you want, will you then go elsewhere?"

"Why is it so imperative that I leave town?" she asked.

"Don't ask me to explain myself. I might be tempted to go for my other solution, one where you won't be able to ask me anything at all."

Even though she couldn't help but wonder why he didn't, she felt it wise not to push him. Did she really want help from someone who made her feel so ill at ease?

"You shouldn't turn me down. I'm not just a vampire. I'm also the master vampire of Hope Acres. Keep in mind, Erin, that whatever your fears are about me, I'm the only man in the neighborhood who might actually be able to help you with your voices."

"I have no intention of finding myself under any obligation to you," she hissed impetuously through her teeth.

"And what if I offered you a job in exchange for my help?"

"I already have a job, see?" She pointed to her uniform.

"Actually your current job might be a plus. I could use someone in security. In fact, you have already aided me in this case while you were working."

She frowned.

"You saved Vincenzo, one of my vampires, a few days ago. He was in the morgue of the hospital," he clarified.

"Okay," she said slowly. "I'm listening."

"Someone is making my vampires disappear. I want to find out who is behind it."

She shook her head. "I'm not a detective. I don't see how I can help you."

"And you're also not a vampire," he said with a smile. "This means that you can do research during the day."

He started the car and drove toward her apartment while she thought over his offer.

When they arrived at her street, she was still considering it.

"So, if I help you with these vampire disappearances, you will help me with my …

problem, nothing else?" She worded her question carefully.

"That's it," he drawled.

Frustrated, she rubbed her temples.

Should I make a deal with the devil? I need help, and my search is going nowhere...

"Fine, I'll see what I can do. Of course, I will need more information. Maybe I can talk to Vincenzo?"

He sighed. "I'll arrange it. I'll pick you up tomorrow."

"I should probably talk to him alone. You might make him nervous, being his boss, right?"

She thought she saw a flash of annoyance in his gaze, but it vanished so fast that she convinced herself she had imagined it.

"Sure," he agreed. "I'll be here around eight."

Her hand moved to the door handle, and she unsuccessfully tried to open the door.

"Sorry." His apologetic expression didn't seem entirely genuine when he unlocked the door with a devilish sparkle in his eyes a moment later.

She climbed out of the car, retrieved her bike and locked it to a stop sign. Then, without sparing him another glance, she ran toward her apartment building.

Her heart was still pounding when she entered her flat. She rested against her closed door and tried to calm her racing pulse as her plump cat sauntered over to her and rubbed its head against her legs.

TOUCHED BY MADNESS

"You're acting out of character," she noted as she bent over to pet the cat. "Do you want me to clean the litter box, or are you hungry?" She peered up and spotted the closed window. "Wait a minute, how did you get in? You weren't in here when I left, were you? Well, I suppose you must have been. Old age is starting to show."

She saw herself in the mirror and froze. Dark hollows shadowed her eyes, and it took a conscious effort to smooth away the almost permanent frown that had settled between her arched brows.

"Altman, I could really use your help right now. Have I made a huge mistake here?"

"I can't tell you anything about Dane," Altman said.

"Can't or won't?" Gideon goaded.

"I couldn't tell you much anyway, even if I wanted to," Altman continued, paying no heed to Gideon. Gideon started to argue with Altman, and Erin tried to block out the discussion.

She sat down on the bed and flopped backward. An orange ball of fur jumped on her bed and delicately pushed her nose under Erin's hand.

Erin turned to face the cat as she stroked it. "Mmm, aren't you being cuddly?"

The creature then leaped off the bed, walked to her bowl and started mewing.

Erin smiled.

At least you're easy to read.

She got up and fed the animal.

Hazel shivered while staring into the dark sky. She felt cold drops of rain splash against her face and roll down her cheeks as it began to downpour.

"And where are you running off to on this wet evening?" a calm voice asked.

She froze and cursed under her breath. She recognized the smooth voice behind her, which had taken her by surprise. When she turned around, Karma was staring at her.

"Shouldn't you be watching Dane instead?"

His mouth twitched. "Maybe I'd rather watch you."

"Is that because you're afraid to confront Dane? Don't you want to be Dane's successor anymore? All you do is make snide remarks at him. I think you're too scared to openly attack him. Scared he'll use his infamous blowtorch on you..."

Karma burst out laughing. "That's what I like about you. You're honest about your dislikes. I find that very refreshing."

"Sorry, I'm not attracted to gray-haired men."

He continued to smile. "You're forgiven. I'm usually not attracted to redheads, but I am willing to overlook that flaw—you haven't answered me yet."

"That's because I don't have to answer to you. Get rid of Dane and maybe you'll get a reply."

TOUCHED BY MADNESS

Before he could reply with an adequate response, she made a run for the car, but his laughter followed her every step of the way.

While she drove toward the cabin, she repeatedly checked the rear-view mirror, expecting to see Karma following her. She gave up when she realized that if he wanted to follow her, he could do so without a vehicle.

Her stomach twisted into a nervous knot while she examined the sky. If there were any large birds out there, she wouldn't be able to spot them in this light. She wasn't able to see much anyway because of the heavy rainfall. The windscreen wipers were working overtime, yet the world remained blurry.

Fearing a car accident, she decided it would be safer for her to wait for the weather to calm down. She parked the car and turned on the radio. After searching for a little while, she finally chose a channel with classical music before closing her eyes, trying to relax. When Albinoni's Adagio came up, she almost smiled as it made her think of funerals, in particular, her own. It dawned on her that she'd be having another funeral if Dane found out she had betrayed him. After a moment, she didn't see the humor of it anymore and quickly turned off the sound.

The noise of the rain tapping on the roof seemed to be diminishing. She scanned the forest surrounding her. Even the dark trees towering over her appeared dangerous. Disgusted, she shook her head at her irrational fears. She wasn't any better than the humans she despised, bathing in light and banishing every shadow.

She grabbed her cell phone, and after a moment's hesitation, put it in her pocket. She decided to overlook the weather, and after one final glance around her, drove toward the center of Hope Acres.

Within five minutes, she had reached the Majestic, where she left her car. She was relieved to find the dingy motel empty, even the reception was unmanned. Using the pay phone next to the reception desk, she keyed in the telephone number that she'd memorized weeks ago to diminish the risk of anyone finding it.

The phone clicked as it was immediately answered.

"Selena, is that you?" Hazel asked.

"Where are you calling me from?"

"Don't worry, Selena. I'm not using my cell phone. They won't trace this call. I'm using a pay phone at the Majestic."

Irritated, Hazel clenched the receiver when she overheard Eartha cursing in the background. "That stupid bitch, as if you can't trace the number from a hotel!"

"Why are you risking exposure?" Selena sighed.

"No, it's just the opposite," Hazel denied. "I'm trying to avoid exposure, right now! Tonight Karma asked me several questions as I left, and I believe he had me followed. I can't see you tonight."

"Yes, you were wise not to come over. We will discuss our final move next week, agreed?"

TOUCHED BY MADNESS

Astonished, Hazel nearly dropped the receiver. "Final move, really?"

"Final for whom?" she heard Eartha snicker in the background.

Hazel inhaled sharply, too horrified to think properly. Eartha must have thought it went unheard, but the comment was not uttered softly enough to be hidden from a vampire with ultra-sensitive hearing. In an attempt to hide her suspicions, she made agreeable noises as Selena suggested a new date before hanging up.

Hazel dropped the receiver back into the cradle, hoping she had fooled the witches when she responded. She tried not to panic and wondered if she might be overreacting. Eartha could just have made a joke, and it might not have been at her expense. If it had been, maybe it was not based on something the witches had planned. God, she hoped not, but the more she attempted to rationalize what she had heard, the worse she felt. What had that offhand comment meant?

She realized that her newfound allies were beginning to look more like her enemies.

The plane was due to arrive at ten-fifteen at the Louis Armstrong airport in New Orleans. Victor wasn't too worried when he finally parked his car around eleven p.m. at the garage. Because of 9/11, airport security had become so thorough that it took foreigners about two hours to go through customs and passport control. He thought it would be nice if all that extra security discouraged foreigners from visiting his country. Although, he was willing to make an exception for his new colleague, whose slight British accent he found sexy as hell. Of course, Erin wasn't actually British, so she wasn't really an exception after all.

When he reached the arrivals hall, a couple of people were waiting at the doors.

Victor took out a sign with the name of the man he had to pick up. He leaned against the wall, hoping he didn't have to wait too long.

The tall, skinny man caught Victor's attention as soon as he walked into the terminal. Instead of looking weary after a long flight, he seemed remarkably alert in comparison to the other passengers.

He wasn't surprised when the man spotted his sign right away and decisively walked toward him.

Victor met the foreigner's icy gray eyes and speculated on what secrets they might hide. He doubted that Jonathan Stratton would tell him much, and the stranger didn't seem very talkative.

"Hi, my name is Victor Nichols. As you can see, I'm here to pick you up. Please call me Victor." He swallowed a growl when the man gave him his luggage. He forced a serene smile. "And what may I call you?"

The man regarded him as if he were a bug he would have liked to step on. His unblinking stare gave Victor the creeps. Then he pointed at the sign in his hands. Victor frowned as he read out the name.

"Mr. Quirkhart?"

The man sighed impatiently. "Doctor, it's Doctor Quirkhart."

SEVEN

Erin deliberately put on a pair of old jeans and a turtleneck sweater just before Dane was due to pick her up. It was probably too warm for a pullover, but she didn't want to flaunt herself to a vampire. It seemed unwise to bare her neck to him, but then she shivered as she remembered his comment about there being other places to bite. The jeans felt safe, because she could move easier in them than in a dress. Not that she ever wore dresses, much to Leila's chagrin. She only put on dresses if someone forced her to, like at Star's party.

"Could you at least put on some lipstick? Or maybe do something with your hair? Wear it down?" Leila whined. She had been nagging the whole evening. Instead of putting her hair in a bun, Erin compromised by wearing a ponytail.

I don't want to send out the wrong signals.

She peered out of her window when she heard an engine roar outside. A black SUV pulled up in front of her building and parked there. She had expected the Mercedes, so she didn't move away from the window until she was sure that it was

TOUCHED BY MADNESS

Dane waiting for her. When Dane got out of the big car, she grabbed her keys and left her apartment.

As she reached his SUV, he regarded her with a mocking smile. "If you want to stop me from touching you, then you should let your hair down." Before she could respond, he reached out. His hand loosened her ponytail, and an instant later, her curly hair tumbled down around her shoulders in glossy tendrils. His hands threaded through the golden tresses with tactile pleasure.

She briefly wondered what it would be like to be embraced in his warm arms before mentally kicking herself and pushing him away from her.

He let her shove him back and pointed at her pullover. "You're going to melt in that. It's been boiling hot all day." He ogled her covered neck. "If you think that a turtleneck will deter me, then you're sadly mistaken."

"I have no idea what you're talking about. I'm only here to assist you with those disappearing vampires, and then you'll help me, right?"

He chuckled. "Right." He walked to the passenger's side of the SUV and opened the car door for her. She shook her head at him, but accepted his invitation and climbed into the car.

He waited for her to sit down before slamming the door shut. "Have you eaten already?" he asked as he sat down beside her.

"Yes, have you?" she retorted.

He roared with laughter.

She stared at him in silence, wondering what the hell he was laughing about. She hardly knew him, yet she knew enough to sense that his cheerful behavior was out of character. Perhaps she had watched too many horror movies and allowed them influence her perception of vampires.

He reached for her hand, but when she tried to keep it from him, he wrapped his hand around hers and drew it toward his chest.

"Erin, if I promise you I won't sink my teeth in your neck tonight, will you promise me you'll try to relax?"

Reluctantly, she nodded. "I'll try."

When he didn't move, she continued, "Can I have my hand back now?"

She was relieved when he released her. It was much easier to breathe when he wasn't touching her. Suspiciously, she eyed him as he started the car. Without thinking, she wondered out loud. "Did you put a thrall on me?"

She didn't trust his smile. It was too much like that of a large cat, which had just spotted a weakened prey. She realized too late what she had just admitted.

"Why?" he mocked. "Do I have you *spellbound*?" His eyes glowed with triumph, and satisfaction curved his wide, sensuous lips into a devilish smile.

She moaned with embarrassment and shrank into her seat.

He winked at her. "Oh, come on, there's no need for shame. I'm a vampire. I see the signs. I detected the response of your breasts when I held your palm against my chest, even through your thick sweater. Didn't you think I'd notice? And when you shift uncomfortably and cross your legs, don't you think I can imagine the response in other parts of your body? Hell, I don't need to imagine it. I can hear your heart racing when you're near me."

Turning her head, she felt her face burn.

What else does he know?

Before she could think of a clever comeback, the car stopped in front of a large gate blocked by several demonstrators carrying placards. They shouted at the car's occupants, and one woman hit the car with a threatening sign, which read:

'Go back to your graves or we'll make sure you do.'

"Fucking Divine Right fanatics," Dane mumbled. Casting a sideways glance at him, Erin wondered if the protesters had a death wish.

She hesitated for a moment before speaking, wondering if it was wise to share her suspicions with Dane. In the end, her dedication to her job decided for her.

"Have you ever considered that they may be responsible for killing your vampires?" she asked.

He nodded. "We did at first, but not anymore. Thanks to your interference with Vincenzo, we now know the killer is working with witches. The Divine Right hates witches as much as vampires, or maybe even more so, believing that witchcraft is a choice, whereas some vampires are made against their will."

She shivered, wondering if he had been one of those vampires. Before she could think of a way to ask him, the gate opened.

136

When he grinned at the demonstrators, they realized he would not hesitate to run them down and quickly moved to the side of the car. They continued yelling as the SUV drove through the gateway that shut automatically behind them.

"Home, sweet home," he said as he got out of the car.

She raised her hand to the door handle, but before she could open the door, he stood in front of it ready to assist her to the driveway.

She shook her head when she caught her first glimpse of the mansion. It looked as if it dated back to the civil war, with white pillars lining the front steps, which led to an ornate veranda. Cyprus trees dotted the vast lawns surrounding the four-story mansion.

She half expected a southern belle to step out of the front doors at any moment.

"I shouldn't be surprised since you drive around in fancy cars. You're filthy rich, aren't you?"

He merely smiled.

Erin walked up to the pond to examine the large carp snapping at invisible bugs in the water.

Dane approached his front door with the sudden realization that he was nervous about showing her his house. He wondered if he could tempt her with its riches, but then resented her for causing such a thought to appear in his mind. He didn't want to feel as if she had to approve of it since she was not going to live here in the future. Or was she? Would he give her a choice?

Keeping her makes me look vulnerable.

But seeing Erin here in his territory made Dane realize that he did not care about what signal her presence might send to his enemies. He entered the building and waited for her to join him. He briefly imagined himself locking the door shut as soon as she set foot in his hallway. He caught her staring at him and beckoned her inside.

Erin felt a little lightheaded while walking into the wide entry hall. It was like stepping back in time and into a luxurious plantation house. He must have spared no expense on his collection of furniture and art. Given that he'd probably had over a century to collect it all, it was no surprise that his collection was so impressive.

Unless he inherited it from the previous master vampire after he had killed him. She immediately suppressed that thought and returned her attention to her surroundings. A warm glow of light illuminated the artwork on the walls. High above the stairs hung a large chandelier, and when she tilted her neck backward, she saw angels painted on the ceiling.

She thought she heard Dane murmur, "Welcome home."

Her pulse jumped. When she turned to confront him, she discovered he had moved on. Worried that she was becoming paranoid, she said nothing and followed him.

They entered the first room on the left. Once inside the room, she spotted Vincenzo seated in front of the fireplace.

Vincenzo jumped up to meet them. "Dane asked me to talk to you. What can I assist you with?" Vincenzo asked.

She opened her mouth, but before she could respond, Vincenzo continued, "Not that I think I can tell you anything that I haven't already told Dane. As a witch, you probably know more about what happened to me than I do."

The day before, she had asked Dane to leave when she questioned Vincenzo, but now she regretted that request.

She peered at Dane. He did not act as if he intended to leave her alone with him anyway. With Vincenzo's hostile behavior, she did not think it mattered.

She sighed. "Fine, just tell me what you told Dane. What do you remember?"

Vincenzo looked at Dane before answering. "I found a note from Dane, saying I had to go to town to get Karma something to eat. It wasn't a weird request. I have to get food for our guests all the time. As I walked to town, I was about to cross the bridge, when I felt something hit me, something sharp. And then I passed out—until you woke me up."

"You walked to town? That's quite a long walk. Didn't you have a car?" she asked.

"Eh, no. I guess not."

"I thought Dane owned several cars. Isn't it weird that they were all gone?"

The vampire shrugged. "Not really, we're all allowed to use them."

"Why?" Dane asked. "Do you think that someone deliberately took the cars so that Vincenzo had to walk?"

She shrugged. "It's a possibility."

Dane nodded. "We'll discuss it with Brock. Come, there are others I want you to meet."

Ignoring Vincenzo, Dane took her arm and led her to an office where a chubby girl was staring at a monitor.

A pretty brunette had her head on the girl's lap, and her long hair was being stroked. They seemed to be in their own world and Erin wanted to keep walking and leave them alone.

Dane, however, had other plans. "I want you to meet Maura and Eve."

"Evening, Dane," Maura said. "So you are finally bringing a woman with you. It's been so long. I don't even remember the last time you did that." She stared curiously at Erin. "Hmm, nice."

"Er, thanks."

"I'm Maura."

"Maura is responsible for the security here. Eve works at Starlight. She dances there."

"Hi, I'm Erin." She glanced at Dane, wondering if she should talk to the women about the missing vampires. As if he'd read her mind, he shook his head.

"You'd better not show her to Hazel. Hazel would go mad," Maura warned.

After Erin and Dane had walked to the next room, Erin asked, "Why would this Hazel character go mad? Is she your ex-girlfriend?"

"Why, are you feeling jealous?"

"No, not at all." She shrugged. "In fact, I think it would be fine if she stayed your girlfriend. Hazel is such a lovely name."

"Coward. You never let me have any fun," Leila wailed.

Dane couldn't quite believe the conversation. Erin seemed perfectly serious, which was something of a blow to his self-image. At least her half-sister was attracted to him.

Suddenly, a horrible thought crossed his mind. Did this mean that if Erin and he were to sleep together, the others would be there too? Appalled, he thought of the other people who had died during the massacre; Altman, Gideon—her mother!

Gritting his teeth, he realized that once more he was visualizing himself sleeping with Erin. And why did he keep undoing her hair?

He thought about the evening they'd first met. He remembered how the voices had been shouting inside her head, and how she had held on to him. He recalled how his touch had made the voices disappear. His lips twitched as he imagined a solution that required a lot of touching.

They entered a formal dining room. A gold chandelier hung above a long, stately dining table.

Dane showed her the kitchen. Her eyes were immediately drawn to a huge refrigerator. Why would a vampire need such a large one?

After casting a quick glance at him, Erin approached the cabinet. She was surprised when she opened it and discovered large pieces of meat, vegetables and bottles of orange juice.

"You'll find what you're searching for in the drawer."

She turned to scrutinize Dane, who grinned at her. "Go on."

She pulled open the drawer of the fridge and found several bags of blood. Unable to control her expression, she felt her nose wrinkle up in disgust.

He laughed. "Don't you wonder what the food is for?" When she frowned, he continued, "We have to feed the people we get to bite."

"There are people who volunteer for this? Never mind!" She raised her hands to prevent him from answering that question. "Aren't those bags sufficient?"

"Yeah, but who would choose canned food when you can have a nice fresh juicy steak?"

Appalled by the idea of people being willingly used as food, she slammed the door of the fridge and was about to leave the kitchen when she noticed a blowtorch standing next to the kitchen sink.

Dane's favorite torture device.

In horror, she stumbled backward to get away from it, right into his chest. She spun around to face him, and their eyes locked. A faint smile played on his lips that made the hairs rise on the back of her neck.

"Crème brûlée?" he joked before walking past her and climbing the stairs. Gritting her teeth, she forced herself to follow him. They reached the top of the staircase and entered a wide corridor with a hardwood floor.

He knocked on one of the doors. After a few moments, a male voice invited him to come inside.

He opened the door and stepped into the room. "Hello, Brock. I'd like you to meet Erin," Dane said.

A tall black man emerged from the bathroom, wearing a pair of jeans and a white shirt. He was nearly as tall as Dane was, but there was a breadth to Dane's shoulders and a hard, lean quality about the rest of him that was worlds apart from Brock's youthful physique. Brock appeared to be in his early twenties whereas Dane had probably been turned when he had been in his mid-thirties. Brock was rubbing a towel against his wet hair.

"Even his bare feet are sexy," Leila whispered.

Erin disagreed, even though Brock was attractive. It was the difference between boy and man, and that difference was power. Erin felt more at ease watching Brock because he came across as a less threatening vampire than Dane.

When she noticed Dane frowning at her, she decided to concentrate on the room instead of on Brock. The modern room seemed very out of place in the dated mansion. The walls were white, apart from the right wall, which was painted a bright orange color. This wall was also covered with at least fifteen African masks. There was a mahogany table against the back wall with two uncomfortable-looking bright green chairs set around it. A pink lamp in the shape of an artichoke hung above the orange bed.

She thought for the second time that evening that the decoration of the house reminded her of pictures from an interior design magazine. The house's lack of a soul prevented it from becoming a home, or perhaps the inhabitants were responsible.

"No coffin?" she asked.

"No, we like to be comfortable when we sleep," Dane explained. "Brock, I've asked Erin to inquire into the vampires who have vanished, so you two may find yourselves working side by side on that issue."

Brock's mouth dropped open with shock, and he froze. After a moment, his expression reset to a serious one.

"You have been investigating it for quite some time now, and I'm sure Erin's input would be much appreciated," Dane continued.

Erin eyed Brock, feeling cautious as she became aware of a growing sense of unease.

"Dane, could I please talk to you alone?" Brock asked.

Dane nodded before leaving the room with the younger vampire.

Erin glanced around still feeling uneasy. She took a seat in one of the green chairs while she watched Brock follow Dane out in the hallway.

Dane noticed his new second-in-command was in fighting form, judging by the glare in his eyes when he closed the door to his room and turned to face him.

After Rafferty had disappeared, Brock had been reluctant to take over Rafferty's position. Dane knew that Brock was a closet nerd and that he preferred numbers to people. He was also aware that Brock believed Maura would have been a better second-in-command after Altman's death and Rafferty's disappearance.

Brock had originally been an exchange student from South Africa, who had been turned the night he had arrived in New Orleans. That had happened in the late eighties, but Dane still thought of Brock as a relatively young vampire.

He hoped that Brock would gain more confidence in his new position as time went by. Unfortunately, in order to hide his insecurity, Brock tended to compensate for it with a bad attitude. As Dane approached him, Brock seemed to stiffen with anger.

"How come you're asking an outsider to take over my investigation? Is this your way of telling me that you are dissatisfied with my work?"

Anger welled in the back of Dane's throat. He wasn't used to having to explain himself, and he didn't intend to start now. After glaring at Brock for a moment, he conceded. These were difficult times, and he couldn't risk alienating the few allies he did trust.

"She's not taking over your investigation. She's merely aiding us. She might be able to follow suspects at times we can't go outside."

"What suspects? I've been busy investigating her!"

Dane gave him a sharp once-over. "Your first priority should be the investigation of the three missing vampires. Weren't you able to get anything sensible from Vincenzo?"

"Has anyone ever gotten anything sensible from Vincenzo?" Brock displayed a dry smile.

"And your investigation of Erin, did you find out anything about her?"

Brock nodded. "She spent most of her childhood in a mental hospital. Are you sure you want me to work with a crazy person?"

Dane thought about the two of them working together, and he had to suppress the instincts that were yelling at him not to leave her alone with any other male, even if that male owned every Star

Trek, Star Wars and X-Files DVD in existence. He realized he didn't know Erin well enough to judge if she had similar interests.

"Although," Brock continued, "if I were to work with her, I would get to know her a lot better. I wouldn't need an additional investigation."

Dane's nostrils flared in annoyance as he exhaled. "There is no need for you to continue investigating Erin. I have decided that you should focus on who is making my vampires disappear. You will, however, work with Erin on the missing vampires. She may not be a professional private investigator, but she isn't like any other human being out there either. That might be useful to us."

"Oh, I almost forgot. You also asked me to investigate her new colleague Victor Nichols."

"Well?" Dane snapped.

"I discovered something strange in his financial records. Jonathan Stratton pays him."

"That's not so strange. Jonathan owns Securistate. The werewolf just started working there."

"Then why has he been paying Victor for five months? Isn't that how long Erin's been in Hope Acres? I wonder what kind of work he did for Mr. Stratton."

"Find out," Dane said. "But investigating what happened to the missing vampires should be your first priority."

Brock nodded. "You're the boss."

TOUCHED BY MADNESS

Nothing more needed to be said. They walked back toward the room where Erin was waiting for them.

Erin stood up when she saw the two vampires re-entering the room. She eyed them with curiosity, but couldn't read anything from the expressions on their faces.

"I don't know what Dane has told you about the vampires who have disappeared, so I'll tell you all I know," Brock said. "Within the last two months, three vampires have disappeared and only one of them has come back. Vincenzo was clearly abducted, and because of the timing, we decided it was prudent to investigate the other two disappearances too. From the information we have gathered, we now believe the other two were murdered. We checked Rafferty's and Jerry's financial records, and so far, they still haven't used their credit cards or bank accounts."

"Do you know if there have been other people or beings in Hope Acres who have also disappeared lately?" Erin asked.

"Er, no." Brock hesitated. "I'll explore that."

She tried not to grin, but failed. She was quite pleased that she was able to contribute.

"The first vampire to disappear was Jerry. We weren't suspicious because he'd only been a vampire for a few weeks. He'd been having problems adjusting. And then, twelve days later, Rafferty disappeared. Dane believed that he probably wanted to be in charge of his own group of vampires, but his absence was unexpected because it was out of character for him to leave without saying goodbye."

Taking a small notepad out of her pocket, Erin quickly scribbled down a few words. She didn't want Dane to complain at a later date that she hadn't lived up to her end of their bargain. Lord knows what payment he would expect if she didn't help him with this.

Payment in kind, probably.

An erotic image of herself and Dane flashed across her mind and taunted her. He was a perfect specimen of male flesh, and she pictured herself crushed beneath his muscled body, succumbing to his devilish touch. The sudden imagery caused every female hormone in her body to wake up and take over her conscious thought. For a moment or two, she felt an almost desperate need for him to grind his hard body against hers.

What would he feel like? Would he handle her roughly or slowly drive her insane?

It was frightening that she was reacting so uncharacteristically toward him. Right now, she could only think of him and the way his eyes watched her, half-closed and sexy. It must be the leopard hormones.

An annoyed cough from Brock interrupted her train of thought. She inwardly winced and felt herself blushing furiously under his intent examination.

For an instant, she was certain he was reading her mind. Appalled by the thought, she shot a glance at Dane. There was something disturbingly sensual about the way he was watching her. In the next breath, she told herself it had to be her imagination.

"I'm sorry, I was just thinking about something. Could you please repeat that?" She was relieved by the steadiness of her voice.

Brock scowled at her. "I just spoke about Vincenzo's disappearance, how it didn't make any sense to us. He wouldn't dare leave us and risk invoking Dane's wrath."

"And he didn't leave of his own volition, he was taken," Dane added. "Thanks to you, we are now a lot closer to finding out what happened."

"Do you have any idea who is behind it, and why?"

Dane sighed. "You mentioned earlier that the cars were perhaps deliberately missing so that Vincenzo was on foot the night of the abduction. If someone here is involved, I'd put my money on Karma. He arrived in Hope Acres a few days after Jerry disappeared and has been openly hostile toward me. It's quite obvious that he seeks my position as master vampire. However, I have other enemies. Humans are often eager to rid themselves of vampires. You saw the vampire hate group outside the mansion earlier. Last month, a woman attacked me with a stake."

"What happened?" she asked, shocked that anyone would dare to attack someone as powerful as Dane.

Dane shrugged. "There were cameras, so all I could do was break her wrist to force her to drop the weapon."

She couldn't help but wonder what would have happened to the woman if there hadn't been any cameras.

"They do seem to have murder on their mind."

Brock shook his head. "That attack was impulsive, unlike the disappearances. Rafferty was very strong and smart. Killing him would not have been possible without a proper strategy. These vampire hate groups aren't organized enough to pull that off."

"Anyone else?"

"I suppose anyone living here could be considered a suspect, even me," Brock stated. "Now that Rafferty is gone, I have taken over his position as second-in-command."

"Yes, but after that Vincenzo got taken, and since you weren't able to prevent that, it made you look bad. I mean, why would you make yourself look bad? Though it reflects badly on Dane also..."

Dane laughed heartily after her comment. She noticed Brock staring at Dane with his mouth wide open before he turned to watch her instead.

Flustered, she averted her eyes. "Sorry, Brock, I didn't mean to criticize your work."

"No, your reasoning is quite sound," Brock agreed easily. "If I wanted Dane's position, going after Vincenzo wouldn't have been such a bad move. It makes him seem an unfit leader." Brock cringed. "No offense, sir."

"You mentioned other people living here. How many vampires are there?" she asked.

"Right now we have seven vampires and two humans staying at the mansion."

"Do all the vampires here want to be a master vampire?"

Brock shrugged. "I doubt it. Some vampires don't have the skill to lead, and I believe they know that. Vincenzo and Eve are followers. So is Hazel. However, Hazel has never forgiven Dane for getting rid of Gregorio, the previous master of Hope Acres, just weeks after he had sired her."

"And the two humans, who are also living here?" she continued.

"Allison cleans the house, and Tamara belongs to Eve and Maura."

Puzzled, Erin wrote down the two names on her list. "Belongs?"

Brock smiled. "Yes, don't worry about Tamara. She's quite happy with the two vampires."

"Don't ask, Erin. Sometimes ignorance really is bliss," Gideon warned her.

"I think you know most of it now," Dane concluded.

"You forgot to mention the witchcraft," she added quickly.

"Ah, yes," Brock said. "Vincenzo showed me the glass jar. He told me that you had performed some magic to make him regain consciousness. What did you do?"

"I just used a simple healing spell with the help of the elements. It's what I had to do before that was actually the hardest part. Someone had put a wormlike creature inside him."

"A dema?" Dane asked. "Where the hell did they find that?"

She shrugged. "To take it out, I had to cut open Vincenzo's mouth. Unfortunately, I got electrocuted every time I touched him."

"Electrocuted? How could Vincenzo end up in the hospital morgue if nobody could touch him?" Brock asked.

"I assume it was a spell to stop witches from touching him, so we couldn't help him."

Brock nodded. "A spell to electrocute witches on touch. That sounds very specific. I'll investigate it."

Dane turned to Erin, who indicated she had no further questions. He nodded at Brock and swiftly left the room, obviously expecting her to follow him without being asked.

Picturing a dog following its master, she fumed in silence. She felt Brock's stare boring into her and decided she had no choice but to follow Dane.

Disgruntled, she followed him out of the room and into the wide hallway. As she walked down the stairs, she glared at his back.

"Master vampire, right! He's not my master!" she grumbled to herself.

The soft knock on her door was the only warning Hazel received before Karma strolled into her bedroom. He didn't spare a glance at her Ming vase on the dressing table or the display case filled with Faberge eggs and marble animal statues from Kenya. His eyes were solely focused on her, as if his gaze alone could pin her to her bed with fear.

She knew he was more powerful than her, but she refused to allow him to walk into her room whenever he wanted to. She sat up on her bed and flung her book onto the floor in anger.

"I didn't say you could come in," she snapped.

He grinned. "Well, fortunately, I'm not someone who waits for an invitation."

"Get out," she ordered.

Appearing unconcerned, he leaned against the door, smiling at her. His light blue eyes seemed to glow.

"Go stalk someone else." She waved him away in a shooing gesture.

"Now why would I do that when it's so much fun to stalk you? You do so many interesting things."

She outwardly scowled, feeling a nervous flutter in her stomach. "What's that supposed to mean?"

Instead of answering her, he walked up to the bed.

She quickly rolled off it and stood in front of him, belligerently sticking her chin out. She was determined not to cower in his presence and glared at him instead. "Stop harassing me."

"Or else what, you'll call out for help? Go right ahead," he mocked.

When she remained silent, he smirked. "I thought so. Who would want to help you?"

"I may not have any allies here, but I am not completely powerless. I'm quite willing to prove that if you need convincing."

"You're a fledgling. Do you think you can fight me? Do you think you can fight Dane?" His smile had faded, and he was studying her face as if he could read things in the back of her mind that even she didn't know.

She squirmed.

Does he know anything about what I'm doing, or is he merely fishing?

"Why would I want to fight Dane?" She forced her voice to remain calm.

"I heard that you're not allowed to feed for a year, because you turned Jerry without Dane's consent. That seems pretty harsh, although the previous master vampire of Hope Acres would probably have killed you for changing humans without his approval. Though maybe not," he thoughtfully continued. "I've been told that the Ancient Gregorio had a soft spot for you, his last child."

She lowered her gaze, but felt her cheeks heat into a blush betraying her discomfort. She could tell that he found it easy to read her. She wanted him to leave before he found out more.

"You've been unhappy ever since Gregorio died," he said. "Maybe you think you can avenge him?"

She glanced up and tried to keep her expression neutral to hide the flicker of anxiety she felt.

He appeared not to notice, but he could have been pretending. "The problem here is not what to do if you get caught. The difficulty lies with succeeding. What happens if you make Dane look so bad that the council replaces him? Who will replace Dane?"

She said nothing.

"You won't be able to replace him. Not even if you were older. You're just not a natural leader."

Wearily, she brushed her hair from her face.

"So they will choose someone else. And that person will know what you did to the previous master vampire, and he won't trust you. The first thing on the new master vampire's agenda will be to make sure that you won't betray him too. And how do you think he'll do that?"

She moved silently backward until her legs touched the edge of the bed. She didn't want to answer him because she thought that would seem like an admission.

He drew closer and pressed himself against her. His body was a solid wall of muscle. "If I were your master, what do you think I'd do?" he whispered.

She shivered at his tone and tried to push him away, but she wasn't able to move him. "Let me go!" she cried. She lifted her eyes and glared into his.

"You know what I would do? I'd make sure you were too afraid to defy me," he continued.

"You don't scare me." Her words came out strangled and husky. Her hands clenched in exasperation.

He grinned. "Yes, I do."

He stepped back, bowed derisively and walked to the door.

"See you later," he said as he left the room.

The door closed behind him with a loud click.

She stood very still, her mouth agape and her mind unable to form any coherent thought. She shook her head, clearing it. Exhausted, she dropped onto the bed with a feeling of defeat.

"Just what I needed, another enemy," she whispered. She curled into a tight ball and closed her eyes.

"So, what do you think?" Dane asked Erin as they entered his room. He rested his shoulder against the ivory wall of the basement room.

She glanced around the brightly lit room. Because of the multitude of white lights embedded in the ceiling, it seemed like daylight even without windows. Lights flickered on the bearskin rug, reflecting the flames from the roaring fire. A leather chair and a white couch faced the fire. It seemed Dane had strategically used pillars to support the house instead of interior walls, to create a large open-plan space. The only walled-off area was the bathroom.

"Are you interested in my Jacuzzi?"

She ignored him and tried to avoid staring at the imposing four-poster bed—she failed miserably. Each dark carved post was adorned with various rings and hooks. Her heart skipped with a combination of fear and excitement.

Noticing her curiosity, he shifted and closed in on her, like a predator with a target in sight.

She felt her skin heat up although the room was pleasantly cool. She trembled with fear and excitement. She shouldn't be attracted to him, and the signs of his interest in bondage should make her run away while screaming hysterically, but they didn't.

She thought about the institution. Doctor Quirky had enjoyed tying her down too. She suppressed her fears and walked toward an impressionist painting of water lilies.

"Nice. I wouldn't have pegged you as a flower-loving guy," she said.

He chuckled. "Did you expect something dark and depressing? It's my home. Would you enjoy living here?"

"No," she answered decisively.

His blue eyes flamed. "No? Why not?"

She shrugged and continued to take in her surroundings. "You need more than expensive furniture to turn your house into a home."

She smiled to herself. "My ideal home would be a little cottage where I wouldn't be afraid to live. I wouldn't want to live in a place where I had to worry about breaking things." She felt her smile fade when she turned to face him. In spite of his blank expression, she felt compelled to take a cautious step backward.

"Uh oh," Leila mumbled.

"What's wrong?" she asked warily.

A dark smile twisted on his lips. "I guess I'm not happy that you're criticizing my house."

His eyes burned into hers, and it felt as if the walls were closing in on her.

Does he think I'm going to stay here? Is that why he wants me to like his home? Doesn't he want me to leave anymore?

"Sorry. The house is stunning, but—"

"You're making it worse," her mother warned.

"Perhaps I should go home," Erin managed. She took another step back, but his hand snaked out with blinding speed and wrapped itself around her wrist.

She was too proud to beg him to release her, but she also realized the danger of standing so close to him with him touching her.

His impact on her senses was devastating. She gave herself a small, imperceptible shake in an effort to free herself from the disorientating sensation that was sweeping through her.

TOUCHED BY MADNESS

She forced herself to act. "Dane, I'm going home now."

He released her, although he appeared reluctant to do so. "Don't you want to talk about your problem first?"

She stared at her arm. The skin was still tingling from where he had touched her. Her instincts told her she should go, but she wasn't getting anywhere with her search. He did seem to be the best candidate to assist her, and he didn't act as if he wanted to punish her anymore for what her father had done.

Isn't my attraction for him worse, more dangerous, in some ways?

She shook her head.

All I need to do is remain sane and not give in to temptation. How hard can that be?

"You've been here now for a couple of months. What have you found out?" he interrupted her thoughts.

"Not a lot." Her voice sounded hoarse, so she cleared her throat. "I couldn't find out anything from the adoption agency. All I managed to find was an article in the library. Apparently, there was some kind of ritual killing where there was one survivor. The—er, voices said that was me, but I don't remember it."

"Do you want to remember?"

She was about to say 'yes', but she hesitated. "I'm not sure. If I could become normal without remembering something traumatic, then I would prefer that. But if the only way for me to become normal is by remembering it, then I guess I'll just have to remember what happened."

He frowned. "What do you mean by normal?"

She pulled a face when she realized that she was probably insulting him.

"You know what I mean."

"You think that if you can undo what happened that night, you'll be normal again when you don't even know what you were before that night?" His voice softened to a velvet murmur.

Defensively, she folded her arms across her chest. "What's that supposed to mean?"

"You must know that the victims of the massacre twenty years ago weren't exactly human. What makes you think that you were an exception?"

She closed her eyes at those smoothly spoken words, shaking her head. A knot of fear twisted in her belly. She opened her mouth, and then closed it again blinking at him.

After a moment, her curiosity got the better of her. "Okay, I'll bite," she said. "What can you tell me?"

He shrugged. "Not a lot, but I can help you remember."

She sighed. "Why do I have a feeling that I'm not going to like what you're going to say next?"

"Because you're clever, Goldilocks," he purred. "I will need to get into your head."

She didn't like the sound of that. "And how do you plan to do that?"

He grinned, flashing his fangs. His canines had elongated into sharp white points.

She shivered, feeling both uncomfortable and intrigued.

What would it feel like if he sank those into me?

"We will have to exchange blood," he said with a wicked gleam in his eyes. He seemed eager to devour her.

She inhaled a short, sharp breath and crossed her arms over her stomach. "Forget it. That's not going to happen."

He cocked his head and strode across the wide room. He stopped in front of her with only an inch between them. She could feel his hot breath on her skin as he stood dangerously close to her. Her breasts brushed against his muscled pectorals as her chest rose and fell when her breathing sped up. Her pulse was racing, and his close proximity played havoc on her body.

A glint of devilish delight appeared in his eyes. It sent a shiver of excitement down her spine. He winked at her, and a mixture of annoyance and desire flushed through her. On the one hand, she wanted to strangle him for playing with her. On the other, she wanted him to tease her more.

"I'm serious, Goldilocks. I'll have to bite you."

EIGHT

Without thinking, Erin followed her instincts as she tried to push Dane away, but she was unable to move him, so she took a step back and turned around to leave instead.

"Good luck with your missing vampires! I will try to solve my own problems another way."

"Why are you so afraid of intimacy?" he asked.

"It has nothing to do with intimacy! Besides, you'd promised me you wouldn't sink your teeth in my neck."

He shrugged. "I said only for tonight."

She scowled. "Well for me, it's never! No one wants to get bitten."

"I will gladly let you bite me, anytime, anywhere," he contradicted in a soft voice.

"Thank you for your generous *help*, but I won't be asking for your assistance in the future. Please don't bother driving me home. I'd rather walk. Goodbye." She went up the stairs and opened the door.

"Erin." Her name was spoken with icy menace that caused her to pause. He was telling her not to move, and she resented him for it.

"I will let you go for now, but the next time you enter my house, I will not."

She spun about and speared him with a glare. "There is no need to threaten me. You won't see me here again."

He slanted his head, and his eyes twinkled with mischief. "I believe that you could resist me, but I don't believe you can resist your own nature."

She felt her cheeks flush. Her chin trembled as she turned her back on him. She walked through the doorway and was about to close the door behind her when she heard the vampire repeat his threat, "Next time, you will stay."

And surrender.

She was shocked when she believed she had overheard his thoughts. Inhaling deeply to calm her nerves, she shook her head.

It must have been one of the voices.

A bell rang as the four witches entered the voodoo store in the French Quarter of New Orleans.

Pauline eyed the closed sign on the door. It told tourists that the place was closed, but the lit candle in front of the window indicated to genuine black magic practitioners that the store was open to them. Apart from the candle on the windowsill, the tiny store was shrouded in darkness. Whenever she visited the place, she felt uncomfortable in the eerie-looking room, which had large voodoo dolls and Haitian artifacts littering every dark corner.

The store provided tourists with harmless products such as voodoo ritual kits, gris-gris bags, candles, incense and books about spells. The harmful products were in the basement, where the witches were headed. The heavy smell of burning incense was giving her a headache, but her stress over the upcoming meeting was probably the real reason for her pain.

She gazed at the other witches and felt disgusted when she saw how eager Eartha was.

Every time they went to New Orleans, they performed a blood sacrifice. Eartha had probably only joined the coven so she could hurt as many creatures as possible. Selena didn't show any emotion, as usual. Aislin seemed sad, but that was probably because her love life had been terrible because of her psychic visions. Knowing beforehand that your lover wasn't going to stay loyal to you did not tend to improve the relationship. Aislin had awful taste in men and in people in general.

Pauline glanced at her coven.

So do I.

Joining Serena's coven three years ago was the worst decision she had ever made. She should have asked Selena more questions about it first, rather than jump into bed with the devil because she was lonely.

The witchcraft Pauline had envisioned had been Wicca; a very peaceful, harmonious and balanced way of living. Instead she was a vegetarian who was about to witness another blood sacrifice. With great reluctance, she walked down the stairs while hoping that the killing of the black rooster would be swift tonight.

Instead of turning on the fluorescent tube that hung above a circle of chairs, they lit candles to create a haunting atmosphere. Dark shadows danced on the walls, and the faces of the coven were all twisted in this light.

The women were dressed in black and they quickly took their seats while waiting for Selena to take hers. She was always the last to join the circle and seemed to enjoy making the others wait for her.

A chill touched Pauline's shoulder when she heard a cat mewing. She spotted the poor creature, locked in a tiny cage. It stuck its paw through the bars and she clenched her fist, fighting her instinct to release the animal. She saw Selena walk toward the cat and lift the cage. The cat hissed.

Pauline hoped it would attack Selena.

Selena flashed a deadly smile at her.

She probably knows what I think of her and finds it amusing.

Pauline was tired of being thought of as entertainment. Ever since Selena had realized that she could not convince her that killing vampires would benefit the coven, Pauline had become the laughing stock of the group. She swallowed, hoping to suppress her nausea.

Selena sat in front of a small wooden table with a big knife and a bowl. She opened the cage and grabbed the cat by the scruff of its neck. Eartha started chanting with enthusiasm.

The sound made Pauline's skin crawl.

The other women joined her, and to avoid being conspicuous, Pauline pretended to sing as well.

She often worried that one day the coven would turn on her, and use her as a blood sacrifice. During these nights in the basement of the voodoo shop, she realized that she stood out.

In order to be less noticeable tonight, she had left her gloves at home, even though her OCD caused her to feel like a germ magnet whenever she had to touch something.

She contemplated her surroundings and expelled a silent sigh. This was the second time in a week that she was in a basement with Eartha.

She thought about the poor werewolf at Star Knight's party. Eartha had convinced both the werewolf and Pauline that she knew how to help him become fully human again. Of course, the blond shrew had lied to them. When Eartha gleefully told her afterward that Dane Lynch had blown the werewolf's head off, Pauline had fantasized about blowing Eartha's head off.

Poor headless werewolf.

She winced as she imagined its blood dripping down the grimy basement wall. She was tired of dingy basements and of feeling so afraid all the time. She'd had enough of this coven.

Selena began to recite a spell, her voice a low litany of words. The cat limply levitated above the table, silent and motionless.

TOUCHED BY MADNESS

It already looks dead.

The group was staring at Selena while they continued their chanting, and Pauline didn't dare to avert her gaze from the intimidating black woman.

Selena raised the knife and cut open the cat's throat, holding a silver bowl beneath it to catch its gushing blood. Selena's eyes then met Pauline's, and her lips curved in an ironic smile. Selena enjoyed making other people uncomfortable.

"Pauline will have the honor to be the first to drink the cat's essence," Selena stated before passing the bowl to Eartha, who was sitting beside her.

Eartha passed the bowl on to Pauline with resentment flashing in her eyes.

As Pauline took the bowl, she wondered why Eartha didn't see that they were no better than vampires, the monsters Eartha claimed they had to destroy.

Pauline closed her eyes as she lifted the bowl to her face. She breathed through her mouth so she didn't have to inhale the metallic smell of blood. She tried not to think about parasites or anything else that might crawl underneath an animal's skin, imagining it was lemonade she was drinking.

When her lips touched the thick liquid, she gagged anyway. She had wanted to take a small sip, but under Selena's probing eyes, her body seemed to have a mind of its own.

After she had taken one large gulp, she returned the bowl to Eartha, who waited for

Selena's approval before she also drank from the blood.

Pauline put her hand on her stomach and silently prayed that she wouldn't throw up. Looking at the dead black cat that had been dropped onto the floor, she realized she would have to cut open the animal later that night. They would use the cat's body parts for potions.

She could easily imagine lying there herself next month.

They are going to betray Hazel, so why wouldn't they do the same to me?

She wondered if she should warn Hazel. Unfortunately, the vampire didn't seem very stable. If the others found out, Pauline would be punished.

She needed to find a way out. Maybe she could tell Dane Lynch what was going on. Could she do so anonymously?

She glanced up to see Selena's steely gaze locked onto her. With her heart pounding, Pauline quickly lowered her gaze and stared at the floor, disgusted by her cowardly behavior.

What was she thinking? She could never stand up to Selena—she never stood up to anyone.

She had let her parents make her turn down scholarships and said nothing. She had let her manager accuse her of theft and said nothing when they fired her. And she would say nothing while Selena slaughtered hens, cats and vampires.

TOUCHED BY MADNESS

Erin woke up around eleven the next morning. She always slept late whenever she had a day off. She would have enjoyed hiding underneath the covers, but had plans to go to the library instead. On Sunday, the public library was open until one o'clock.

Her room was in a state of total chaos, as usual. She considered cleaning it later that afternoon, but finding out about her past was her top priority today. She was relieved not to have had any nightmares last night and smiled as she saw her cat lounging on the bed.

Erin squatted to pet the animal. "What is going on with you? Have you finally decided to like me after all?"

"At last she's acting like a proper familiar."

"I'm not so sure, Mom."

As if to prove Erin's words true, the cat ran off the bed and jumped on the windowsill.

Erin laughed as she left her bed to open the window for her mewling pet.

The cat pranced out of the apartment without sparing Erin another glance. "She only slept there, because a bed is more comfortable than a floor or a wooden chair."

Erin went back to her bed and lay down to stare at the ceiling.

"So, what are your plans for today?" Leila asked.

"I was thinking about going to the library again," Erin said. "To see if I missed anything the last time I tried to investigate what happened to us."

Nobody said anything.

"Unless you have a better suggestion?" she asked. "Maybe I should go back to that vampire and let him bite me, so he can examine the inside of my brain."

"No, you don't want Dane to ferret around in your head," Altman advised. *"But he is right about you needing to remember what happened. Maybe then, you can reverse the ritual. I'm sorry I can't tell you more about that night."*

"Is it really a blur for you all?" she asked.

"I remember Dad—" Leila stopped talking abruptly.

"Our father, what do you remember?" Erin sat up when the others remained silent.

"Don't stop talking in order to spare my feelings. We came here to get answers. If any of you could tell me more about that night, then he or she should have done so as soon as we left the asylum. You know very well that I don't remember a thing."

Due to the fact that her nightmares kept changing, she doubted that they truly reflected what had happened during the ritual.

She rubbed her face and closed her eyes. As usual, whenever she tried to think of her father, she drew a blank.

"I'm sorry, honey," her mother said gently.

"Me too. It's just that I thought my last memory of that night wasn't useful," Leila justified herself. *"I only remember him telling us that he had a surprise for us at the church. You were giddy with excitement.*

TOUCHED BY MADNESS

I was terrified. I knew from experience what Dad's surprises were like."

Erin felt herself growing cold. Had she really been excited about her father's 'surprise'?

She opened her eyes, got up and discovered that her legs were trembling. Her stomach heaved. She grabbed it and tried to swallow the acidic fluid finding its way up her throat. She failed.

After flushing the toilet and rinsing her mouth, she took a long shower. When she stepped out of the shower, she felt a wave of dizziness wash over her and gripped the sink to steady herself.

She caught a glimpse of her reflection in the steamed-up mirror and wiped away the steam to study her face. Her features seemed to belong to a stranger. Her human face had an alien appearance. She frowned when she realized the irises of both her eyes had dilated, and the white around her cat-like eyes had disappeared. She covered her golden eyes and prayed they would turn human again.

"Please, please, please," she muttered.

"I shouldn't have said anything," Leila said.

Erin opened her eyes and shook her head. "Don't blame yourself. You only did what I asked."

She cursed when her eyes continued to be inhuman. She couldn't go out looking like this.

She wondered if other people had noticed that she didn't look entirely normal. Doctor Quirkhart had known she was different.

Is this how he had known?

She shivered, trying to suppress thoughts of her sadistic psychiatrist. She shook her head. "Never mind, I'll just wear sunglasses."

Still slightly shaky, she put on a pair of jeans and a black T-shirt, leaving her hair to fall down her back. She was relieved that Leila made no comments about Erin not tying her hair back. It had nothing to do with Dane, who seemed to enjoy watching her hair move around freely. She just couldn't be bothered to deal with it right now.

She put on a pair of dark glasses and left her apartment.

The library was quiet when Erin walked into the building. She saw only a plump librarian, who appeared to be in her late forties putting away books on the shelf.

She walked toward her. "Hello. I'd like to visit the archives again if it's okay?"

The librarian nodded, and after laying down the books, she moved to the counter, took a key out of a drawer, and handed it to Erin.

Erin smiled at her while taking the key. "Thank you."

"Please let me know if you need any help," the woman kindly offered.

After thanking the librarian again, Erin opened the door to the archives and searched once more for articles about the murder. Like last time, she only found one. It was in the same drawer she had left it in a few months ago.

She took the article and made a photocopy. After that, she sat down and reread it.

RITUAL KILLING LINKED TO BODIES FOUND IN DEVEREAUX CHURCH

Last Saturday, police entered the Devereaux church in Hope Acres to find four bodies pierced with swords. It has been confirmed that these were the victims of a voodoo-style ritual killing. There was one survivor. A seven-year-old girl who has been hospitalized.

Officers from New Orleans aided their Hope Acres' colleagues to investigate the Devereaux church after a phone call alerted the policemen that illegal activities were taking place that evening. Because of Halloween, the police decided to take extra precautions. Philippe Lepareur, chief of police, stated that he had expected more problems because of Hope Acres' large supernatural community.

"I was informed by my forensic colleagues that the wounds in the ritual killing appear to be self-inflicted," he told reporters today. The police have a description of a sixth person whom they believe to be involved in the ritual killing. The chief would not confirm whether the bodies found were human or other. The police are looking for witnesses.

When Erin glanced up from the article, she noticed the librarian regarding her with a smile. "Were you able to find what you were searchin' for?" the woman asked.

Erin was about to answer affirmatively, then she hesitated. "I—maybe you could help me. I'm doing some research on a killing that took place here about twenty years ago. Perhaps you remember something about it?"

The librarian nodded. "You mean at the Devereaux Church? Yes, I remember." When she spotted the puzzled expression on Erin's face, the woman laughed. "It's not hard to remember somethin' like that, honey. We're a small town. Fortunately, we don't get a lot of murders here. So when they do occur—well, you know."

The woman saw the copy of the article from the New Orleans Telegraph and nodded. "I'm afraid that the article you found is the only article that was written about the killings."

"Really? That's weird. I'd expect more of a fuss since something like this had never happened in Hope Acres before. Wouldn't the reporters consider it big news?"

The librarian seemed flushed. "Well, I'm afraid that the whole affair was kinda covered up."

When Erin frowned in confusion, the woman pointed at the article. "My husband, the chief of police of Hope Acres, kept it quiet."

"Why would he cover it up?"

"In those days, there was an economic crisis, and we needed all the tourists we could get. The mayor was afraid that bad press would chase them away, and he asked Philippe to..." The woman trailed off.

"Yes?" Erin asked.

As if realizing that she was giving information about her husband to a stranger, and probably worrying that her husband wouldn't approve, the librarian seemed reluctant to continue. "I'm sorry, do you mind telling me why you are investigating something that happened over twenty years ago?"

Erin weighed her options and decided to tell her the truth, hoping it wouldn't turn out to be the wrong decision. "I'm the seven-year-old girl they mention in the article."

The woman surprised Erin by starting to laugh. "Omigosh, but that's wonderful news! Philippe always said he wanted to know what'd happened to you. After you left the hospital he tried to find out what happened to you." She eyed Erin's sunglasses with curiosity, but shrugged when Erin made no attempt to remove them.

"Perhaps you wanna meet my husband? I'm sure he'd love to meet you. You come over tonight, we gonna ball some crawfish. I'm Betty Lepareur, by the way." The woman held out her hand and Erin shook it.

"Erin Holland." Erin was about to accept Betty's offer when the sound of a book falling on the floor startled her. They both spun around to see Victor standing behind a bookcase about three feet away from them.

"I can't believe we didn't notice him!" Altman complained.

"I wonder how long he's been standing there." Erin's mother sounded worried.

Silently, Erin agreed with them.

Victor raised his hands in the air and tried to appear innocent as he apologized. "Sorry, I know—library, shush."

"What are you doing here? I didn't think you could read," Erin sneered, causing Betty to frown at her.

Victor chuckled. "You're right. I don't read. But they also have DVDs, and I thought I'd check them out."

"No we don't," Betty contradicted.

"You don't? Oh, that's too bad. Perhaps you have books with lots of violence that you could recommend?" Victor went on.

"There are some books in our horror section that you might find interestin'. The recommendations are on top."

Betty waited for Victor to leave before she continued talking. "Your man is very handsome."

"Oh, he's not my man," Erin hurried to explain.

"But he's very attractive, don't you think?"

"He's not my type," Erin whispered fiercely. She couldn't see Victor, but she was convinced that no matter where he stood in the library, he would be able to overhear them with his werewolf senses. "Listen, I've got to go now, but I'd love to come over tonight and talk to your husband, if he won't mind seeing me."

"Great. Let me just write down the address." Betty walked to her desk again.

Erin turned around to find Victor, but he seemed to have disappeared.

"As if I would be that lucky," she mumbled to herself.

Betty returned to Erin and handed over a piece of paper with the address. Erin took it and thanked her.

"Can you be there at seven? And try not to eat before comin' over. I'm a great cook," Betty proudly declared.

Erin waved at the librarian before leaving the building. She had only taken two steps when she heard a familiar voice behind her.

"So what are you up to now?"

Irritated, she turned to face her pesky colleague. "Victor, could you please stop sneaking up on me? Isn't seeing me at work enough?"

"Ah, but during the weekends, I miss you," he drawled.

"You're not denying that you're following me?"

He shrugged casually. "You're right. I wouldn't have gone into the library if it weren't for you."

When she frowned at him, he continued, "I saw you from across the street entering the library, and I suddenly realized that I owe you an apology. That's why I followed you."

"An apology, what for?" She could think of many situations where his behavior had been less than honorable, and wondered which one he planned to apologize for.

He avoided her gaze. "I should have helped you at Star Knight's party, and I wanted to say I'm sorry."

"Wonders will never cease!" Altman exclaimed.

She silently agreed with her vampire companion. She was about to say Victor was forgiven when she realized that Victor had been in the library for at least fifteen minutes without making himself known. The only reason she knew he'd been there was that he had dropped a book on the floor.

What if that book hadn't fallen?

"Why didn't you tell me you were sorry straight away?" she demanded.

"You mean last week at Star's party?"

"No, I meant when you got to the library. I was there for quite some time, and you hadn't made yourself known to me. In fact ... I think you would have stayed hidden, had it not been for that book you dropped."

"Okay, you caught me," he responded breezily. "I was curious when I overheard you saying you needed to search the archives. I wondered why someone from out of town wanted to see records of a killing that took place twenty years ago."

"But you didn't know then that I was investigating a killing," she retorted.

"You go, girl!" Leila encouraged her.

"Okay," he admitted. "I thought I would be able to find out more if I stayed hidden. It was only curiosity... What were you trying to investigate?" he asked when she didn't say anything. "I know you think I'm worthless, and my actions haven't always been ... helpful, but I'd like to make up for it. You know I'm a werewolf, so you know I'm super-strong, right?"

179

She nodded but remained silent.

He chuckled. "Good. If you need to intimidate someone, so that he or she can tell you what happened all those years ago, you could use someone like me, right? I can be very intimidating."

She laughed. "I'm afraid that the only person who needs to tell me what happened during the ritual killing twenty years ago is me, and I don't believe intimidation can make me remember what happened."

"Oh, honey, I'm not sure you can trust this man," her mother warned.

"Too late, but maybe he can help her. He should be part of a pack. Maybe their Alpha can help her. Not Victor, though. He's obviously a bum," Altman concluded.

"Really?" Victor sounded shocked. "Are you telling me that you survived that?"

"Don't act so surprised!" Her lips curved in an ironic smile. "You managed to overhear everything else we said. I suppose I have your werewolf senses to thank for that!"

He didn't deny it. "And how about your senses?" he murmured coaxingly.

"What about my senses?" She tried to sound casual, but the tremble in her voice betrayed her discomfort.

A grin curled the corner of his lips as if he derived enjoyment from unnerving her. She glared at him while her heart thundered.

He took a predatory step closer, but she stood her ground. She refused to feel intimidated, even when his eyes drifted shut, and he leaned over her.

She could feel the heat coming off his body. He was so close. His nose was only inches from her neck when he inhaled.

"You don't smell human," he said.

She willed herself not to move, run or show any emotion at the werewolf's comment even though he had just given utterance to her greatest fear. She thought of the remark Dane had made the previous night. What if she miraculously managed to undo what had happened all those years ago only to discover that she had never been normal to begin with? She frantically shook her head. She refused to believe that.

"I am human!"

His nose touched her skin as he continued to breathe her in. "I smell cat on you. I also smell magic and power. I even smell death—vampire?"

Frustrated, she pushed him away. "Fuck off! Don't be ridiculous! How can I smell like a vampire when I'm clearly very much alive?"

He opened his eyes and let his gaze travel over her trim figure. "Yes, you're right. You are indeed very much alive. I hear your heart thundering in your chest. Thanks to my inner wolf, I know your heart has been beating in a nervous gallop ever since we started this conversation about your otherness."

He continued to ogle her as if she were a tasty morsel.

TOUCHED BY MADNESS

She crossed her arms so tightly over her chest it was a wonder she could breathe.

"My otherness? It's only because of that ritual that—that I smell this way. Once I know how to undo it all, I will smell just like anyone else."

"Really?" he taunted her. "And how will you undo the ritual?"

She sighed. "I need to remember what happened. Maybe I can turn the ritual around, somehow...?"

"And what, make those who died come alive again?"

She shook her head. "No, but maybe I can help them cross over or something like that."

"Cross over? What the hell is that supposed to mean? I'm not going anywhere!" Gideon complained.

"Hey, me neither," Leila protested.

"Shut up, you two, what did you think would happen?" Altman asked.

"Why would the other victims need to cross over? Are you seeing their ghosts?" he asked curiously.

"I'm going home. I'm getting a headache. I'll see you tomorrow at work."

"Well, I'm going home too, and as it happens, I live in the same building." He managed to walk beside her in silence for only a few minutes. "You know, I've been thinking—"

"Can't you shut up for a little while?" she grated through set teeth.

"No-no-no, this is a good idea, I swear!" He rushed out the words. "I think I know how you can make yourself remember what happened."

"How?" She couldn't hide her skepticism.

"With hypnosis! It's very simple. I can't believe you haven't thought of that."

"I don't..." She hesitated.

"Fortunately, hypnosis isn't like religion. You don't have to believe in it for it to work. All you need is a good shrink."

She was unable to suppress a flinch.

He continued as if he hadn't noticed her discomfort. "In fact, I even know a shrink. He works on the fourth-floor in our hospital. Isn't that a coincidence?"

She studied him with suspicion. "Yes, that is a coincidence, very much so. How come you know a shrink?"

"Oh, come on," he joked. "Someone as fucked-up as me must have seen a shrink at some point in his life, don't you think?"

"He's right," Altman said. *"However, I don't think you should see the same shrink he went to see. Obviously it hasn't been working!"*

She giggled, and Victor pulled a puzzled expression.

"I don't think you should see a shrink. You don't want to end up in an institution again. What if we end up with another Doctor Quirky?" Leila asked.

She shuddered when she thought of her old nemesis and shook her head. "I'm glad you've seen a shrink, Victor. Although somehow I doubt it helped much. Thank you for your advice, but I don't do shrinks. I'd rather not remember."

She had been so caught up in their conversation that she was startled when she realized that they had already arrived at their apartment building.

"Well, as always, it's been a pleasure," she said in front of the entrance.

"I'm going up too," he said with a smile.

She groaned when he let her walk in front of him. She rushed up the stairs in an attempt to leave him behind.

When she turned at the top of the stairs, she noticed that he was still smiling. The pervert had probably been enjoying the view. She stopped in front of her door and opened her mouth to say goodbye, but he interrupted her before she could utter a word.

"I understand that you don't want to try hypnosis. But I wish you would let me help you."

"Maybe he's not so bad after all," Leila mused. *"You should reconsider sex with him."*

"Leila! Stop it!" Erin's mother countered.

Erin squeezed her eyes shut when she noticed the eagerness on Victor's face. "Hmm. Okay, I might be able to use you after all."

When he nodded, she continued, "Good. I'd like you to get my records out of the archives. They are on the fourth-floor."

"What file? And why can't you get it yourself?" he asked.

"I want to know what the doctors wrote about me when I arrived at the hospital twenty years ago. Maybe I remembered more then."

"And what makes you think that those records are on the fourth-floor?"

"Because Nikko told me they were. He said when he hired me that I wasn't to go to the psych ward on the fourth-floor. Security guards aren't allowed in there unless it is an emergency. The ward is off limits because they want to protect the patients' privacy and also because the records of all patients are kept there."

"Can't you try breaking into the hospital computers instead?" he proposed.

"Oh my God, the werewolf has a point!" Altman sounded shocked.

"But I could be wrong," he rushed to add. "Computers can easily be broken into, so they probably only use paper records. I think we should go to the fourth-floor—Oh, and X-rays. Those can't be put into computers, right?"

"No, you were right. It was almost as if Nikko was telling me to go there."

When Victor frowned, she added. "Reverse psychology. If he says 'don't do this' then I will do it, so for some reason, he wants me to enter the psych ward."

"So they can lock you up when you get there? Erin, you're such a paranoid idiot!" Gideon complained. *"What's next, you seeing Doctor Quirkhart?"*

"No. I'm not going in there," she said. "And you don't have to either. You're going to help me break into the hospital computer."

He slowly shook his head, and she grinned as she opened the apartment door. "Why the sad face, Victor? I thought this would be right up your alley. You like breaking the rules, right? So let's break them," she dared him before slamming the door shut in his face.

Erin stared up at the faint moon in the darkening blue and pink sky and inhaled deeply as the twilight air whipped softly around the gray house. Like her, the Lepareurs lived on the bad side of Hope Acres, but she could tell by the fresh coat of paint on the walls that Betty and her husband had taken good care of their house.

The hedge around the house had been neatly trimmed and a pile of colored leaves from the trees surrounding the small yard had been swept off the lawn and into a corner, to be disposed of.

She drew in a ragged breath. Even before leaving her studio apartment, a quivering tension had begun coiling in her stomach. It was a mixture of exhilaration and apprehension. She was finally going to hear what had happened from someone who had actually been there. The thought had crossed her mind several times that she probably wasn't going to like what the policeman would tell her, but even bad news was better than the unknown.

She lifted her hand, but before she could knock, Betty opened the door. Erin was surprised by what appeared to be genuine joy in Betty's expression.

"Omigosh, I'm so glad you came!" Betty exclaimed. "I've been countin' the hours all afternoon." She opened her arms and Erin couldn't avoid enduring a long motherly hug from a woman she hardly knew. She expected Betty to release her as soon as she realized the stiffness of the person she held. Instead, Betty said, "Oh, you poor girl," while stroking Erin's curly hair.

Erin felt a lump develop in her throat, and tears pricked her eyelids.

She swallowed a few times and blinked back the unshed tears before she managed to gently push herself away.

I don't even want to know where that came from.

"Is she here yet?" a man grumbled from inside the house. "You tell her it's impolite to show up ten minutes late when someone invites you over for dinner."

Betty winked at Erin. "Yes, Grumpy," she yelled out. "He's stone-deaf," she whispered to Erin.

"There's nothin' wrong with my ears," the man shouted from another room.

"Never mind him, honey." Betty patted Erin's arm.

Erin frowned at Betty's hand, still feeling uneasy when someone touched or comforted her.

TOUCHED BY MADNESS

Betty continued as if she didn't notice her discomfort. "Philippe hasn't been the same ever since they forced him to retire."

They entered the cozy front room. The centerpiece was a fire burning in the fireplace. Soft jazz music played in the background, creating a warm and relaxing environment.

The former chief of police sat in a comfortable lounge chair.

"Those Divine Right bastards! They didn't approve of my connections within the supernatural community, that's why I'm retired! Where yat? I'm Philippe." He introduced himself by getting up and shaking Erin's hand. He examined her in silence before nodding. "Yes, you have the look of her."

"Of the girl you saw survive the ritual killing twenty years ago?" she asked.

"No, of your mother. Spitting image, you are, apart from the eyes. I suppose they are like his," he said.

She hesitated. "You—you mean my dad, right?"

"Yes, but let's not let him ruin dinner," he grunted, walking over to the set table. "We'll discuss him after the meal."

During dinner, it struck Erin that Betty ensured that the conversation remained pleasant by keeping the subjects neutral to all parties. They mainly discussed safe subjects, such as books that had been adapted for the big screen.

Philippe had asked Erin a couple of questions about what had happened after she left Hope Acres, but the moment she mentioned the asylum, Betty interrupted her and changed the subject.

The food had been excellent, a traditional Louisiana dinner. After having much enjoyed the crawfish, Philippe and Erin left the table to discuss the past.

He moaned when he sat down on the lounge chair in the front room. "Don't get me wrong, chère. I don't want to be a vampire, but sometimes I wish I didn't age. Arthritis," he explained. "The doctors try to get me hooked on drugs, but I prefer the pain."

She took the photocopy of the article from her coat and sat down on the couch next to the former chief of police.

She gave him the piece of paper, and he put on his glasses to read the article. He nodded. "Yeah, I remember this. Fortunately, I haven't got Alzheimer's yet."

"So, what happened?" Every sense heightened, she waited for him to continue.

"We got a call that day about Merenda. She said that he was fixin' to do somethin' huge on Hallows' eve."

"She?"

"We always assumed it was your mother who had called us with the warnin' because we traced the call back to your house."

"Mom?" she whispered.

"We'll talk later," her mother said softly.

"Yea, someone we interviewed afterward told us that your mother'd been tryin' to leave Merenda for a while. Merenda'd been married before and his wife had mysteriously disappeared. Merenda'd been pushin' your mom to marry him for a long time, and she had found it more and more difficult to turn him down. She'd been terrified of him, and she'd worried that he would take his anger out on you or on Leila. I couldn't blame her—he also gave me the creeps."

Erin's voice shook slightly, when she asked. "Are you sure this Oliver Merenda was my dad?"

He contemplated her question and sighed. "Yea, it was common knowledge, even if you're a blonde—unless your mother had an affair. *Mais non*. I don't believe that. Merenda was obsessed with her, and with gettin' power. He always had her watched. Besides, you have his eyes."

She drew in a deep quivering breath. "What did my mom say exactly, during the call?"

"She said that she had overheard Merenda makin' an appointment with Altman, the second-in-command vampire of Hope Acres, for later that evenin' at the Devereaux Church. She had also noticed him putting several swords in his car. I wanted to nail the bastard so badly that I called the master vampire."

He chuckled briefly. "I knew that Dane wouldn't tolerate anyone meddlin' with his second-in-command."

"Dane? You mean Dane Lynch was there?" She widened her eyes.

"Yea, that's right. I also called in the cops from New Orleans, in case Dane didn't succeed. I didn't think they would be necessary, though," he added with a wry smile. "Dane can be quite ruthless."

She shivered uneasily and rubbed her arms.

"So, that evenin', we had the buildin' surrounded. Dane was the first to enter the church. The event was supposed to have started at midnight. Too bad Merenda decided to move the ceremony forward..."

She frowned. "So what happened when Dane entered the church?"

The ex-cop shrugged. "Dane only told us that Merenda had disappeared. The ritual must have gone wrong. We kind of hoped that he'd exploded or somethin' like that. There was no trace of him. There'd been a pentagram drawn on the floor, and at every point of the star, there was a body pierced by a sword. You were one of them, but the sword had miraculously missed your heart. Or maybe it wasn't a miracle. You were wearing some creepy kind of amulet around your neck. It looked more like a weapon—not really fit for a child, so we got rid of that. And Dane, well, I thought that Dane..." He trailed off into an uncomfortable silence.

"You thought that Dane what?" she persisted with a sense of urgency. Dane hadn't mentioned any of this to her.

"Well, I thought he was acting a little odd," he admitted. "I only knew Dane as someone cold and ruthless. With you, he acted just weird. I could be wrong. It's been twenty years, and we were all under a lot of stress that night. Life in Hope Acres is generally uneventful."

"So how did he seem different?"

"When we entered the church, it seemed as though he was fixin' to bite you. He seemed almost possessed."

When Philippe spotted the panic-stricken expression on her face, he quickly shook his head. "But I must have imagined it. Dane won't allow any of his vampires to bite anyone who isn't a consentin' adult. He punishes his vampires severely for breakin' those rules. He's very different from the previous master vampire. The ancient Gregorio allowed his vampires to turn children."

The chief hesitated briefly before continuing, "In fact, I'd even suggest that you contact Dane about that night. He could probably tell you more."

"What?" she yelled incredulously. "So he can finish the job?"

"Hey! Don't overreact," Philippe complained. "As I said before, I'm sure I was wrong. Actually, Dane seemed very concerned about you that night. He let you go without a fight when I told him you had to go to the hospital. As a matter of fact, of all the people I know, I'd say that Dane is the most reliable. You just don't want to fuck with him, is all."

She shot him a skeptical glance. "Really? I guess you don't know a lot of people then. I met Mr. Lynch about a week ago. I told him I needed to remember what had happened that night, and he never told me that he had been present at the scene of the crime. That doesn't seem reliable to me. The only thing he suggested was letting him bite me so he could try to retrieve memories of what had happened that night."

He shrugged. "Well, I don't know why he didn't tell you that he was there that night. Of course, he wasn't there durin' the ritual, because he was with us. You're probably better off not knowin' what happened. The idea of your dad forcin' you to kill yourself—nobody needs to remember somethin' like that."

"But I must," she said. "You didn't interview me afterward?"

"No," he murmured. "You were too traumatized. You'd repressed the whole ceremony."

She sighed, frustrated.

"If you really need to know what happened, then the only thing I can recommend is lettin' Dane bite you," he went on. "Your dad was never seen again, and the only remainin' witness is you. You're the only one who knows what occurred that night. However, if I were you, I'd count my blessings. In this case particularly, I'd say that ignorance really is bliss."

Let Dane bite me.

After Philippe made his suggestion, Erin had been in a hurry to leave the Lepareurs' house. She hoped the others didn't agree with the former cop. She was afraid to ask them what they wanted her to do. She couldn't afford one of them taking over her body one night to go see Dane.

As she entered her apartment, she thought about what her next step should be. Either she could let a shrink try to hypnotize her and pray that he wouldn't lock her into an institution again, or she could allow Dane to bite her and pray that he wouldn't make her his in return.

She cursed briefly, dropped herself on the bed and curled into a tight ball. Her dream of finding out how to get rid of the voices had never seemed more impossible.

NINE

How do I get Erin to come to me?

Dane had been trying to find an answer to that question ever since Erin had left his mansion in a hurry, the previous night. Brooding over the same question had kept him awake for a good portion of the day.

He'd forgotten about the problem of the vampires disappearing as he had been consumed with thoughts of Erin. Still, he refused to think of her as a liability. He could always decide to get rid of her after she had entertained him.

Damn it, but it had been a long time since he had been this intent on having a woman. He knew what it meant to desire a woman physically, but he was rapidly coming to realize that what he wanted from Erin Holland amounted to something much more complicated than physical satisfaction. He found her intriguing.

He had been interested in her when she was a little girl, gazing up at him as if he were someone she could trust. She had grabbed him then and hadn't wanted to let go. She must have felt instinctively that he would protect her and that he would never purposely hurt her.

His intimidation tactics over the last couple of days must have destroyed those feelings. However, he could make her feel that way again and more so. He wanted to create a bond between them, one not easily broken.

Exchanging blood would establish such a bond, and as a bonus, he would be able to delve into her memories. He would resolve her issue with the voices, and in return, she would give herself completely to him—no more secrets.

Such a bond would make killing her harder, and he was not so far gone not to realize that someday he might be forced to do so, but he refused to worry about that now.

He would make her welcome the bonds closing in around her, and seducing her in her dreams would be a step in the right direction.

He rejected the thought that he might be betraying her trust by invading her sleep, a time when she was the most vulnerable. He told himself it was in her best interest if they established a blood bond. Not only would he find out what had happened the night of the massacre, but he would also sense it if she got into trouble.

He was just about to leave his quarters when he heard someone knocking on his basement door. The door opened and a familiar face appeared.

He kept his face expressionless as he watched Jonathan Stratton enter his room. Stratton looked all business in his tailor-made suit and expensive Italian shoes.

"Good evening, my old friend," Stratton said, greeting him with an easy smile.

Dane wondered if the Las Vegas vampire was aware that he had asked Brock to investigate him.

"Good evening, Stratton. I'm surprised to find you here. I would have thought that you'd be too worried that the press will find out your terrible secret," he mocked.

Stratton flashed a shark's grin at him.

Most men would be trembling in Stratton's presence. There was a harsh ruthlessness to the man. His steely eyes peered over a hawk-like nose and aggressive jawline. His dark hair was slicked back, revealing a slightly receding hairline, colored only with a touch of gray at the temples.

Usually, no one could intimidate Dane, even if that person had the power and reputation that Stratton had. However, Stratton was known for his erratic behavior and would turn on anyone at a moment's notice, especially if that person was considered an old friend. Since this was an unexpected visit, Dane decided to tread with the utmost care.

Stratton shrugged. "It's all about priorities, Dane. Seeing you now is more important than the chance of getting caught in your lair by a pesky reporter."

"They are bound to find out you're a vampire anyway, or are you going to dye your hair completely gray? I always assumed you were too vain to make yourself appear older."

Stratton chuckled. "Probably, but we are lucky to be living in an era where nobody needs to age as long as they are rich enough, and everyone knows I'm loaded."

Dane walked to his fridge and opened it. He took out a bag of blood and waved it at Stratton. Stratton shook his head and theatrically shivered.

"No, thank you. I don't understand how you can stomach the stuff. I only drink directly from the source." Stratton grinned. "Fortunately, I know I can trust the people around me. They are too afraid to tattle on me to the press."

Dane poured himself a glass and waited for Stratton to sit before he sat down on the padded leather chair opposite to him.

"So, what's the emergency?" Dane queried, his curiosity getting the better of him.

"We share similar interests, or so I've been told," Stratton answered. "I heard that you've been in touch with one of my employees."

Dane nodded as he took a sip from the blood. "I won't deny it. I'm just wondering why you are showing such an interest in a small-town security guard, considering you must have over a hundred thousand people working for you."

"But Erin is such an extraordinary girl. I'll let you in on a secret. I'm very pleased with the way I managed to have her work for me," Stratton drawled.

"What the hell is that supposed to mean?" Dane couldn't hide the hostility in his voice.

"It means, old friend, that I have invested a lot of energy in her, and I will not allow anyone to interfere with my efforts. I have plans for Erin Holland."

Dane nearly broke his glass when he put it down on the table. "And what exactly are your *plans*, old friend? Not one of your sick jokes, I hope."

Stratton sighed with disappointment. "I hope we aren't going to fight over a girl. We're not are we? I always thought we were more civilized than that. You can't be sweet on her, can you? I thought more highly of you."

Dane clenched his jaw, and his expression must have become stony because Stratton groaned.

"There's no need to give me the evil eye. You're terrifying enough without that expression."

Dane continued to stare at Stratton in silence.

"Okay. The thing is, I—I knew her father," Stratton faltered. "In fact, I was supposed to have been there that night twenty years ago."

Shocked by Stratton's admission, Dane stopped glaring.

"Merenda tried to lure me with the promise of a very powerful gift, and I would have gone there, had it not been for someone trying to kidnap me the previous night. It seemed unwise to leave my home. I never would have thought I'd be grateful to a bunch of kidnappers," Stratton joked. "I can't help but wonder what would have happened had I gone there instead of Altman. Would I have died, or would I have ended up like Erin Holland? I kept wondering how the experience had changed her."

"So that's why you hired Victor to watch her? To see how the ritual had affected her?" Dane asked.

Stratton nodded. "That too, but I also wanted to test her, to see if she got the powers from your vampire, like the powers her father tried to steal from me. And if I can't get back at her father for what he tried to do to me, I can at least get her. She's mine for two years. I want to make sure that I can use her to the fullest extent of her abilities. Besides, everyone knows that knowledge is power." He laughed.

Dane's gaze slowly ran over Stratton. His jaw tightened and anger welled up deep inside him, eating away at him while he pondered Stratton's words.

She's mine for two years.

Dane flexed his hands into fists, but he wasn't going to attack Stratton, not yet. Stratton was right about knowledge being power. He needed to know more about the other vampire's *plans.*

Stratton seemed oblivious to Dane's turmoil and continued with his explanation. "The contract I made her sign is impossible to get out of. Unfortunately, I haven't seen her in action yet..." Stratton's lips curved in an ironic smile.

"Although I heard she put on quite a show at Star's party last week. Weren't you there? I should have put cameras there. I usually have them everywhere."

He'd gone too far. Stratton's amusement at Erin's misery undid Dane's last fragment of control. His gut clenched in fury, and his entire body went rigid. His eyes flared, and he growled as he flew at the other vampire, the need to kill strong in him.

Stratton's eyes grew wide, and he tried to remove Dane's hands from around his neck by grabbing his wrists while struggling to get free.

Dane couldn't choke him to death since vampires didn't need air to breathe, but he could use all his strength to try to rip off his head. It felt to Stratton as if Dane was trying to do just that.

Stratton wouldn't have thought it possible, but as he stared into Dane's eyes he realized that he had underestimated him.

"W-what?" he uttered with difficulty. "Stop," Stratton gasped.

The fire didn't leave Dane's eyes, but he did finally release him. Dane stepped back and glared down at him with a look of murder in his eyes.

"I always wondered why Merenda didn't contact you for the ritual. I guess, I finally have my answer," Stratton jested. "You didn't need any additional power."

Stratton rubbed his neck while he continued to remain seated. "Well, this conversation sure didn't go as I expected."

"No." Dane's expression was set in stone.

"Shall we just forget this conversation ever took place?"

"No," Dane repeated in a cold voice. "You will break off whatever plans you have set up for Erin Holland, and you will call off your watchdog. If I see that werewolf sniffing around her ever again, I'll neuter him before I finish what I started tonight."

"Now, wait a minute—"

"Do you understand me?" Dane interrupted.

"Yes," Stratton replied with reluctance. "Could he at least finish the job at the hospital? The other guard should return next week."

"No." Dane's voice refused argument. Any sign of weakness was absent from his reply to Stratton's request. "Get out."

Stratton seemed to waver before rising from the couch, keeping his eyes fixed on Dane.

Dane realized that Stratton was probably expecting to be attacked again, a thought that forced him to suppress a smile. He waited for the Las Vegas vampire to leave the basement before allowing himself to relax.

He pondered over the way he had reacted to Stratton's words. Even without the physical bond with Erin, he had completely lost his cool. He wasn't too worried that he had gained another enemy—it went with the territory. He was, however, annoyed that Erin had managed to draw the attention of the

Las Vegas master vampire. She didn't know it yet, but he felt he had just done her a huge favor.

And I don't do anyone any favors for nothing, he told himself as he left the basement. He was going to collect, and he was going to do it right now.

Jonathan Stratton told his chauffeur to hurry to the New Orleans airport. He didn't want to spend any more time than necessary in Hope Acres. He cursed when the conversation with Dane preyed on his mind, but he wouldn't admit defeat.

Stratton hadn't made it to the top without fighting for his success, and he wouldn't let a small-town vampire get the best of him. For now, he would do what Dane had told him to do, and let him think that he had beaten him. He would tell the werewolf to lay low for a little while. Then, when Dane would least expect it, he would strike.

Dane hadn't told him to fire Merenda's daughter, so Stratton would continue to keep her working at the hospital where an old acquaintance of hers was also present.

A tiny smile tugged at his lips. Dane hadn't mentioned the shrink that he had flown in, so he wasn't aware of his involvement with the good doctor.

He decided not to send the doctor back to Europe just yet. His encounter with Dane had taught him that the vampire had a soft spot for the girl, and if he wanted to hurt him, the best way would be through her.

His smile widened. Over the years, he had often wondered how to play one of his pranks on Dane and now, thanks to his sweet employee, he finally could. All he had to do was see to it that the girl and the shrink were reunited.

Dane was deep within the body of the bald eagle when he landed on Erin's fire escape. This time, she had closed the curtains before going to bed. He closed his eyes as he pictured her there, waiting for him.

He wished he could open the window and enter the apartment.

Patience.

He knew she would never forgive him if he forced his way in now. Fortunately, she didn't know how easy it was for him to enter her dreams.

He opened his mind and concentrated on Erin asleep inside. He waited for an image, a sensation...

The cloying, pungent odor of antiseptics mixed with the smell of fear assaulted Erin's senses. She had that familiar heavy, distorted feeling as if she were sinking in quicksand, struggling to get loose. The headache and nausea were present, as they were every time she awoke in the white room.

They had been drugging her every day for weeks now or maybe for years. She had lost all sense of time ever since the Johanssons had left her at the institution. She couldn't even remember the last time her body had been free of numbness. Her ears felt muffled and she could barely hear. Her vision was also blurry. However, her nose worked perfectly as usual, and she knew that he was there.

He had her strapped down to the table, and her legs had been pried apart. She was grateful that he had let her wear her nightgown this time. Unfortunately, her legs still felt uncomfortably bare. She wished she could sink into the cold metal table, trying in vain to make herself invisible from the doctor's gaze.

If only she could draw her knees up to her chin and wrap her arms tightly around them, not that it would offer her much protection against the shrink's probing eyes. If only she were lucid enough to think of one of her mother's spells, one that would release her. She would even settle for one of Gideon's dark magic spells, to kill the doctor.

"Ah, you're awake." Doctor Quirky's voice slithered through her haze in a whisper.

She felt a pat on her head, and she let out an aggressive growl. If only she could pass out again.

"You still haven't given up fighting me, I see," he went on thoughtfully. "Well, today you can tone it down a bit. The biting didn't work."

She tried to take in the white figure standing next to her. She had a hard time focusing, but could see the white bandage on his hand where she had bitten him.

She briefly wondered what he was talking about, but got distracted when he started waving something at her that looked suspiciously like a syringe. She had been afraid of needles before going to the hospital. Now she was glad to accept the numbness the injection would bring.

"I'm not going to draw blood today. That didn't work either. We're going to try something completely different." When she frowned, the doctor explained, "Today, we're going to try to create life."

In her haze, she watched as the doctor hovered over her. She squeezed her eyes together to try to read his face. Doctor Quirkhart studied her with an intense, analytical expression.

"So much power in such a frail body," the doctor whispered as he touched one of her legs. "Tell me, Erin, how do you feel about motherhood?"

Confused by the odd question, she started to struggle. She wanted to change into the leopard and rip out her tormentor's throat. She didn't care about exposing herself, since the doctor had seen her change before.

For the first time since they had tied her down, she heard one of the straps tearing. A sense of euphoric triumph flowed through her, but she heard the doctor curse.

"Those idiots. They haven't given you enough drugs," he muttered.

She refused to pay any attention to him. She was finally going to get loose and rid herself of Doctor Quirky once and for all!

She felt a sharp sting on her arm. Everything was dimming. She felt an instant of panic, but a swirling blackness beckoned.

"No," she heard herself murmur. A cold-gloved hand spread her legs wider. She felt something hard enter her. 'No, please don't...' she thought, and then she thought nothing at all.

I should have interfered, was Dane's first thought as he opened his eyes. Still in the body of the bird, he stared at the window, wishing Erin had left the curtains open.

Is she still asleep, stuck in that awful dream?

He should have emerged in her nightmare, grabbed that doctor and ripped his intestines out.

As soon as he had caught the first images from the dream, shock had coursed through him like a jolt from a power line. All thoughts of seduction had dissipated within seconds.

He flapped his wings in frustration, anger still festering in his gut. He felt as if his head was about to explode. He was disgusted with himself. While she had been strapped on the hospital table, he had felt her desolation. When the syringe filled with semen had penetrated her, he had experienced the violation with her. Why hadn't he done anything? The shock had paralyzed him too.

He wondered briefly if the nightmare had been imaginary or if it had been a memory.

TOUCHED BY MADNESS

It couldn't have been real, could it?

It was hard to believe that a doctor would act that way. If a licensed psychiatrist succeeded in getting one of his patients pregnant, he would not only risk losing his license, but also his freedom. He wouldn't be stupid enough to risk jail, right? Thoughts spun in his brain. Dane knew he wouldn't be able to let this go until he had asked Brock to investigate what had happened to Erin at the institution.

A hissing sound above him interrupted his thoughts. Remaining in the body of the bald eagle, he moved his head backward.

Three steps away from him, an overweight orange cat glared at him. Its back was arched while the tip of its tail twitched. The creature acted as if it were on the prowl and had spotted its prey. It made a clicking noise with its teeth, and its ears flattened to its skull.

Even though he wasn't really worried about the cat, he decided to change back into his human form. His body had just started growing when the large feline surprised him by launching itself at him at full speed. It managed to sink its claws into his eagle chest and sink its teeth into his wings.

His body started to tear and blood leaked from his wounds. When he had finished changing back to a human, the cat fell on the steps with a loud thump. It hissed at the vampire with its mouth covered in blood.

"Okay, Fatso! You think you'll have me for dinner, eh?" he goaded the animal. His fangs

208

elongated, and he grinned at the creature. "How about if I eat you instead?"

The cat started mewing at the top of its voice.

He clenched his fists in anger. His nostrils flared, promising retaliation. He opened his hands and reached out for the cat, but then he heard a soft voice from inside the apartment.

"Hey, cat, can you please make your noise somewhere else?" the voice pleaded.

The cat refused to move and continued meowing while staring at the vampire.

"So you're protecting her, are you?" he noted. "Well, I guess I can't punish you for that."

He heard Erin's bed creaking as she got up. Ignoring his wounds, he forced his body to change back to an eagle and flew up into the sky. He managed to land on the lamppost, before she opened the window. She had turned on the lights.

"Puss, shut up! They will kick me out of the building if you won't be quiet. Do you want to come in?" Erin hesitated for a second. "Why couldn't you make this racket while I was having a nightmare?" The cat walked up to the window, silent this time.

Erin frowned when the light touched the animal's face.

"Are you covered in blood? Oh, yuck! You haven't been catching mice again, I hope. You'd better not bring them in here." The creature entered the apartment, and Erin shut the window.

Dane waited for Erin to turn the lights off before spreading his wings and launching himself up into the sky.

TOUCHED BY MADNESS

"Get up, get up, get u-up!" Leila's whiny voice tormented Erin. In the background a country song was playing.

"Oh, five more minutes," Erin moaned.

"You've already had five minutes and many more."

Erin groaned as she forced herself to open one eye to peek at the time on the radio alarm clock. She was already twenty minutes late.

"Just turn off that horrible sound!" Gideon complained.

Reluctantly, she got up and turned off the music. She opened one of her drawers to search for a painkiller and sighed with relief when she found two pills. She filled a glass with water and swallowed the aspirin, hoping it would prevent the migraine that was threatening to ensue. She was already seeing white spots, probably brought on by the nightmare and the restless night that had followed it.

After waking up from her nightmare at three a.m., she had been unable to fall asleep. Every time she managed to doze off, she awoke a few minutes later. She felt exhausted. She had probably finally sunk into a deep slumber a couple of minutes before the alarm had gone off.

She dragged herself to the bathroom and splashed some cold water on her wrists and face, before pressing her fingers on the bags under her eyes.

"Bad night, eh?" Gideon established gaily.

She refused to answer.

"It was all that talk about seeing a shrink yesterday, right? Well, you don't have to do anything you don't want to do," her mother soothed.

"Yes, Ann, she does," Gideon contradicted.

"I can't see a shrink. I just can't." Erin's voice came out low and husky.

"You mustn't let Dane bite you," Altman warned.

"What do you want me to do, then? Don't let Dane bite me. Don't see a shrink. What I do, or don't do, affects us all. I can't just decide to do nothing!" she snapped.

"Just don't do anything rash. Let us think this over carefully, so we can all decide what the next step should be," her mother suggested wisely.

"I agree. We've been with you for so long now. It's all right if we get to stay with you a little while longer," Altman said.

Erin smiled. Altman always knew just what to say. She then nodded to herself in the mirror and went back to her front room.

"Shit," she muttered upon noticing the time on the clock. After hurriedly tugging on her uniform and pulling her hair back in a ponytail, she ran out of her apartment leaving behind the grumpy cat she had forgotten to feed that morning.

Without protecting herself against the heavy rainfall, she pumped her legs while riding her bike to work as fast as she could. An SUV overtook her and carved arcs of water from the gutter, which drenched her.

Cold water slapped against her face, flooding her eyes. She swallowed a curse and wished she'd worn a raincoat. So far, the weather in October had been quite calm with few thunderstorms. She didn't really mind the rain. It was refreshing and made most people go indoors, which meant they weren't in her way.

In spite of having been allowed out only on rare occasions, she had gotten accustomed to living in a bad climate while staying in England, but she preferred the weather in Louisiana to that of London, even hurricane season.

When she arrived at the hospital, she locked her bike without taking any additional time to chain the vehicle to a lamppost. At full speed, she rushed into the building.

"Finally!" Victor said as he heard her enter the small office. He frowned when he turned around to face her. "What the hell happened to you?"

"What do you think?" she grunted as she squeezed the water out of her hair. "I decided to take a swim with my clothes on. How come you're not wet?"

Victor grabbed a towel and threw it at her. It was still damp, but she decided not to think about where it might have been before.

"I've got to go. Nikko needs to see me straight away, so I'm afraid you're on your own today."

"Ah, that's just too bad," she said with as little sincerity as possible.

He blew her a kiss as he put on his coat. "I'll miss you too." He left the room while she continued to rub herself dry. She was imagining a peaceful day without pesky werewolves when the phone rang.

"Hey, old colleague," Frank said cheerfully when she greeted the caller.

"Hi, Frank. Am I glad to hear your voice! Please tell me you'll get back to work tomorrow!" she begged, sitting down at the monitors.

"Yes, afraid so," Frank answered. "Daphne can't leave the hospital yet because she's still weak, but the doctors think we can take her home by the end of this week."

"I thought you wanted to stay with Janice as long as the baby needed to stay in the hospital." As she spoke, she reviewed what was appearing on the different screens.

"Yeah..." He sighed. "I guess the replacement really sucked. Nikko threatened he would get me sacked, and now that we have a baby, I just can't risk it."

"I'm sorry, but I'm happy that you'll be back."

"That bad, eh?" Frank joked. "I also wanted to ask you if you'd like to see Daphne tonight. I can't believe you still haven't seen her! Fortunately, she looks just like her mom, so she's gorgeous. You'll come?"

She was about to think of an answer when she saw a vaguely familiar young woman in her early twenties standing on the second floor in front of the door leading to the medicine supply. She seemed nervous. She kept inspecting her surroundings and constantly fidgeted with her purse.

The woman closed her eyes, and Erin saw her lips move even though there was no one standing next to her.

"Erin, still there?" she heard Frank ask.

"Ah, I've got to go. Talk to you later," she replied, distracted by the activity on the security monitors.

"I will see you to—" Frank was cut off mid-sentence as she hung up the phone.

Erin wasn't allowed to run inside the hospital, unless it was an emergency. Her instincts told her this was one of those situations where running was allowed. She was also glad to have an excuse to ignore Frank's request to go and see his daughter that night. She didn't want to worry about the pain it might cause her to see someone else's baby.

She quickly pushed away the memory of her pregnancy. She would focus on work instead.

She had just reached the second floor when she spotted the woman opening the door and entering the room reserved for hospital personnel. Convinced that this woman didn't work at the hospital, she followed her into the room.

She had to breathe through her mouth to keep her eyes from watering when the chlorine smell pricked her nostrils. She watched the mysterious woman put her gloved hands on several small bottles.

Erin saw sodium thiopental written on the labels of the tiny bottles. She squinted while she tried to place the woman. She had seen someone with the same short black hair a little while ago. If only she could remember where...

The woman dropped five medicine bottles into her purse before turning around to leave the room. She shrieked when she saw Erin standing by the doorway.

Erin folded her arms across her chest and shot her a disapproving glare.

All color drained from the thief's face.

Erin wondered what kind of excuse the woman would come up with and waited for her to say something. She was surprised to discover that the woman had not prepared a speech at all, but seemed frozen in shock by her arrival.

Didn't she think about getting caught? Is she that brazen or that naïve?

Upon first inspection, she seemed harmless. Erin continued to study the woman. She couldn't shake the feeling that she had seen her before. She thought the thief was quite pretty. Even if her haircut was rather masculine, her elfin face was pretty enough to pull it off. In a moment of clarity, it dawned on her where she'd seen her before.

This was one of the women from Star Knight's party, one of the people who had been in the basement.

TOUCHED BY MADNESS

The woman finally opened her mouth. "I—I came in here to hide from my boyfriend."

Erin smiled, impressed. "That's good."

The woman frowned. "Is it?"

Erin nodded. "Oh, not that I believe you of course, I just thought it was a good lie."

"What makes you think it was a lie?" The woman's voice rose a little as if she was fighting to keep calm.

Erin raised an amused eyebrow. "I saw you put five medicine bottles in your purse."

The blush colored the thief's face, and her eyes widened in innocence. "Oh, I see. What if I put them back?" She opened her purse and put her hand inside.

Erin raised her hand as she strode toward the woman. "No, wait!"

However, Erin was too late. The woman had removed her hand and thrown a red powdery substance in Erin's face while saying, "Stiff as a statue!"

Erin inwardly struggled, as outwardly she was unable to move.

The woman still appeared nervous as she walked past her. "I'm so sorry," she whispered. "Please don't worry. The spell will wear off in about half an hour." She left the room in a hurry while Erin remained frozen to the spot, feeling extremely pissed off.

"I can't believe that witch outsmarted you!" Gideon laughed.

"A witch! We've finally seen a witch—a real one!" Erin's mother sounded like she wanted to celebrate.

"And she's getting away. Do something!" Altman ordered.

Erin tried to open her mouth, but nothing happened. Even her lips were paralyzed.

"Oh, well. Let's see... Allow Erin to move and be free. As is my will, so mote it be," her mother tried. She started to apologize for her horrible spell, but then Erin let out a growl. Her hands started to shake, and her mother cheered.

Erin shook off the uncomfortable tingle of her limbs waking up and forced herself to run out of the room. She was on the prowl, and she refused to let her prey escape again.

She ran downstairs at full speed. She nearly burst through the automatic doors because they opened too slowly.

One of the voices tried to warn her against exposure, but she was too wrapped up in the hunt to care. She also ignored the wind tugging at her uniform. In spite of raindrops streaming down her face, her vision was good enough for her to catch sight of the thief. The woman appeared to be in a hurry as she opened the door of a ramshackle green car.

Without hesitation, Erin jumped on the wet roof of the car. Hearing her prey shriek, she leapt on the hood of the vehicle. She peered into the car and saw the black-haired woman shaking behind the steering wheel. The corners of Erin's mouth twitched into a smile.

TOUCHED BY MADNESS

"Get out," she growled.

"H-h-how?" the thief stammered as she left the car.

Erin shook her head. "You'll be doing the talking," she said as she jumped down in front of the terrified woman.

Erin grabbed her and dragged her back into the hospital. She pushed open the door to the office and ordered the woman to sit down, then waited for the witch to obey.

"Talk," Erin ordered.

"What—what do you want me to say?" the woman asked, picking up her purse. Erin snatched it away from the thief, both to avoid another trick and to examine the medicine that had been stolen.

"You can start by telling me your name," Erin commanded while she carefully removed the five bottles from the purse. She made sure to avoid touching the pouch with the red powder.

The woman tried shrugging casually. "Sure. It's Pauline Johnson."

Erin opened the purse again and took out a wallet. She opened it and read the driver's license of the woman in front of her. She sighed and saw Pauline flinch.

"Let's try that again, shall we?" Erin suggested.

"Sorry—it's Pauline Collins," Pauline mumbled without meeting her eyes.

Erin frowned while trying to analyze the thief. "I must admit you don't come across as a junkie. Did you want to use this on another unsuspecting werewolf?"

Pauline gasped as she recognized her. She let out a nervous giggle and shook her head. "No, far from it."

"Sodium thiopental," Erin read out loud, picking up one of the bottles. "What does it do? Does it get you high?"

When Erin saw Pauline hesitating, she forcefully set down the medicine on the table.

"There's no need to lie to me," Erin snapped. "We're surrounded by doctors. I'm sure one of them can tell me what this stuff is used for. Hell, I could probably search online and get a straight answer there."

"It's an anesthetic. You use it for operations," Pauline admitted softly.

"And is that what you're going to use it for?" Erin asked when Pauline fell silent. "Are you going to use it for some kind of operation? So many bottles, are you going to operate on an elephant, or is that what you would need for a werewolf?"

Pauline put her shaking hands underneath the table. They were trembling so badly that they made her entire body shake.

Erin turned away, picked up a jug of water from the table and poured Pauline a glass.

The thief tried to steady her nerves by taking a small sip and looked as if she was trying to concentrate.

"No, I'm not going to use it on a werewolf—oh, my God, she's going to kill me!" Pauline despaired.

Interested, Erin leaned forward. "Who? That blond witch?"

219

TOUCHED BY MADNESS

"Please..." Pauline tried to speak, but the word came out only as a weak, incomprehensible gurgle.

Mercilessly, Erin waited for Pauline to continue.

"Please don't make me tell you," Pauline begged. "Can't I just return the medicine? I promise I won't come back."

Pauline closed her eyes, but was unable to stop the tears that flowed down her cheeks. She lapsed into silence for several minutes, lost in her own thoughts while Erin watched her.

"There's no need to act like a victim. I remember you torturing that werewolf," Erin said. "You and that vile blonde."

Pauline's cheeks glowed with a fierce blush. "No," she contradicted. "We ... I-I wanted to help him. Eartha said that she knew how to turn him human again. We believed her. The guy—he really didn't want to be a werewolf anymore."

Her words sent a prickle of recognition down Erin's spine. "You think there is a way to make such a creature human?" she asked, intrigued.

Is there a way you could make me human?

Pauline wavered and Erin's hope disappeared. "I'm not sure. I have spells for werewolves to help them master their animalistic nature, but they would still turn furry during full moon. Lycanthropy is not like a spell," Pauline explained.

"Every spell has a counter spell, so if someone casts a spell or a curse, it can be broken. When someone has the strain of a werewolf in their DNA, then it's part of their genetic make-up. I don't think it's possible to change someone's DNA."

Deciding not to pay any heed to the theft for the moment, Erin tried to find out more about witchcraft. "How about counter spells? Have you ever performed any? And did they work?"

Pauline relaxed in her chair, appearing slightly more at ease, probably because of Erin's interest in magic. "Well, someone I know was bragging about a piece of jewelry she had cursed to punish the woman who had married her ex. The woman refused to take off the diamond necklace, and it was seeping away her energy. It was slowly killing her, and her husband and the doctors were mystified. So, one night I snuck out of the house, and I entered the hospital."

Erin frowned. "You had to sneak out of your own house?"

Pauline chose to ignore Erin's question and went on with her story. "When I got to her room, I was very fortunate to find her alone. I cast the paralysis spell that I used on you and removed the necklace. To undo the damage that the cursed diamonds had caused, I reversed the spell. It was easy because the person who had cast the spell had told me exactly what she had done. After I had performed the counter spell, I witnessed the woman's health returning right in front of my eyes. It was amazing. That's the real reason I wanted to be a witch, so I could heal people."

Pauline didn't have to add that she wasn't healing people now.

"The person who told you about the curse, I'll bet she was that Eartha from the party, right? You're living with her, aren't you?" Erin queried.

Pauline seemed reluctant to answer at first, but eventually nodded.

"You're in a lot of trouble, aren't you?" Erin continued.

Pauline refused to answer.

"Well, so am I. Maybe we can help each other out," Erin proposed.

Confused, Pauline raised her eyes to stare at her.

"I'll return the medicine bottles, and I'm willing to overlook that you tried to steal them. In exchange, I want a couple of things," Erin said.

Eager, Pauline nodded even though she didn't know what Erin would want in return for her silence.

"First, I don't want you to steal any anesthetic medicine anymore. I can't set you free knowing that my silence might hurt someone. If Eartha needs to use those drugs, she should get them herself. You mustn't get involved." Erin's voice was resolute.

"Second, I want you to help me with a counter spell. I think I've been cursed. Unfortunately, I don't know what the original spell was, but maybe we can find out."

"Third, if you agree to my terms, I can't let you get in any more trouble. I'd feel responsible, because I hadn't turned you in. So you'll have to stop living with Eartha. That woman is clearly a bad influence on you."

"Oh, honey! I'm so proud of you! Yes, witches should stick together!" Erin's mother praised her.

"Oh, but where am I supposed to live, then?" Pauline asked.

"Oh, whatever you're thinking, please don't!" Altman complained.

Erin suppressed any feelings of doubt and ignored Altman.

"I guess you can stay at my place." Erin sighed. "Temporarily!" she was quick to add.

Pauline couldn't believe how fortunate she had been. During most of the conversation, her stomach had felt as though a thousand tiny snakes had been coiled within, wriggling and biting. And now this security guard, who had the power to turn her life into a bigger mess than Pauline had created herself, was offering her a way out.

She briefly considered warning the guard about Selena and the others, but decided it might frighten her away. It was hard to picture the woman frightened of anything, though. She seemed so tough.

She recollected the way the woman had leapt on the hood of her car and wanted to cheer. Although, not at the time. At the time, she had been frightened out of her wits.

She decided she would find a way to make herself indispensable to the security guard, and

TOUCHED BY MADNESS

together they would fight Selena and the rest of the coven.

TEN

Back on the second floor, Erin walked slowly toward the medicine store. Her steps echoed through the wide hallway. She could find her way with her eyes shut. All she needed to do was follow the smell. Pauline's disinfectant odor was still lingering in the building, and it was far more pungent than any of the chemicals used by the hospital.

The first thing she would have to talk about with Pauline was her choice of soap. She decided that when she got home that night, she'd suggest the witch use a different scent.

She heard the five medicine bottles that Pauline had stolen clinking together in the overly-stuffed pockets in her uniform. With every step she took, she could hear the glass of the bottles bang against each other. She covered the bulging pockets with her hands to muffle the sound as she continued down the hall.

There were two nurses murmuring in a doorway at the end of the corridor. Fortunately, they weren't paying any attention to her. They were facing one of the wards instead of the main corridor.

After one final peek that no one was taking any notice of her, Erin unlocked the supply room door and silently slipped inside. Making as little noise as possible, she closed the door behind her. If nobody entered the room now and no one spotted her leaving, then she was in the clear. The camera wouldn't see her either, not since she had tampered with it.

She took a deep breath and pulled the bottles out of her pockets. She put them back on the shelf next to other bottles with the same label, exhaling a sigh of relief. Now nobody would suspect a thing.

"I can't believe you gave your apartment key to a thief." Gideon laughed. *"How stupid can you get?"*

"A witch could never undo a spell a voodoo priest cast!" Leila added.

"Hey!" her mother shouted in protest.

"Sorry, Ann. I know you tried, but—"

"Shut up Leila, this isn't the time," Erin said.

Relief washed over her when she opened the door to find the hallway deserted. She stepped out of the room and placed the key in the lock. She was about to lock the door when she noticed the two nurses from earlier turn around.

She held her breath, and her pulse raced until she realized they weren't looking in her direction. After letting out a reassured sigh, she finished locking the door and made her way back downstairs to the security office.

After returning to her office, she unfroze the security camera on the second floor. The voices in her head started to complain again, causing her to feel the beginnings of a headache. Her mother and Altman were the only ones with anything positive to say.

"Listen," she tried to reason with them. "You know we need help to undo what happened to us all those years ago. It was some kind of ritual. She's a witch. She should know something about rituals, right?"

"Yeah, but she was talking about helping people," Gideon said, sounding disgusted. *"We need someone who knows about black magic, voodoo magic. White magic is too weak."*

"White magic isn't weak!" Erin's mother was quick to object. *"White and black magic are both equally powerful."*

"I don't understand why you're not all happy! At least now, I don't have to see a psychiatrist or accept Dane's help. She could perform a counter spell for us!" Erin exclaimed. "Besides, I don't want to go to someone who deals in black magic. I'm not sure those people can be trusted."

"Quite right!" Altman agreed.

"But do you know what it's like to share a tiny studio apartment with a stranger?" Leila asked. *"Especially a female stranger?"*

"It will only be for a week or so, maybe two weeks. Oh crap, she'll probably have a heart attack when she sees the mess," Erin realized. She became conscious of another problem that might arise from Pauline's stay.

"Guys, you need to promise me something."

"I'm not going to promise you anything!" Gideon protested immediately.

"What is it, honey?" her mother asked.

"I don't want you to take over my body when I'm asleep. Well, I never wanted you to take over my body, apart from the one time where you attacked Doctor Quirky," Erin rushed to add. "I just can't have you do anything weird while that witch is staying with me."

"Ah, you're no fun," Gideon whined.

"I can't vouch for Gideon, but I can safely say that the rest of us will behave. Won't you, Leila?" Altman reassured Erin.

She thanked them, feeling relieved when even Leila and Gideon agreed that they wouldn't try to repossess her while Pauline resided at her studio apartment.

"There's no need to sound so pleased," a familiar voice behind her remarked.

Taken by surprise, she nearly fell out of her chair when she spun around to see Victor standing in the doorway.

He was watching her with an amused expression on his face.

"You shouldn't sneak up on people!" she snapped.

"Really? I think I should do it more often! You never know what you might catch people doing..." His voice softened to a velvet murmur.

"I—I was just talking to myself," she was quick to explain.

"I heard you. Good news travels fast." His voice turned bitter. "You were thanking God that I got fired, weren't you?"

"What? No! Of course not!" she denied.

"So what were you doing, then?" he asked.

Frustrated that she couldn't answer him, she clenched her fists. What was she supposed to say?

I was thanking the voices in my head for not taking over my body?

No wonder her foster parents had decided to have her committed.

When she remained silent, Victor spoke up, "I came here because I wanted to let you know that I'm still willing to help you break into the hospital records." A wicked smile appeared on his face. "Now more than ever."

She grinned. "Revenge?"

"Abso-fucking-lutely!" He grinned back.

She nodded at the computer on her desk. "Do you think we can try to break into the records on this computer, or should we try from another location?"

"Oh, w-well," he stammered. He appeared a bit flustered. "I'm not really that computer literate, so I guess we really need to break into the records on the fourth-floor."

She frowned and stared at him feeling suspicious. "Why are you suddenly so keen on us going to the fourth-floor? I told you I didn't want to go to the psych ward!"

TOUCHED BY MADNESS

Is this a trap?

"You don't have to do this, honey," her mother advised. *"You've got Pauline's help now."*

"Don't be so paranoid, Erin! The more information we get the better," Gideon objected.

"If you want me to help you break into the hospital records, it's best to do so while I'm still wearing the uniform," Victor reasoned. "Today we can walk freely around the hospital without raising any suspicions, but tomorrow, I won't have this uniform anymore."

She had to admit that the werewolf was right, and so was Gideon. They could use more information. She was tired of being suspicious of everyone. Besides, Pauline might not succeed in undoing her father's ritual.

She nodded at him.

What the hell, if I want to be normal, I need to start trusting people.

"Okay, let's go then," he urged her.

"You want us to go up there straight away, without any preparation?" Suspicion clouded her mind again, and her voice sounded nervous.

"Yeah, Nikko wants me to hand over the uniform before five o'clock today."

She felt pressured to rush when she didn't want to. She needed to mentally prepare herself before going to the psych ward. She wanted to have at least an entire day to steady her nerves before she did this. She couldn't afford to have a mental breakdown up there.

And what if the keys on my key ring don't open all the doors?

There were so many things that could go wrong. She thought about Pauline standing in front of the locked door that led to the medicine supply.

Had she used a spell to unlock it?

A good witch might be able to assist them.

She glanced at her watch. They had four hours left. "It's only one o'clock, so if I want to go home first, there is still time, right?"

He shook his head. "Why do you want to go home? Let's go up right now. I don't want to postpone this."

"What's the rush?" she asked. "I know someone who might be able to help us. I want to see if she can."

He emphatically shook his head. "I don't want to involve anyone else, what if that person talks? It's not just your neck on the line here, you know?"

She raised her hands. She didn't want to get into a deep discussion. "Fine, I won't tell anyone else about this." She had to treat the situation like tearing off a Band-Aid. It might be less painful to do it in one go.

At least I won't have time to worry about it.

"Let me do my rounds. It will help me clear my head, I hope," she grumbled. "Can you stay here until I get back?"

"Sure," he answered as he looked at his watch. "Just don't take too long, okay?"

She nodded without any enthusiasm.

This is going to suck.

Victor sighed with relief as he watched Erin leave the office. He prayed she hadn't lied to him about not getting in touch with anyone else about her problem. He knew that Stratton wouldn't thank him if he let Erin bring a third party on their little assignment.

He briefly wondered whom Erin had considered contacting. He felt that he had been very vigilant while keeping watch on her. Had there been a girl or woman he had failed to notice? He didn't like this feeling of uncertainty, of self-doubt.

As a matter of fact, the whole situation made him uncomfortable. He usually had to investigate people from a distance, take some incriminating pictures of his targets and then move on to the next case. He rarely had to get involved.

His head started to pound, causing him to swear and rub his sore temples. He didn't know exactly what Jonathan Stratton's intentions were for Erin, but he was relieved that he could plead ignorance about it all. He couldn't imagine it was anything pleasant. Stratton's remark about having something planned which would have her screaming for help didn't inspire good feelings about his role in this.

He tried to tell himself that Stratton had probably arranged for them to find a fake file, one that would be frustrating, but it wouldn't cause pain.

He didn't want to hurt Erin. He'd been shocked to hear of the ritual killing she had survived. Something in her eyes had told him that the tragedy hadn't ended there. He didn't want to have to introduce Doctor Quirkhart to her. That man would probably take pleasure in dissecting her.

He shivered as he thought about the cold, unblinking gaze of the doctor. He hoped that the man would never level that flat, icy stare on Erin. He closed his eyes and groaned.

What have I got myself into?

He wondered if today was going to be the day that Stratton would make his final move, so that Victor would be allowed to close the case and leave Erin in peace. For the first time in his career, an assignment made him feel guilty. He really didn't like the feeling.

Unfortunately, he knew that the events of that afternoon were only going to make him feel worse. Fake file, he knew he was lying to himself.

He was going to hand Erin over to the shrink with dead eyes.

God knows what will happen to her after that.

Erin stood in front of the office where Victor was waiting for her. She blew out a frustrated breath.

TOUCHED BY MADNESS

She'd hoped she would run into problems while doing her rounds, anything to give her an excuse not to go to the psych ward that day. Even throwing people out of the hospital for lack of insurance would have been preferable.

When she left the institution seven months ago, she had promised herself she would not set foot in one of those places ever again.

The managing director from the institution had told her that she hadn't believed her to be cured, but she didn't think Erin would cause harm to herself or to others and had therefore decided to let her leave.

Erin wasn't an idiot. She knew they had let her leave because they were worried that she might press charges against them for allowing Doctor Quirkhart to carry out his twisted experiments on her, and for getting rid of the evidence of his last experiment without asking for her permission.

Of course, the managing director had also mentioned that if she thought about going up against them, she would advise against it. The courts wouldn't listen to someone who had spent most of her life in an asylum.

At that time, she hadn't wanted to fight them. She had been too numb, too stupefied from the abortion forced on her in the twenty-third week of her pregnancy. She hadn't wanted to analyze then how she felt about her baby. Even now, she didn't know if she could have loved it.

She had to think of the child as an 'it'. But she was probably better off not thinking about the baby at all, especially if she was going to enter the psych ward and be confronted with her past.

"Ah, there you are," Victor said as he watched her hovering in the doorway. "Are you ready?"

"Sure." She was proud to hear how calm she sounded.

"Will you be okay?" her mother asked.

"She'll be fine. She's not alone," Altman answered for Erin. *"We're all here with her."*

"She might end up missing us when we're gone!" Leila tried to lighten the mood.

It helped.

Erin even managed a smile as she followed Victor up the stairs.

On the fourth-floor, they stopped to peer through the window of the psychiatric department. The corridor appeared empty.

Victor glanced at the electronic lock on the door and cursed when he realized that the keys on his key ring couldn't unlock it. "Damn, I forgot about that!" he confessed. "Do you want me to call my shrink to let us in?"

She sighed. "No need. I got hold of an electronic card."

She was about to put the card in front of the box next to the door when she hesitated.

"Now what?" He sounded impatient.

"We need a story. If someone asks what we're doing there, what are we going to say?" she asked.

He shrugged. "I could say that I'm introducing you to that shrink I know. Can we go in now?"

TOUCHED BY MADNESS

She nodded. She took a deep breath to steady her nerves and unlocked the door. Her first impression was that the corridor of the psych ward didn't seem any different from the other corridors in the hospital. The smell was the same, and there wasn't any noise. She could hear some people talking in one of the rooms, but there wasn't anyone crying or screaming.

"That's odd," she mumbled.

"What is?" he whispered.

"The silence," she answered. "Where is everyone?"

"They've probably drugged all their patients so they could go home," he joked as they moved on.

Each room had a small plaque outside the door with the patient's last name as well as the doctor's name.

Victor didn't glance at the plaques, though.

"You seem to know where we need to go for the hospital records," she said. "Have you been here before?"

"Yes, I told you, I've been seeing a shrink here," he replied without looking at her.

"Convenient," she muttered.

They were about to pass the nurses' station, which was situated near the end of the hallway, when they were spotted.

The pretty young nurse sitting behind the desk widened her eyes when she noticed them. "What are you doing here?" she asked. "Oh, hi Victor." She smiled with recognition. "Are you here to see Doc—?"

"Yes," he interrupted her. "We're in a bit of a hurry," he said, nodding at his watch.

"Well okay, see you later," the nurse replied, appearing slightly disappointed.

Erin raised an eyebrow as they walked on.

"We went out once. She was very clingy," he explained.

At the end of the hallway they turned right, only to find another long corridor.

"It's the final room on the left," Victor said, continuing to move forward.

Erin paused for a moment. Her throat tightened and her stomach clenched with anxiety. Was she finally going to discover what had happened all those years ago? She dragged in another deep breath and gritted her teeth. It was time to face her past. She purposefully strode after Victor.

Unease gnawed at her gut when she stopped in front of the room. The door was marked with the word 'Archives'.

Victor fumbled with his key ring, trying out different keys in the lock.

"Oh, please don't tell me we've got this far just to have a stupid lock stop us," she moaned.

"Why don't you try your keys?" he suggested. "You had the electronic card. Maybe they gave you more keys. I'll go have a chat with Samantha." He gestured back toward the nurses' station. "And see if I can steal a set of keys while she's distracted."

She frowned.

"Samantha, that nurse we just spoke to," he explained.

With great reluctance to be left alone, she eventually nodded. "Oh—right, okay."

"Unless there's a problem?" he asked.

"Don't be such a coward," Gideon nagged.

"No, of course not. No problem at all." She let out a nervous laugh.

Does shit scared class as a problem?

He didn't seem to notice her discomfort. "I'll be right back," he said before he left her standing at the door, watching him walk away.

"Don't just stand there! Try the damn keys," Gideon demanded.

"Right," she muttered and took out her key ring.

She looked around and again found it hard to believe how fortunate it was that the hallway was deserted, but she refused to tempt fate by hanging around.

Her hands shook a little as she rushed to try each key in the lock. She was able to get some keys inside, but when she tried turning them, they wouldn't move.

She was beginning to believe she'd never unlock the door when the sixth key she tried turned in the lock with a loud clunk.

She grinned at her success. She left the key in the lock while she hurried back to the nurses' station to tell Victor. She peeked around the corner, hoping to see him, so she could signal for him to return, but he seemed to have disappeared.

"Come on! We don't need him. Just open that door," Leila urged Erin.

"Where the hell is he?" Erin whispered. She could see Samantha's hands busily typing, but nothing indicated that Victor was trying to steal the nurse's keys.

"We're better off without him," Altman agreed with Leila. *"It's safer for you inside that room than standing out here in the hallway."*

After one final glance at the nurses' station, Erin turned to walk back to the archives. Without giving herself any time to hesitate, she pushed open the door.

She let out a loud sneeze when stale air welcomed her into the room. She snapped her head around in alarm, but no one appeared to have heard her.

"Stop acting so jumpy," Leila said.

"Right," Erin mumbled. A fluorescent lamp flickered briefly before coming on automatically when she entered the room.

She peered around, trying to get her bearings. The room had no windows, and it made her feel slightly claustrophobic. She spotted seven long rows of cabinets almost touching the high ceiling. Between each row, there was a narrow aisle. Each cabinet was labeled with a date. She walked toward the third row and grabbed a nearby stool to stand on in case she needed to open one of the drawers at the top.

The records of the patients were put into the archives annually, and within each year the documents were filed alphabetically, so she quickly opened the drawer of the year in question and easily found the file that was labeled 'Holland, Erin.'

She inhaled sharply when she picked up the dusty yellowing file. Her knees felt weak when she removed the folder from the cabinet. Overcome with dizziness, she sat down on the stool and tried to calm her rattled nerves.

This can't be any worse than what I already know.

It was very likely that Mr. Lepareur had already told her the worst of it. But what if he hadn't?

"Go on then, open it," Leila said impatiently.

"You're right. There's no point in putting it off any longer," Erin agreed.

She opened the file and was startled when a disc in a plastic cover fell out. Then she studied the typed pages of the file. The document started with general information such as her parents' names, her home address and the type of injury sustained.

She shivered as she turned to the second page to find an X-ray of her chest that the doctors had obtained while the sword had still been stuck inside her. It was difficult to imagine anyone surviving that.

She moved to the third page, where there was information from the psychiatrist who talked to her after she'd woken from surgery.

Engrossed in the document, she wasn't alarmed when a rush of air and a whisper of sound indicated that someone had entered the room. She assumed it was Victor.

The blood drained from her face when she heard a familiar British accent that chilled her down to the bone.

"Hello Erin, miss me?"

The hackles on the back of her neck rose as she recognized the voice of her old enemy.

She jumped from her seat while cold terror shuddered through her body. She wondered if she was having another nightmare when she glanced back to find Doctor Quirkhart grinning behind her.

She dropped the file, becoming paralyzed with shock.

It can't be him. It just can't be!

His wiry long arm wrapped around her waist and jerked her back against his boney body. The speed and strength of her assailant was surprising, given his skeletal physique.

She opened her mouth to scream, when something sharp dug into her neck. Overwhelming clouds of darkness rose before her eyes, pushing out all rational thought, pushing away the paralysis.

She reacted like a wild animal, hurling herself backward with all her strength and trying to knock her attacker off balance. His cold hand clamped over her mouth. She arched, kicked, clawed, fought and bit, anything to free herself of his iron grip.

Her punches and kicks weakened as the drugs began to affect her system. Everything seemed to dim, but she continued to struggle, attempting to dislodge the hand over her mouth so that she could at least call for help.

Where the hell is Victor?

She writhed in anguish when her muscles relaxed and the world around her dropped out of focus.

She growled and jerked her head backward seeking to smash it into the doctor's mouth or jaw, but her strength was nearly gone and the impact of the blow hardly seemed to affect him. A feeling of abject helplessness added to her panic as her senses reeled.

"Change, Erin!" Altman yelled.

"Yes, fight back!" Leila added.

She moaned as she fought the effects of the drugs, twitching one last time to try to change. She realized with a sense of defeat that it was too late when a dark chill seized her brain. She surrendered to exhaustion, feeling heavy with weariness. Her body went limp as her eyes dropped shut, and mercifully, she sank into the shadows.

ELEVEN

Never had Pauline been more thankful for her gloves than now. She stood in the doorway of Erin's small apartment in shock. The room probably hadn't seen anything resembling a cleaning product for at least a year.

She gagged at the sight of it and wondered if she was finally going to experience what it would have been like to live as a student. She had always imagined students living in a pigsty, which fitted the description of this room to perfection.

Great, I can experience the only part of college I'd have gladly missed.

She began picking up the empty packaging she found scattered around the room. The table was hidden underneath a pile of bills and leaflets. She dropped the rubbish she'd collected and decided to search for garbage bags first, but after going through the pantry and finding nothing, she settled for carrier bags.

She stepped on a pile of paper that stuck to her shoe. After trying to shake it off for a moment she reached down to pluck it off her foot.

TOUCHED BY MADNESS

She gulped back an acid reflex when she peeled chewing gum off her shoe and the paper. She stared at the document and discovered she was holding Erin's Securistate contract. She shook her head and placed it on the bed to be filed later.

She decided to make several piles; one pile for dirty clothes, another for administration, one for garbage and a final pile consisting of clean clothes. The latter were hanging on a clothesline but she suspected that they had probably been dry for quite some time.

There weren't any paintings, posters or even calendars on the wall. She felt a thrill of excitement over the idea of making the apartment into a beautiful home and couldn't wait to use her magic touch.

She switched on the clock radio next to the bed for some music and hummed as she cleaned the studio apartment. She was happy that she could immediately start making herself indispensable to the security guard.

She glanced at the single bed with a frown. Somehow, she doubted that Erin would appreciate sharing her bed.

She decided to go shopping for a new bed as soon as Erin returned from the hospital, preferably one without centuries of dust mite in it.

She glanced at her watch to see how much time she had left to clean up the apartment, before Erin would be back. Surprised, she noticed that it was already six-thirty. Erin had told her that she would finish work at five.

Where is she?

She walked up to the window and pushed it open. A loud mewing sound caught her attention. She looked down to see a fat orange cat approach her. It barely gave her a second glance, as it jumped through the window and into the apartment.

"Ah, so I guess I have you to thank that there aren't any rats running around," she joked. She entered the kitchen, searching for something to feed the cat. She picked up an empty bowl and filled it with milk. When she put it in front of the animal, the cat started to lick it up eagerly.

She squatted next to the cat, clearly interrupting its meal, judging by the annoyed glance it gave her. The animal stopped drinking and moved to the bed with an angry flick of its tail.

"Oh, I beg your pardon! I'm good enough to feed you, but I can't be near you, can I? Well, thank you very much." She raised herself.

"I'll have you know that I've never injured a cat in my life. Selena was the one who enjoyed hurting creatures, and I've left Selena now."

But had she really left the coven?

Again, she wondered where Erin was. What if Selena had gone to the hospital and run into Erin? Would she punish Pauline by going after someone who had aided her?

Feeling anxious, she walked back to the window.

Why didn't I warn Erin?

The security guard had seemed so fierce when standing on the hood of her car in the pouring rain.

She was still impressed by how fast Erin had managed to break off the paralysis spell. She had believed that anyone who was that strong might be able to fight Selena and win.

And now ... if Selena had hurt Erin it was all her fault. She should have told Erin what she was getting into.

The cat meowed right after the door downstairs shut with a bang.

She rushed to the apartment door, opened it and waited for the person climbing the stairs to reach her floor. She prayed it would be Erin.

Disappointed, she saw a handsome man in uniform making his way upstairs. About to close the door, she heard him ask, "Hey, what are you doing in Erin's room?"

Reluctantly, she reopened the door. "I'm a friend."

The man chuckled. "Erin doesn't have any friends."

She folded her arms over her chest and scowled at the man. If that were true, then it wouldn't be a laughing matter. "Well, she can count me as her friend. And who exactly are you? Clearly you are not a friend if you claim that she doesn't have any."

The man abruptly stopped laughing. His expression appeared solemn for a moment. "No, I'm not a friend."

The cat walked up to the doorway and hissed at the man. He glanced at the cat and growled in response. The cat ran out into the hallway and fled downstairs. Lips twitching, the man turned and moved to the next flight of stairs.

"You're wearing the same uniform. Are you colleagues?" she called out.

She believed she heard him mutter, "Not anymore." She wanted to ask him what he meant by that peculiar comment, but he'd already left. Had Erin been fired? Had they found out that Erin had let her go after catching her stealing drugs from the hospital?

Nervously, she walked up to the window and looked outside, searching for Erin again. The street was empty.

She noticed the canals running with torrential rain, but she couldn't believe that Erin would try to avoid bad weather. The girl seemed strong enough to face anything.

But why isn't she home yet?

She heaved a sigh of resignation as she closed the window and grabbed her coat off the chair. She would have to return to the hospital. If Erin had gotten in trouble because of her, she would never be able to forgive herself.

No, I'm not a friend. The words continued to echo in his mind as Victor entered his apartment. Frustrated, he slammed the door shut before walking to the fridge and taking out a beer can. He stood at the kitchen counter and drained the beverage in one long gulp. Next, he opened a second can, downing that too in the hope it would drown the guilt that was twisting his stomach into a heavy knot.

I'm not a friend.

He couldn't undo that last statement even though he desperately wanted to. It had been an honest assessment. This afternoon he had sold out someone he secretly admired. He told himself Erin Holland had only been a case, a way to make some money. If Jonathan Stratton hadn't hired him, he would have found someone else to spy on her, but Victor's actions hadn't consisted merely of spying on someone. He had actually helped someone to kidnap her, a person who had made his instincts scream from the first time he had laid eyes on him. A chill trailed down his spine. He'd lured Erin into the hands of a real monster.

He shook his head, trying to shake off the image of Erin tied up in a straitjacket at the back of Doctor Quirkhart's truck.

But then Jonathan Stratton's words plagued his mind.

I have something planned that will have her screaming for help.

Victor wanted to have no part in it anymore. He refused to think about his boss's reaction, grabbed a bag and started packing.

The werewolf was convinced the whole situation would blow up before long. And if it wasn't Erin breaking loose, it would be Dane Lynch who would unleash the blood-fury boiling inside him when he discovered someone was threatening a girl he seemed to consider his. It would be best if the master vampire of Hope Acres never discovered his role in the kidnapping.

In spite of the staff meeting that had been held at the time of the abduction and the switched-off security cameras, the service elevator that he and Doctor Quirkhart had used when sneaking Erin out of the building had not been deserted. There had still been some people who had caught sight of them. Patients and hospital staff had glanced at them inquisitively while he carried an unconscious Erin outside.

The scary psychiatrist had walked beside them at a calm pace, acting as if he didn't have a care in the world. The doctor didn't seem worried about witnesses. He was obviously completely out of his mind.

And now Erin is tied up somewhere with him.

He suppressed his feelings of guilt. There was nothing he could do, it was too late.

The only thing he could do now was get the hell out of here.

Dane entered Brock's room after only one knock on the door. Brock looked up from behind his mahogany desk and nodded a greeting to him while he continued his phone conversation.

TOUCHED BY MADNESS

Dane narrowed his eyes with impatience while he waited for Brock to finish the call.

Ever since he had shared Erin's horrific dream Dane had been feeling on edge. This nightmare had a greater effect on him than the one he had forced Erin to have about her father. He began to pace up and down the room as images of Erin strapped on a hospital table haunted him. If only he had been able to find her twenty years ago. He should have tried harder. But at the time, he had not been so interested in helping her. Perhaps it was for the best that she had disappeared.

Brock thanked the person on the phone, hung up and rose to face him.

"So what was it?" Dane asked without elaborating on what he needed to know. "Fact or fiction?"

Brock stared at his master with a grim expression. "Fact."

Dane clenched his fists so loudly that his knuckles cracked. He turned his back on the other vampire in an attempt to control the anger boiling up inside him. Before Erin, he hadn't ever had to worry about showing signs of weakness. Now he was struggling to keep his emotions in check.

"I want you to find the shrink for me." Something about the angry command in his gravelly voice made the other vampire take a step backward.

Brock seemed to gather his courage. "I-I believe he started his own practice in London."

"I don't want you to believe. I want you to know!" Dane growled. "I want you to tell me as soon as possible where that bastard is."

A few seconds later, the door opened and a dark figure slipped into the room. "No wonder your vampires keep leaving you," Karma drawled as he approached Dane.

"Be careful what you say," Dane threatened. "I'm in no mood for your games."

Karma shrugged. "You never are."

Dane took two steps in Karma's direction, fuming with anger.

"I overheard what you said to your second-in-command," Karma said as he studied Brock. "Really Dane, you should always stay calm when you're dealing with your subjects."

Dane scowled at the older vampire. "What do you want?"

"I want you to focus on what matters," Karma said. "Your vampires are disappearing. Someone is obviously trying to make you look bad, and you're letting that happen."

"What are you complaining about? Isn't that why you're here? That's what the council wants to hear, right?" Dane snapped.

Karma's lips twisted in a cold smile of triumph. "You're making it too easy, Dane. If I wanted your position I could just take it."

The air between them trembled, raw with tension.

"So why don't you?" Dane goaded.

"Dane!" Brock exclaimed in warning.

"You should listen to Brock, Dane. All these emotions..." Karma shook his head in disgust. "What has happened to you?"

Dane remained silent.

"You were the one who defeated the ancient Gregorio! Gregorio defeated by a vampire a little over two hundred years old. You were amazing!" Karma complimented. "Afterward everyone was afraid of you. Your *piercing* regard could reduce older vampires to puddles of obedience. But now I wonder. How did you manage it?"

Dane's lips curved in an ironic smile. "Why? Are you thinking about getting rid of another powerful vampire? Do you need any pointers?"

"Why so evasive?" Karma turned to Brock who stared at the door with longing. "Why doesn't your master give me a straight answer? Come on Brock, tell me. How did your master fight such a powerful opponent?"

Before Brock could think of an answer, Dane intervened, "You don't need to question my vampires. If you really want to know what happened, I'll tell you. Afterward, you can run to your council buddies and tell them all about it."

When Karma didn't respond, Dane continued, "It wasn't a fair fight. I murdered him."

Karma shook his head. "If you're trying to shock me, then that won't work. If you *murdered* him, as you say, I'm sure he had it coming."

Dane raised his eyebrows in surprise. "I'm not convinced the members of the council would share your opinion."

Karma shrugged casually. "I ran into Gregorio a couple of times. Calling him a sociopath would be too kind. So, how did you do it?"

"We were outside the cabin next to the bayou. Gregorio had summoned me, and I knew beforehand that it wasn't going to be a courtesy call," Dane told Karma.

"Rafferty was there and so was Altman. Gregorio said that he had overheard that I wanted to take over his position. He wanted me to know my place, and Altman and Rafferty were there to teach me."

"Hmm, and what method of persuasion did he use that time?" Karma queried.

"He told Altman to burn his initials into my flesh, but as you know vampires heal too fast for that to be much of a punishment," Dane said. "Altman was told to use the fire and a 'special' brand from the barbecue that Gregorio had brought especially for the occasion. Gregorio said a mark like that would burn for eternity and bind me to him. I suspected a witch had cursed the brand in some way. I knew full well that Gregorio regularly enjoyed the company of witches. From what I learned afterward, the brand would have permanently neutered me of my free will."

"What happened to the brand?" Karma asked.

"I had it destroyed. It was my first act as master vampire of Hope Acres," Dane replied with a scowl.

"A shame, such objects are rare," Karma commented.

"Such objects should not exist at all," Dane replied.

"Probably, please continue."

"Rafferty was told to hold me down, but before Rafferty could touch me, I had knocked over the barbecue and it set Gregorio on fire."

Karma frowned. "That doesn't sound like murder to me."

"Oh, but it was," Dane drawled. "When he tried to get away, probably to jump in the bayou, I grabbed the barbecue and used it to push him into the cabin. Then I locked the door and waited for the pounding to stop."

"And the other vampires let you?"

"They weren't able to pull me away," Dane defended them.

"Really?" Karma didn't sound as though he believed him. "And after the pounding stopped?"

"I unlocked the door," Dane continued. "Gregorio had set the whole room on fire, and we had to leave. We let the cabin burn down. Nothing remained."

"And then you told the others that you were the new master vampire of Hope Acres. No one dared to defy you?" Karma sounded surprised.

Dane chuckled. "It's what you said. They were all afraid of me. Sure, some weren't happy about his death. They adapted."

Silence filled the room while the three vampires were lost in thought. Dane was the one to break the silence. "So now you know, you can tell the council all about it."

"I might," Karma said. "If you manage to solve your little problem with the missing vampires, I will keep quiet. But if you keep focusing on less important things, you will force me to do something about it."

A tiny smile was tugging at Dane's lips. "Now why do I think that you are not telling me everything?"

Karma walked to the door. "Because you're not stupid."

"But you won't help us with the missing vampires. You want to tell the council Dane failed," Brock said.

Karma opened the door and turned to face them. "I'm not the enemy here. Think about it."

Karma shut the door leaving behind two mystified vampires.

"So..." Brock hesitated. "Do you want me to stop focusing on Erin?"

"I still want you to find that shrink," Dane ordered. "Other than that, I will deal with her. In fact, I will deal with her right now."

He was tired of vampires telling him how to act. What was the point of being a master vampire if he could not do as he pleased? Of course, Erin would attract the attention of his enemies once his interest in her was known, but Dane refused to worry about future battles. He had earned his reputation the hard way, and if others needed convincing, he was looking forward to the fight.

"And the missing vampires?" Brock asked.

"I am not going to take orders from Karma. I will investigate that in my own time," Dane said in an empty voice.

"Yes, Sir."

Dane ignored Brock and left the room. He should have bonded with Erin twenty years ago. She needed him. Her time at the hospital—hell, even her time in Hope Acres— proved it to him. She might need some convincing, but he was not going to use kid gloves just because she had been through hell. He didn't have that in him. He was a killer. He would get rid of her tormentor, and then they would focus on the future—their future.

Karma strolled through the front door on his way out of the mansion. He hesitated for a moment when he glanced down to find Hazel sitting outside on the stone steps waiting for him. The determined expression on her face made him sigh.

"Did you have a nice conversation?" she asked.

"Yes." The single word of agreement was dragged from him.

"You're not going to follow me around anymore?"

"It seems that you're the one doing the following," he said.

"Fine." She stood up and turned around. She was about to go back inside when he grabbed her wrist.

"Wait," he ordered.

Her eyes narrowed on his hand as it held her. "What?"

"I didn't tell them anything about you," he confided.

She pulled herself loose and snorted. "There's nothing to tell."

"I noticed you've stopped leaving the house. Are you afraid to, Hazel dear?" he asked, offering her a coaxing smile.

"Don't be ridiculous!" Her laugh came out as nervous yelp while she wearily brushed her red hair from her face. "I'm avoiding temptation, that's all."

"Ah, because Dane told you not to bite anyone for at least a year," he said.

"That's right."

"And what do you think of his punishment for turning Jerry? Quite harsh, wasn't it?" he asked as though he were sympathizing with her.

She shrugged. "I guess."

"I wonder what Gregorio would have done—he was very strict, right?"

She jumped up. "Y-yes," she stammered.

He stared straight into her green eyes, which she quickly averted.

"But he was never strict with you, was he? He didn't have to be. You would never do anything against his wishes. He had you properly trained," he mocked.

She looked up, appearing furious. Her eyes were shooting daggers at him, but she didn't contradict him.

"You know what I find strange?" he murmured. "I find it strange how someone who is so used to following a leader, someone like you, completely changed her personality the minute that leader was gone."

"Maybe the leader replacing him is a bad one!" she snapped as she turned around.

"Why would you deliberately defy the new master? It doesn't make sense. Why would you turn Jerry, knowing how Dane would react?" he went on as if she hadn't spoken. She rushed back into the house.

"But you didn't, did you?" he called out. She froze in the doorway.

"You didn't turn Jerry," he stated without doubt.

She slammed the door behind her as she entered the mansion. He smirked as he watched her flight.

"Thank you for that confirmation," he mumbled as he walked up to his car. The council would be very interested in his findings.

Pauline felt ill at ease when she entered the hospital for the second time that day. Fortunately, she didn't seem to be attracting anyone's attention. Her heart accelerated as she approached the office where Erin had interrogated her. Not for the first time in the previous thirty minutes did she debate the wisdom of returning to the scene of the crime.

What if Erin had changed her mind and called the police? What if Selena and Eartha had gone to the hospital to find out why she hadn't come home? What if they were waiting for her to arrive at the hospital?

She closed her eyes and took a deep breath, hoping it would relax her nerves. It failed miserably. She pushed all doubts aside and forced herself to knock on the wall next to the open door of the room where a security guard was observing the monitors. Disappointed, she realized it wasn't Erin. The overweight male security guard seemed to be in his late forties.

He frowned as he noticed her. "Yes?"

"H-hello. I'm looking for Erin." Her voice shook.

"She's not here." The man turned his back on her and stared again at the screens on his desk.

Resenting her dismissal, she clenched her fists. "I-I..."

"What?" the man called out.

"H-have you seen h-her?" she persevered.

"No, I haven't! In fact, when I arrived, there wasn't anyone here. I guess she decided to play hooky, just like that colleague of hers," he ranted. "Hell, maybe they were off playing together. I don't give a fuck! Will you get the hell out?"

Without responding, she left the office. She thought about walking through the building. Maybe

TOUCHED BY MADNESS

Erin had never left the hospital. She considered doing a location spell.

She watched a security camera that was pointed right at her. If something had happened to Erin in the hospital, a camera should have witnessed it.

She winced as she pictured herself asking the security guard to show her footage of Erin. It would show if anything had happened to Erin while she was working, but it probably wouldn't reveal where she was now. Also, that security guard was an ass.

Doing a location spell was an easier solution. It'd be nice to use her magic for a good cause. She hoped it would work.

She decided it would be best if she returned to Erin's apartment. The hospital made her feel nervous, especially under the close scrutiny of the cameras. She needed a quiet, undisturbed place to scry for Erin.

She left the building, and as she drove to Erin's studio she mulled over the mystery of what had happened to Erin.

Maybe Erin's colleague was right and Erin had gone out to play with the other security guard. She hoped that Erin had returned to her studio apartment, but a part of her was convinced that she would have to stand up to Selena alone.

Ten minutes later, she entered an empty apartment. She turned on the lights and glanced around hoping Erin had returned. The apartment looked exactly the same as it had when she had left.

There were no indications that anyone else had been here.

She sighed and peeked out of the window examining the street below. The road was dark and empty. When she glanced down, she saw Erin's cat walking up the stairs of the fire escape before stopping in front of the window. The animal raised its paw as if it wanted to get in, but she shook her head.

"Sorry, cat. I can't afford any distractions."

She went into the kitchen to search for candles for the location spell. She was surprised to find a whole pantry filled with candles in different colors, incense, herbs, ribbons and mood stones.

She laughed. "That's great! She's a witch too."

She took out four blue candles, a match, jasmine incense and a glass. She peered out of the window one last time, still no Erin in sight.

She filled the glass with water and set it down on the bathroom floor. She left the room to fetch the other items before returning to the bathroom and sitting down facing the glass. She placed the four candles around her. One candle facing north, the others facing south, east and west. She turned in the direction of the west and lit the candles and the incense.

"Where are you, Erin?" she whispered. She closed her eyes, concentrating to calm her mind. When she felt she was ready to receive the information, she opened her eyes and stared down into the water.

TOUCHED BY MADNESS

"Powers That Be, show me where Erin is. As is my will, so mote it be." She repeated it four times, staring at the water and waiting. Unfortunately, patience wasn't something she excelled at, but with some effort, she managed to keep herself focused and bided her time.

The loud drip from a leaky tap grated on her nerves while she waited for something to happen. She was beginning to wonder if she'd lost her touch, when she felt something.

Her mouth dropped open in surprise as a picture started to form in her mind. She wasn't a visual person, and the few times that Selena had made her do a location spell, she had only gotten a feeling of a location. Maybe she was more motivated now.

Her first impression was that of a fog, out of which, tall brown shapes emerged. She squeezed her eyes shut to concentrate harder on the image. The faintest whiff of spicy wood entered her nostrils. She smiled when she recognized the smell of burnt leaves. A surge of excitement raced through her when the mist stirred, and the objects solidified. She recognized the forest because she had lived in it for the past three years, ever since she had joined Selena's coven.

She shivered when she saw an isolated cabin. The vision was still a little bit blurry, but she didn't need to see any additional details. Even though there were several cabins in the forest that looked like the bungalow she had shared with Selena and the others, she felt certain this was the same one.

Selena must have gone out to the hospital to search for her after she hadn't returned with the drugs. Maybe Selena had put Erin under a truth spell and found out that she had offered her a way out of the coven. What if she was going to put Erin through the same torture that the vampires had gone through? Or worse, what if Selena had decided to punish Erin by handing her over to the thing...?

"I'm sorry, Erin," she whispered as the vision faded away. She blew out the candles, but let the incense dissolve.

Leaving the items on the floor, she stood up on shaking legs. She caught her reflection in the mirror and flinched when she saw the terror in her gaze. She approached the mirror and touched its cold surface.

There she was, a pale coward. She had known all along that running away wasn't the solution. She must undo the evil she had committed as a puppet in Selena's coven. Her cowardly behavior had endangered another innocent bystander. Turning on the cold water, she splashed it on her face and berated herself for her conduct.

"No more," she said to her reflection. "I'm going to find a way to finally rid myself, and this earth of an evil witch."

But how was she going to do that?

She wiped her face on a towel and waited a few seconds to embolden herself. Straightening her shoulders, she felt some of her doubts dissipate, as she stood tall. She hurried out of the apartment before she could change her mind.

TWELVE

"Erin, open your eyes."

When she did, she found herself lying in bed in her apartment. A strange man stood propped against the wall across from her with his hands shoved into the pockets of his jeans.

The stranger was a large man with pale skin, short ginger hair and light gray eyes that shimmered in the light.

He crossed the room and walked toward her bed.

"Do you mind?" she muttered as she sat up straight.

She glanced down and saw she was wearing her favorite Garfield nightgown. It was a very modest nightshirt, but she still felt uncomfortable. She tugged the covers up to her chin.

The man hesitated before leaning against the wall again. He appeared flustered.

"I'm sorry. I didn't mean to intrude. I just thought that this time the situation really warranted it."

"What situation?" She frowned as she studied him. He was an ordinary-looking man, who seemed to be in his early forties. She couldn't remember if she had ever laid eyes on him before, but somehow he seemed familiar.

"I know you, don't I?" She gave him a nervous smile. "Or am I imagining things?"

"On the contrary," the man said as he drew his hands from his pockets and pushed away from the wall. He moved closer. "You are one of the sanest people I know."

She closed her eyes while the stranger talked, focusing on the man's voice. With sudden recognition, she realized whose voice it was.

"Altman, is that you?"

Altman nodded with a somber expression.

"How...? Why are you here?" she asked.

"Don't you remember what happened? You were at the hospital..." he reminded her.

She shivered. "Doctor Quirky," she whispered with a feeling of doom. "He found me at the archives. What about Victor?"

He pulled a face.

"H-h—he betrayed me?" she stammered.

When he remained silent, she frowned. "And then Doctor Quirky drugged me. So I'm with him now?"

"Yes." After his single word of agreement, a body-shaking wave of revulsion swamped her entire being.

"Then what are you doing talking to me?" she demanded angrily. "Aren't you fighting him now?"

The vampire sighed. "We tried, but something is blocking us."

"Really? You can't take over my body anymore when I'm asleep?" She had wanted them to stop possessing her, but the timing could not be worse. "Did Doctor Quirkhart do something to stop you?"

"No, we think that you're doing it. And by the startled expression on your face, I guess that you weren't aware of it," he said.

"That doesn't sound right. I've been trying to stop you from taking over my body. Why would I suddenly be able to do so now?" she protested.

He shrugged. "I don't know. Maybe you've become more powerful."

"Just like that, after twenty years?" she asked.

"Well, in a couple of days it will be Halloween. Then it will be exactly twenty years since you got our powers. And magic is usually stronger during Halloween. The reason isn't important, though. I'm just speculating. Whatever it is, it feels as though it is blocking us from the inside," he clarified.

"Do you know how I can undo whatever it is I did?" she asked, panic-stricken. "Maybe I can talk to my mom? She might know a spell."

"No, I'm sorry. Only vampires and warlocks can enter other people's dreams."

"Warlocks as well? So Gideon could show up now too?"

He shook his head decisively. "No, he won't. Don't worry about that. We won't let that happen."

A frightening thought entered her mind. "So vampires can enter people's dreams? Can all vampires do that?"

"The older vampires can, yes. It's quite easy," he said. "All you need to do is concentrate. I could probably teach you how to do it too, considering you also have a couple of my other talents."

"Do you think that Dane Lynch could enter my dreams?" she asked.

"Oh! Well, I guess..." He looked away, sounding uncomfortable. "Maybe we should first focus on the problem at hand."

"I don't know about that. I don't want to think about problems that I don't know how to solve. Let's discuss something else. So you can enter my dreams, but you've never done it before, right?" she continued. "Why haven't you?"

"I felt you needed at least that much privacy. I know you didn't ask us to join you. Even during the day, I try to give you some time on your own. I guess you didn't know," he said.

"You're right. To me it seems like all of you are always there." She smiled. "So where do you go when you're not with me?"

He swiftly moved to her bed and settled next to her on the mattress. He shot her a reluctant glance. "A dark place."

"That sounds terrible," she said. "Do you see my mom and the others as well when you go there?"

"No. I'm always on my own." He appeared sad for a moment before continuing, "But let's concentrate on Doctor Quirkhart."

"All right," she agreed, although her mind was still busy with the image of Altman stuck in a dark place.

What if that was what awaited them when they crossed over? She didn't care about Gideon, but she *didn't want the others to end up spending their afterlife there.*

"No, stay focused," she mumbled. Altman was right. She had to keep her mind on the issue that they first needed to resolve. She pictured herself unconscious with Doctor Quirky hovering over her, and a violent shiver shook through her.

"What do you think I should do?" she asked hoarsely.

"Try not to resist us. We all want the same thing here. Even Gideon can't wait to go after the shrink."

"Fine, please possess my body," she ordered.

A smile lit up his serious face and she grinned, pleasantly surprised.

"I'm happy to meet you like this. Let's do it again someday, after we get rid of the psycho!"

"Yes, try positive thoughts," he joked. "Maybe that will help us get rid of the obstruction. Good luck!"

"Yes, you too," she said.

He turned, and within two steps, completely disappeared into the shadows.

A sliver of light across her eyes woke her. Erin came to with a sour, chemical taste in her mouth that confirmed her suspicion of being drugged. She felt the familiar immobility and heaviness in her limbs.

An unfamiliar odor of wet, mossy wood pervaded her nostrils. She kept her eyes closed and tried to keep her breathing even, in an attempt to assess as much of herself and her surroundings as she could. She didn't want to inform anyone watching her that she was conscious.

She was barefoot and cold, but relieved to find that her uniform hadn't been removed.

Her heart sank when she recognized the binding feeling of a straitjacket.

She lay perfectly still and listened with her vampire hearing. Bullfrogs were calling out nearby, anoles were hissing and mosquitoes were humming. If Doctor Quirky lurked, he was taking pains not to betray his presence.

Okay, time to confront my fears.

She opened her eyes and blinked up into the flame of a candle.

"Ah, finally! I was getting afraid that I had given you too high a dose," a cheerful obtrusive voice said.

She jerked her head around as her heart frantically hammered.

"I was worried you might be playing dead."

She slowly sat up on the hard sofa. She felt dizzy and swayed, nearly tumbling backward. Her gaze swept the room. Seeing the doctor wasn't something she was anticipating with pleasure, so she decided to check out her surroundings instead.

She was in the front room of what appeared to be a small cabin. She was surprised to discover that the doctor had used candles to light the room. There was a tiny kitchen on her left. Instead of a dining table, she noticed a desk with an open laptop on it. She squeezed her eyes to see what was on its screen, but her vision was still blurry.

TOUCHED BY MADNESS

When Doctor Quirky noticed her interest, he walked up to the desk and shut the laptop.

She breathed in deeply and straightened up from the sofa, wishing she could press her hand to her upset stomach and rub it. The straitjacket made every movement awkward.

She raised her head in the doctor's direction. There was no use putting it off anymore. She had to confront her old enemy.

The drug was beginning to wear off, and her vision started to clear, but her tongue still felt thick and dry in her mouth.

Her first impression was that the shrink hadn't changed much. He was still tall, skinny and ugly. He hadn't stopped using the same awful cotton candy comb-over. She noticed that his eyes were gray, just like Altman's, but ironically, unlike the eyes of the vampire, Doctor Quirkhart's gray eyes were dead.

She cleared her throat and struggled to find her voice.

"What the fuck do you want from me?" she rasped.

The psychiatrist leveled a disdainful glare at her. He opened his bag and removed surgical instruments that he put on a white cloth on the desk next to him. The glimmer of the silver tools laid out on the surface seemed to be standard torture fare.

Her stomach clenched.

He removed a box of salt, a box of matches and some lighter fluid from his bag.

Puzzled, she shook her head as she stared at the suspicious-looking items. He placed them next to the surgical instruments.

He caught the confusion on her face. "Shall I tell you what I have planned for us?" His voice was soft.

She was about to tell him she wasn't interested when he retrieved the last items from his bag, a syringe and a gun. He put them next to the laptop.

The hackles on the back of her neck rose. "So you've decided to use guns now? Aren't you tough?"

"It's just a precaution," he replied.

"Against me? Poor defenseless me." She laughed. "I'm tied up in a straitjacket! This doesn't seem like any therapy I have ever heard of, *Doctor Quirky.*"

He stiffened at her taunt.

"Shall I tell you what kind of therapy I have envisioned?"

"Yes," she said resolutely. If she knew what to expect, she could prepare herself.

"Well, too bad. I don't answer to you." A smile was tugging at his lips.

She nodded at the gun. "I thought you wanted to be me. Now you want to kill me?"

"Be like you," he sneered. "You're an abomination! And I'm not the only one who believes that. We will get rid of all the monsters, and you're the biggest freak of them all! Ha! Be like you," he repeated. "I did those things to find out if you could contaminate others."

TOUCHED BY MADNESS

"So you sacrificed yourself, is that what you're saying? For science, and—and the other things you did?" She couldn't say it.

"The pregnancy?" he jeered. "You didn't really believe that I would use my own seed, did you?"

A lump rose in her throat. "Is that what you tell yourself, or is that what you want your Divine Right buddies to believe?" Her voice started shrieking while her gaze collided with his. She laughed a hollow, mocking sound that tore at her chest as it escaped. She didn't care if she sounded hysterical. She didn't feel reasonable at the moment.

"The Divine Right knows the danger of allowing freaks to mingle with humans. We have to kill you before you kill us."

She gazed at the closed door. The windows were also shut, but she supposed that if she used enough speed, she would be able to break through the glass.

"Don't try to escape, Erin."

She turned to her tormentor and felt her body tense at the twisted expression on his face.

"Why not? You're going to kill me anyway!"

"Maybe not, we're going to do a couple of tests first. You could try to change our minds." He smirked.

The words struck like a blow to her chest. More tests. Panic flashed up and crested as he lifted one of the surgical knives from the desk.

"I've read up on ways to test many creatures. Unfortunately, I find the methods to be so uncivilized and tiresome. I would rather not exert myself. Alas, my new friends are unable to trust anyone but me, so I'm afraid that I will be the one doing the dirty work." With a sigh of resignation, he walked toward her, his step purposeful.

She met his mocking gaze with her stomach twisting into knots. Her bravado faltered when she saw him play with one of his knives, and then crumbled.

"It's a pity the hospital caught me before I could do more tests. I never found out what your pain levels were. I know that sunlight doesn't hurt you. We need to know more."

She struggled to stand and moved away from the couch. Her eyes remained centered on the knife. In the flickering candlelight, the silver blade seemed to glow with a strange red luminescence as if it were coated with her blood already.

She tasted bile as the doctor drew closer to her, his gray eyes glittering. She took one look at his crazed expression and recognized something far worse than insanity in it. He was pure evil.

He knew the power he had over her and looked as if he couldn't wait to exercise that power. He was prolonging it only to toy with her a little bit more.

Breathing was almost impossible. She felt as though she were going to fall to her knees at any moment.

"It will be interesting to see whether you heal as slowly as we humans or as quickly as the monster you are," he said, his voice calm and pleasant.

"Just do it and stop gloating," she snapped. Her nerves were too raw to contain the protest.

Seeing her concern, he smiled.

Nervously licking her lips, she exhaled another hard breath while making her way to the door. She came to a hard stop when he grabbed her around her waist. Her body went rigid with fear.

"You don't do this for science. You do it because you're a sadist!" she shouted, her voice now burning with anger.

The doctor remained quiet and forced her back to the couch. He reached out to touch her face with his bony fingers.

She jerked back, trying to sink into the couch to get as far away from him as possible.

"I was wondering whether to give you more drugs before my first test, but I enjoy your screaming far too much." He sat down on her legs.

Tied up as she was in the straitjacket, she couldn't move. Paralyzing fear flooded her, the kind she remembered from her time at the mental hospital.

He raised his knife as he slid down to sit on her feet. Without taking off the trousers, he cut through the sturdy fabric on her left thigh.

She felt the knife slice through her skin. She swallowed a scream.

He ripped open the hole in her trousers to investigate his handiwork.

The sight of the thin cut as the blood spread, welling in liquid lines down her pale skin broke through her paralysis. She kicked him, and he cursed when her leg hit his groin.

He quickly retreated and moved to the desk, rubbing his injury. Silently, he picked up the syringe, returned to the couch and unhesitatingly jabbed it into her arm.

"W-what is it?" she asked.

"The first test," he whispered in her ear. Then he let go, and she slipped to the floor. The coils of fear that had been twisting inside her bowels turned into shards of glass grinding up her insides.

"Stop fighting us," Altman said.

"I-I'm—I'm not," she replied, her voice soft as the contents of the syringe began to affect her.

"Huh? You're not, what?" The psychiatrist bent over her.

"Fighting..." she muttered.

The doctor laughed. "You're right. You're not fighting at all!"

He stared down at the leg he had cut and frowned. The leg had begun to heal, the skin reknitting as he observed her.

"Freak," he said.

She watched as he left the cabin, her mind and her emotions thrown into turmoil. She remained on the floor, her hair tangled around her face.

"Embrace it," Gideon encouraged. *"Embrace the power."*

"Tired," she whispered. She closed her eyes.

"Fight the drugs, but not us," Altman said. *"You know he will cut you open when he gets back."*

But there was no fight left in her, only a vast emptiness. She knew she was probably going to die tonight, but somehow that knowledge did not quite touch her. Nothing touched her.

"Think about the baby," Leila suddenly blurted.

"I don't want to think about, the baby," Erin whined.

"You have to. You have to get even," Leila said.

"Stop acting like a stupid victim! He's here. No witnesses—kill him!" Gideon yelled.

Erin's eyes remained closed and she pictured herself as she had been, strapped on the hospital table. Her body had changed. For the first time, she had breasts and a belly. A baby was living inside her. And they...

"They killed her," she cried. She finally realized that in her mind, the baby had been a little girl. The child had never been an 'it'.

"Then punish them!" Leila said. *"Get even!"*

With great effort, Erin got to her knees. She had to get out of the straitjacket. She was going to get a handle on this, she promised herself—for her daughter.

She found strength in pushing the memories aside and going on. Now she realized that she needed to seek the part of her that she had suppressed, and accept it. She couldn't remember ever being this furious. She embraced her fury now.

Her anger seemed to minimize the influence of the drugs. Her chest felt tight, a lump locking in her throat as she pushed back the impulse to sob in rage.

She would stop running. She was going to fight the crazy doctor and rid herself of him once and for all.

Her breath caught at the prospect of the battle ahead. No more tests, she told herself. She broke off the thought as sickness roiled in her stomach, and nightmares threatened to replace determination. She could do this.

"Try a spell to take off the straitjacket," her mother suggested.

"Where is Doctor Quirky?" Erin asked.

"Who cares? Just get ready for him to come back. Call out the leopard. The change will get rid of the straitjacket," Leila told her.

Erin preferred the quickest solution, and since she didn't feel creative enough to think of a good incantation, she opted for Leila's suggestion.

She closed her eyes as she called on the powers she had long considered a curse. As always, the leopard was eager to respond.

The first things to change were her arms. She fell down on the floor and groaned while her confined body tried to make the transformation into an animal.

It was a very unnatural position for a leopard to have its front legs tied behind its back.

Fortunately, the legs were very thin compared to the arms of a human and she managed to pull all four legs out from under the jacket. Now the garment was stuck around the upper level of her body and, combined with her uniform, it felt as though the straitjacket was choking her.

TOUCHED BY MADNESS

Her face had finished shifting, so now her leopard's teeth could bite through the cloth around her neck.

She was so involved in the task of biting through the straitjacket that she didn't notice the doctor's return.

He stood, observing her.

"Well, well! I only have to leave the room for a few minutes for you to show your true face." When he finally spoke, the sound of his voice sent a shiver down her spine.

She refused to let him distract her and continued with her task. She tore once more into the garment. Cloth ripped.

He grimaced. "I guess I should have given you a higher dosage."

Still in leopard form, she slipped out of the jacket and her ruined uniform. Her leopard's teeth had also torn through the blouse, and her shape-shifting had caused the seam of her trousers to come apart.

She felt his gaze slicing into her. She glared at her tormentor, growling deep in her throat. It was an animal sound.

"You sound like a rabid dog," he mocked. "You know what we do to rabid dogs, don't you?"

She forced herself to transform back to her human form and got up. All she wore were stretched out panties, but she faced her tormentor unashamed. She didn't want there to be any misunderstandings when she spoke to him.

"Why don't you try to give me another shot, asshole?" she goaded. Anger pumped inside her body, filling her eyes and her voice. The pitch of her voice was lower than usual, but the words were comprehensible. She staggered over to him.

He smiled, eyes gleaming. "Good idea." He raised his arm, which was holding a gun.

"I'm going to bathe myself in your blood," she rasped into the charged air. Fury spilled from her tense body.

"Stop talking, let's have some action!" Gideon screamed.

She was about to tell Gideon to shut up when, without warning, Doctor Quirkhart fired several shots in her direction, clearly sensing her distraction.

She gritted her teeth in annoyance as one of the bullets hit her arm. The adrenaline headed off any feelings of pain. She felt invincible.

Her nostrils flared, and her back teeth clenched. She leapt at him, beginning to shift in mid-air. Then she was on the ground with him beneath her. He seemed stunned by the force of the blow and lay on the floor, shocked and unable to move.

The cat, however, wanted to play with her food.

"Fight me," she purred. Her voice was half human and half growl. She felt the familiar sensation of her teeth elongating and licked his neck with a wicked grin.

He screamed and moved his arms to push her leopard body off his own. Irritated by the hands waving in front of her face, she sank her razor-sharp canines into his right wrist.

The psychiatrist's blood spattered on her face, and he seemed to be shouting his lungs out. He attempted to pull his arm out of her muzzle, but she refused to let go and his hand was torn from his arm.

She would have expected him to scream even louder. Instead, a small sound escaped his throat, very much like a whimper, and then he fell silent. She let go of his arm and licked the blood from her cheeks.

He tried to pull the injured arm to his stomach, and his breathing was irregular.

She stared at him again, hesitating when she saw the stricken expression on his face.

"No doubts!" Gideon said.

"Kill him," Leila yelled.

She heard the sound of metal sliding over the wooden floor and turned her head to determine where it came from.

She grunted when she saw the doctor quickly retracting his remaining hand from the gun.

She moved closer, invading his space. He swallowed hard, and her gaze slipped to the base of his throat where she knew his pulse beat hard and fast.

Doctor Quirkhart saw the leopard's lucid stare and flinched. Why weren't the drugs affecting her as they had before? He had injected her with the same medication when he had been her psychiatrist at the institution. She should have been out like a light even before he had left the cabin. Had returning to her birth town increased her powers in some way?

The animal's breath touched his neck, and he shuddered in revulsion. His fist clenched at his side. He was about to throw up. He eyed the tiny camera next to the laptop. Where were the others? Why weren't they intervening?

It had been so nice to talk to people who had agreed with his actions at the hospital in England. He was a visionary. He should have been given a medal instead of being fired!

Before he had received the call inviting him to go to Hope Acres, the Divine Right followers had always seemed to him to border on maniacal. The man on the phone, however, had been calm and remarkably well-spoken.

The doctor's ego had taken a heavy blow when the managing director of the institution fired him. He wondered what she would say if she could see Erin now.

As the leopard licked the blood off his skin, he found it difficult to stay focused. His skin felt cold and clammy, and he experienced a weakness that worsened as his breathing became shallow and irregular.

He noticed that the leopard had moved to lick his left hand. Her tongue was scraping off the skin of his fingers and she purred, nibbling on the flesh as if it were a delicacy.

He hoped that if he stopped moving, the large animal would lose interest in her prey and move away. Then the creature glanced up at him with blank golden eyes. He realized that there was nothing of Erin left. The cat had completely taken over.

His heart skipped a beat as it dawned on him that it wouldn't matter what he did. She was going to consume him, one bite at a time.

The horrific image broke through his numbness. As his mind rebelled, his body managed to fight back. The arm that wasn't being gnawed at started hitting the leopard. But since blood loss had sapped his strength, his handless limb could not do much damage. The leopard growled and subdued him by biting through the other wrist. Blood spilled over him in a hot arc. He screamed and prayed for oblivion.

Unfortunately for him, he stayed conscious through most of his ordeal, even when the claws of the animal slid straight into his abdomen.

It was at that point that he had his most lucid thought. He realized why no one had come to rescue him, and also why the drugs he had been given hadn't been strong enough to knock Erin out. No one was coming for him. Not because they hadn't wanted to test Erin, but for a more horrifying reason.

He was the test.

Darkness came. It swallowed up the leopard and left him alone, floating in the dark.

The leopard tilted her head as she observed the food, puzzled that it had stopped moving. She poked into the flesh of the stomach. The body was still warm and smelled fresh.

"He's gone now," someone said.

"It never hurts to be sure," another voice added.

The leopard looked up, confused when she couldn't find the source of the voices. The darkness inside her mind wavered. Something was trying to break through.

"Erin, you can stop now," a familiar female voice said.

The leopard peered down at the body that had been torn to pieces, and then at the dried blood on her own fur. She whimpered as her human mind rushed back to her.

"No regrets," Altman said. *"It was either him or you."*

She slowly crawled away from the body.

Erin was still in animal form, but her thoughts were now human. At first, they were a vague blur, and then she remembered. The clawed hands, the hunger for flesh...

The leopard had roamed freely. She had finally managed to tear down her shields and was now witnessing the results.

TOUCHED BY MADNESS

"You should make sure that he's really dead," Gideon said.

"Oh, come on!" Leila exclaimed. *"Look at him!"*

For once, Erin agreed with Gideon. She didn't want there to be any more surprises. The good old doctor had given her enough surprises to last a lifetime. Still in leopard form, she prodded the body. It seemed lifeless. She walked up to his face. The doctor had his eyes closed and made no sound.

"Maybe he fainted," Gideon said.

Then, without remorse, Erin tore out his throat.

THIRTEEN

Erin's stomach growled. She opened her eyes to narrow slits and blinked at the dead doctor lying beneath her naked human body.

She tried to push herself off him, but her left hand slid straight into his abdomen as if it were Jell-O. She retched as she quickly withdrew her hand from where it lay, buried in the corpse. The sound of slimy flesh sticking to her limbs made her feel worse.

She swallowed to suppress the bile rising in her throat. She assumed that her stomach was upset because it had had to digest a human being. She swore she could still taste him. She had never eaten a human before, and sincerely hoped that Doctor Quirky was the only human she would ever eat.

She didn't want to get up, but she wasn't comfortable lying on top of the man she had just eaten. Groaning, she managed to crawl toward the bathroom and leaned against the doorway. She really needed to take a bath. Her stomach, left arm and legs were covered in the psychiatrist's blood and flesh.

TOUCHED BY MADNESS

She touched her face and was surprised that it felt clean. Her right arm wasn't covered in gore, either. Appalled, she realized that she had probably licked them clean. She wondered if by fighting monsters, she was becoming one.

She stared at the corpse in front of her. Before she could wash away the evidence, she needed to get rid of the doctor. If she touched him after she had bathed, she would get dirty again.

She dreaded having to touch him, but had to decide what she should do with the body. She considered burying him somewhere in the forest, but understood that if his body were discovered there, the police would know he had been murdered. Going to the police herself and claiming self-defense wasn't an option if she wanted to avoid exposure.

The bayou seemed the best solution. She hoped the alligators would finish off the body. Then if anyone ever found remains, the wildlife would be blamed.

She pushed herself up with the help of the doorframe and staggered over to her old enemy. In spite of the drugs still pumping through her system, she managed to lift what remained of him off the floor. She was surprised that his body didn't weigh much at all. She felt strong enough to easily carry several bodies, but she prayed she would never require this kind of strength again

She opened the door. The night was nearly pitch-black with only the pale moon lighting the dark sky. Dense forest surrounded the cabin, which she stumbled toward as she carried the body out of the cabin and into the darkness.

Wind rushed along the ground, and the air smelled of rain. The distinctive odor of the bayou pinpointed its location to her heightened senses. The sounds and smells of the bayou were all around her. She could hear night birds calling, the rustling of snakes and the stench of decayed vegetation. The body also gave off a distinct odor, which made her gag in revulsion.

As she left the cabin, her feet sank into soft mud, making a sound of suction every time they got stuck, and she had to pull them free. The cypress trees ominously swayed. Shades of gray cast eerie shadows over long strands of moss sweeping the water below the trees. Twigs snapped as she moved to the water, praying she hadn't dropped any body parts along the way.

When she reached the water's edge, she hesitated. She didn't want to just throw him in the bayou in case he would immediately drift back to the shore.

She moaned when she saw snakes plop into the water from low-slung branches. The sounds of the wilderness carried in the stillness of the swamp. She tried not to think about the deadly creatures as she stepped into the marsh. She felt crawfish against her skin when she waded through the shallow water.

The water wasn't cold, but her teeth were chattering all the same. She found it difficult to see what was in the water with her in the dark.

TOUCHED BY MADNESS

Every time she moved forward, murky ripples surrounded her. Her bare feet were sucked down into the muddy soil of the bayou, and the darkness around her was smothering. It was like being buried alive.

"Just drop him," Altman said.

"He'll drift back to the shore. They'll find him too soon and know a leopard attacked him," Erin whispered.

"Why are you whispering?" Gideon complained.

"He wasn't alone," she explained. "He said that *they* were going to do tests on me. The others must have been members of the Divine Right group."

"Why did they let you kill him, then?" Leila asked.

"I—" The sound of a loud splash near her interrupted what she was about to say. She stopped to listen. Her gaze searched the woods near the bayou. She had to wait a moment before she could hear anything besides the sound of her own heartbeat and labored breathing.

"It was probably an alligator sliding away from the shore into the water," Gideon said.

"Thank you," she mumbled. "You know what? I think you're right. I'll just dump the body here. There seem to be enough alligators in this area to deal with it." The creature must have smelled the blood trail that she had left as she entered the water.

She suppressed a shriek when something cold and rough glided against her left leg. She quickly dropped what remained of the psychiatrist.

She spread her legs, lifted her arms and stared down into the dark water. She felt her arms transform into paws, while the rest of her remained human. She imagined an alligator with glittering silver eyes. She squeezed together her eyes and could have sworn she saw a snout opening and teeth gleaming.

"It's just a piece of wood," Gideon grunted.

"Thank God," her mother said. *"Just get out of there."*

She didn't need anyone else to encourage her. Without hesitation, she turned around and waded back to the shore as fast as she could.

The slippery moss on the ground made her fall back into the bayou. Her head was immersed in the slimy water. For a moment, everything went silent.

She swallowed a large amount of the vile liquid when attempting to inhale frightened gulps of air. She burst to the surface and coughed, managing to grab the trunk of a tree and pull herself out.

"I thought you wanted to be quiet," Gideon sneered.

"Shut up, asshole," Leila defended Erin.

Erin didn't say anything as she walked back to the cabin. The small building was easy to locate because she hadn't switched off the lights before carrying the body out, and the door was still open. She refused to worry about the doctor's possible accomplices. She entered the hut, closed the door and moved straight to the bathroom.

TOUCHED BY MADNESS

After rinsing her mouth with mouthwash, she bent over the bathtub to turn on the tap. She stepped into the bathtub without adjusting the heat.

She lay in the tub with her back pressed against the cool porcelain. She stuck the heel of her foot into the opening to prevent the water from draining away and closed her eyes as she felt the water rise. Occasionally, she lifted her foot, watching the murky water swirl away, refusing to linger in the dirty bathwater longer than necessary. She preferred taking showers, but after the day she'd had, she doubted she would be able to stand.

"Uh, I don't know how long you plan on staying here, but you did mention there could be others, right?" Leila asked.

"Fine, let them come. I would prefer to face them now. I don't want to have to worry about them coming after me later," she answered. She felt reckless. She'd faced her biggest fear tonight and embraced the darkest side of her nature. But at the end of it all, she was the one who'd survived.

"But you could use help," her mother said. *"The witch might be able to assist you."*

"And I'm sure that the master vampire of Hope Acres would love to help you out. Of course, you'd owe him big time!" Leila joked. *"But that wouldn't be so bad, would it? If you're honest, you'll admit you want him. You'd have to be made of stone not to be affected by his hot eyes devouring you."*

When Erin refused to respond to Leila's comment, her mother continued, *"And what about Frank? You've never tried asking Frank for help."*

Reluctantly Erin opened her eyes.

She sighed. "I don't want to tell Frank about me. I like being friends with someone who doesn't think I'm crazy."

"You're not proper friends if he doesn't know who you really are," Leila said.

Erin stared at the tap. The water had cooled down and she lifted her foot to let it drain away. She turned off the water, and silence filled the room. She turned her head to face the empty hallway.

"No one is coming," she whispered.

"No, and thank God for that!" her mother said.

"You sound almost disappointed," Gideon said. *"Believe me, it's better this way. You're in no condition to fight."*

Erin slowly lifted her wet body out of the bathtub and took a deep breath. A draft caressed her bare torso. The room dipped and swayed, and her knees folded. Only the wall behind her prevented her fall.

"Just look at you!" Gideon continued. *"You can't even stand on your own two legs!"*

"It's the drugs," Erin grumbled.

She pushed herself away from the wall. Standing with trembling limbs in the tub, she grabbed a towel. She lifted the cloth to her face and smelled it. It seemed clean. She imagined Doctor Quirkhart using the towel, and her mind rebelled at the image of the psychiatrist wiping his bony bum with the same cloth.

When she was dry, she climbed over the brim of the bathtub. The room was cold, and the mirror had steamed up. She wiped the mirror with the damp towel and glanced at herself. She remembered getting shot in her arm. The bullet must have gone straight through, and her leopard genes must have healed it.

While her arm didn't have any marks, her face was pale and drawn. She schooled her face until it looked back at her with complete and remote indifference before she returned to the front room. Aching from head to toe and reeling with dizziness and exhaustion, she moved forward.

There was blood on the carpet, but she didn't see any remaining body parts. She pictured herself devouring it all and trembled as she got herself under control.

She saw her torn uniform and remnants of the straitjacket lying on the floor. She searched the room, trying to find something intact to wear. She found nothing in the front room and moved to the bedroom.

In a drawer, she found a couple of underpants in her size, no jeans, but there were socks and T-shirts that fitted her. She wondered how long the doctor had planned to keep her there.

She saw a pair of trousers that must have belonged to Doctor Quirkhart lying in a heap in the corner, and she snatched them up. She had to roll up the legs when she put them on. She was tall for a girl, but the doctor had towered over most men.

The drugs had weakened her so much that it took several attempts before she managed to finish dressing. Returning to the front room, she found her shoes and put them on.

She was about to leave the cabin when the blue light on the laptop caught her attention. Walking up to the desk, she touched the computer.

"Leave it," her mother said.

She briefly hesitated before she decided to disregard her mother's warning.

She opened the device and glanced at the screen. Wide-eyed, she took a step back, surprised to see her own face looking back at her.

Wavering, she approached the computer again and watched her movement on the monitor. She glanced up and noticed a hole in the wall with a cable sticking out of it. Frowning, she lifted her hand and pulled at the wire. Sure enough, a tiny surveillance camera fell out and landed on the desk.

A chill slid down her spine. Her throat tightened, and she tasted bile at the back of it.

She briefly cried out in fury, her face hardening. She was seriously pissed now, and she let instinct take over.

"I hope you enjoyed the show," she growled through clenched teeth at the camera. Then she threw the laptop onto the floor. It skittered across the wood and landed with a thump against the sofa.

The thought of being watched as she had eaten a human being made her gorge rise, but she forced the nausea down. She squeezed her eyes shut, feeling like digging a grave and throwing herself into it.

TOUCHED BY MADNESS

She had given Quirkhart's Divine Right friends the evidence they wanted. She was indeed a monster. She wished she could justify her actions and explain that she had been forced to defend herself. However, she remembered how she had toyed with her old enemy. She hadn't killed him with one blow, but had enjoyed his suffering.

"Just go home," Altman told her.

She pointed at the blood on the floor and nodded at the surveillance camera. "What about all the evidence? There is no body now, but any idiot can see that a crime was committed here. Hell, they taped me committing it!"

"You did the world a favor, Erin," Altman said.

"You're not going to whine about not being a regular human again, are you?" Gideon asked. *"If you are, please warn me, so I can try to block you out."*

Erin shook her head as she walked to the doorway. Once she reached the threshold, she turned to take a final glance at the room.

"Don't worry, Gideon," she replied. "You're right. No more whining, so what if I'm a monster?"

She shrugged. "The humans I'm dealing with are just as bad—maybe even worse because they have no excuse for their behavior. With me, it's just part of my nature."

She eyed the bloodstains. "Let them clean up their own mess. Hell, let them go to the police and tell them that I killed their friend, a kidnapper. They were his accomplices, and they let him die. They're as guilty as I am!"

"Speaking of accomplices, what if they decided to show up, after all? Can we go now?" Leila asked impatiently.

"Yes, let's go. You know, there is at least one accomplice whom we're all acquainted with. What do you think about giving Victor a little visit?" Erin asked, smiling bitterly.

The smile faded as the thought crossed her mind that Victor had probably been observing her while she had devoured Doctor Quirky. He would have enjoyed himself while doing so, the creep.

She did not know if male werewolves were stronger than female leopards, but she refused to worry about it. She would find out soon enough. She didn't care that the drugs were still in her system. All she wanted was to vent her rage on him.

She turned off the lights and finally walked out the door. Several blue herons silhouetted against the horizon crept slowly through the shallow edge of the water. She searched the woods near the water's edge.

"Is there anyone there? Are you waiting for me?" she called out. A bird squawked in the distance, but no one replied.

It had started to rain again. She closed her eyes, expelling a relieved sigh and throwing her head back as the drops fell on her. Even though she enjoyed the water sliding down her face, the cool rain didn't lessen her desire for vengeance.

"Victor, here I come," she whispered. "Be ready for a serious butt-kicking."

TOUCHED BY MADNESS

Jonathan Stratton smiled as he watched Erin leave the cabin. He rewound the scene to his favorite moment. It had been a brilliant idea to put a second camera in the room. He wished he hadn't hesitated when he had considered setting up surveillance cameras in every room of the building.

Unfortunately, he had decided not risk antagonizing the psychiatrist by invading his privacy in the bathroom and bedroom, but next time he wouldn't hesitate to do so.

The vampire thought over the reunion he had arranged between Erin and her enemy. She hadn't disappointed him. When she had finally stopped fighting herself, she had shone with power.

Usually, he found strength annoying when he tested people. He preferred it when they broke down. There was something about the transition from just a slight discomfort to full-blown panic that he found fascinating to observe.

When someone truly experienced fear, the widening of their eyes, the instinctive rise of their upper lip. It was something an actor could never portray properly.

Tonight Erin's performance had not been as he had expected, but he couldn't wait for an encore. She would make him a perfect weapon.

Stratton understood Dane's obsession with her. He froze the image on the screen when Erin had finally stood up to Doctor Quirkhart after she had changed back to her human form. Half-naked and full of glory, she was amazing. He touched the screen in awe.

"Mine," he whispered. *At least for the next eighteen months.*

And now that he knew what she was capable of, he had to think about how he could use her to her full potential.

Hazel was in a hell of a predicament. Karma was on to her, and the only people who could protect her were busy plotting her demise.

She felt trapped. In her stomach, a battle had erupted, and the sensation of unease and anxiety had not lessened as the night had continued.

She had tried to keep herself busy with cleaning her bedroom, a task she usually found very relaxing. Unfortunately, because she was always very organized, there hadn't been much for her to clean. She couldn't clean any other parts of the house because she didn't want to raise anyone's suspicion with behavior that was out of character. And even if she had been able to occupy herself with cleaning the entire mansion, she believed that nothing could distract her from the sense of imminent doom.

Because of her anxiety, she had not been able to relax. She couldn't stop trembling, and the lack of food made her feel weak.

Karma knew.

TOUCHED BY MADNESS

It wasn't the first time she had resented the position she'd been forced into. When Gregorio had first revealed himself to her after his *death*, she had felt honored. When he had told her to spy on Dane, she had been happy to do so. She had always disliked Dane for his arrogant behavior toward her. She had looked forward to teaching him a lesson. He would never underestimate her again.

However, when she thought about the situation she was in now, she had to admit that Dane had been right to belittle her. She should have confided in someone as soon as Gregorio had approached her. No one could serve two masters at the same time.

She wished that Selena and her creepy coven had never rescued Gregorio. If he thought he was powerful enough to be the master vampire of Hope Acres, why couldn't he have confronted Dane face-to-face?

The cowardly way they had made vampires disappear had the effect of making Gregorio appear weak rather than Dane. Of course, she wouldn't dare to say that to the ancient Gregorio. She wasn't suicidal.

But if she were to go up to the cabin to warn Gregorio, wouldn't it be like committing suicide? Sadly, if she stayed at Dane's mansion, she might as well stake herself. Her betrayal was certain to come to light in the near future. Running away might have seemed like a good idea, had it not been for the witches with their nasty location spells.

There was no simple solution. She had considered going up to Karma and begging him for mercy. However, she didn't think he had any mercy in him.

It was no use for her to continue to dwell on her situation. Her options were limited and not one of them appealing. After spending her first wakeful day since becoming a vampire, she finally reached the conclusion that it was best to appease the person who terrified her the most. She just had to be certain that Gregorio's allies wouldn't kill her when she did.

She panted slightly as she picked up the cellphone. She hadn't called the witches' cabin from her own phone before, but realized that the secret was about to be exposed and there was no point wasting time trying to locate a safe line.

She braced herself while she waited for someone to pick up the phone, hoping it would be Pauline because she acted less annoying than the other witches.

"Yes?" a cold voice asked.

Hazel suppressed the urge to hang up as soon as she recognized Eartha on the other side of the line. The vampire moved toward the closed window, away from the door and lowered her voice. "I need to talk to him."

"Him who?" Eartha snickered.

"Why are you such a bitch?" Hazel sighed.

"I decided to be just like you," Eartha replied. Then, strangely enough, she became polite. "I'm afraid that he is not to be disturbed right now. He—Selena is alone with him."

Selena had promised Gregorio that she would heal his burnt flesh, and after each session, the leathery flesh on his face did appear smoother.

Hazel knew from experience that when you touched that callous flesh you discovered that the healing was merely an illusion. She hadn't mentioned this to Gregorio, though. He must know. He must occasionally rub his skin. She couldn't believe that the witches were able to deceive him, but if they were fooling him, she didn't want to be the one to inform him of that.

"I know that we aren't allowed to disturb him, but this is an emergency," Hazel explained.

"What's the matter? Maybe I can help," Eartha offered.

Hazel frowned. Even if she had never overheard Eartha discussing her murder, this offer would have made her suspicious. The witch would never offer a vampire any assistance unless doing so gave her the opportunity to hurt it. She believed the only reason Eartha hadn't turned on Gregorio was because Selena would kill her if she did.

Hazel hesitated for a moment before answering. "We let the cat out of the bag." She let out a sigh and gazed at the door. "Karma knows he's alive."

Hazel expected Eartha to explode and start yelling at her, but Eartha surprised her by being silent for a little while.

"I don't want to know how he found out. Sometimes you're better off not knowing..." the witch eventually said.

"You must tell *him* what's going on right now," Hazel demanded. "He has to prepare for an attack."

"Well, I don't want to be the messenger," Eartha dawdled.

"Then put him on the phone!" Hazel demanded.

"Aislin interrupted his session a few weeks ago, and he used one of his sharp fingernails to cut open both her cheeks. If you want him to know this now, you will have to come over and tell him yourself," Eartha countered.

"Fine." Hazel sighed. She was probably going to fall right into their trap. Hazel could only hope Eartha realized that Gregorio would want her to investigate Karma's plans. He would not appreciate them killing his only vampire ally.

She glanced at the door and told herself it would be safer to leave through the window. Opening the window, she climbed out onto the ledge and let herself drop, landing gracefully on the gravel driveway below.

She decided to leave the car behind to prevent alerting the others to her departure. If she hurried, she could reach the cabin in a little under forty minutes.

Hazel ran up to the fence and turned around for one last look at her home. She surveyed the house and was pleased to see no one following her.

TOUCHED BY MADNESS

It was unfortunate that she forgot to examine the sky. A large bird flew high above her head, circling while observing her every move.

Erin raced through the woods, forcing herself to keep going. Several times branches smacked her face and scratched against her skin. Her legs were so wobbly, she collapsed and stumbled twice, but she kept going no matter what. It was as if she was running on a shot of pure adrenaline.

She was tempted to become a leopard because it would enable her to leave the scene of the crime at a much faster pace, but decided against it.

She feared that if she did change, the animal within would completely take over. Ever since she had killed her old nemesis and finally embraced her primal side, she could feel the leopard on the edge of her consciousness, waiting just below the surface. It was the leopard that anticipated lashing out at Victor for his betrayal. The human had no say in it. She knew that if she allowed the animal to reappear so soon after being unleashed, it would not leave without a fight.

She breathed a sigh as the trail to the city came into view, and she broke out of the bayou. She pumped her arms and legs as hard as she could, aching to reach the safety of her home and leave this insane nightmare behind her.

It wasn't long before she could see her building just ahead. She slowed down to glance up at the thick gray storm clouds that hung low in the dark sky.

She trembled with exhaustion, and then jogged across the street to her building. One of the apartments downstairs caught her attention as the light of the lamppost lit the clock inside. It was nearly midnight.

She smiled when her mother murmured, *"The witching hour."*

The street was deserted, and rain had begun to create pools of mud on the road. She was about to open the door to her building when an orange ball of fur walked up to her.

The cat meowed.

Erin bent over to pet her, but nearly fell over when a bout of dizziness washed over her.

She sighed. "Sorry, but whatever it is, it will have to wait. I have some butt to kick," she told the cat. She glanced up at the floor above hers and let out a low growl.

Victor.

She shrugged when the cat started mewing again, and she opened the door to enter the building, letting the cat inside at the same time. She waited a moment for the animal to follow her up the stairs, and then shooed her away when she neared her own apartment. It would be best if the cat wasn't anywhere near her and Victor during their confrontation. She might end up getting hurt.

TOUCHED BY MADNESS

Erin didn't want to waste time conversing with Pauline in her own apartment, so she continued up the stairs, leaving an angry cat clawing at her front door behind her.

She had just reached Victor's floor when it dawned on her that her cat was probably unhappy with their new housemate. She hesitated, wondering if she should go down to Pauline first after all. Then she heard the door downstairs slam shut. Heavy footsteps resounded through the building.

She gazed down the stairwell. It wasn't Victor. She turned around to face the traitor's door and pounded vigorously on its surface.

"Think before you act," her mother advised.

"Don't be too careful," Gideon contradicted. *"You can't let that fleabag get away with it."*

"He may not have known what would happen if he turned you over to that—" her mother began. *"However,"* she admitted reluctantly, *"ignorance is no excuse."*

"He must have realized that Quirky didn't want to kidnap her, so he could give her a present," Gideon grumbled.

Encouraged by Gideon's support, Erin started to bang on Victor's door again, this time with all her strength.

The door fell open as the frame around it splintered under her fist. Startled, she peered inside. She expected to find a mess similar to her own studio apartment, but the walls were bare, and so was the rest of the apartment.

There wasn't any furniture, curtains or carpets. She wondered for a moment if Victor had lived here at all. But of course he had, she'd seen him taking women up to this apartment on numerous occasions.

Had he left? Who was he really? Was his name even Victor?

It became clear to her that he had not been here by accident. Had he left because his job had been successfully completed when he handed her over to Doctor Quirkhart? Perhaps he was frightened that she might escape and come after him.

Her mouth edged up slightly at the corners. She hoped he was terrified.

She examined the room one last time, trying to find a clue to his whereabouts. There weren't even any garbage cans to search. The room had been wiped clean. She couldn't even smell him with her superior leopard senses.

She left the apartment, carefully shutting the door behind her.

Would she ever have the opportunity to make him pay?

She sighed as she reached the door to her own apartment. She knocked and waited for Pauline to open the door, frowning when no one appeared to let her in.

"Pauline, are you there? I gave you the key, remember?" she said.

She quickly lost patience and tried turning the doorknob. The door opened. With mixed feelings, she entered the room.

TOUCHED BY MADNESS

Her first impression on entering the apartment was that she must have made a mistake and entered the wrong place. The walls of her room were yellow, not white, and so were her curtains, weren't they?

She walked up to them and touched the material. It was slightly damp and smelled like flowers.

"Hello?" she called out. "Pauline?"

She recognized the bed and the radio alarm, but her bedcovers seemed unfamiliar. Had Mary Poppins decided to visit her while she had been tied up?

When she entered the bathroom, she was relieved to find that not everything had been tidied up. As she turned on the light, she noticed several candles, the ashes of burnt incense and a cup filled with water lying on the floor.

"Great, she must have used some spell to make the dirt disappear. Only the spell backfired, and now she's gone too."

"*Erin, I can't believe you are my daughter,*" Ann complained. "*You know what spell she performed. A glass filled with water, incense and blue candles... Please stop embarrassing me.*"

"All right, she must have tried to find me," Erin concluded. "Oh, well." She shrugged. "When she doesn't find me, I'm sure she'll return."

"*Erin!*" her mother said, sounding horrified. "*What if the people who were watching you went to the cabin? If she gets hurt trying to help you, then I'm not talking to you anymore!*"

"And that is a problem because...?" Gideon taunted.

Erin picked up the box of matches. "Please stop arguing. I'll check it out." She sat down next to the toilet and lit the candles.

"What are you doing?" Ann asked. *"We need to go to the cabin straight away."*

"I just want to be sure that I'm going to search for her in the right location," Erin explained.

She closed her eyes to clear her head in order to concentrate on what she wished to accomplish. Calling up her magic, she let it build within her. She felt herself grow unnaturally calm and serene.

She opened her eyes, gazed down into the glass and was about to utter the words that would show her the whereabouts of the witch, when an image appeared in the water.

"What the—"

"What is it?" she heard Leila ask.

"I-I see the cabin. It's as if I'm lying on the ground, looking up. It must be from Pauline's perspective."

"Without using a spell? You must be getting more powerful," Altman said.

"It's strange though..." Erin frowned with confusion. "The lights are on."

"So whoever was watching you did go to the cabin," Altman said. *"Maybe to clean up the bloodstain."*

She continued to examine the picture and shook her head. "No, that's not it. This is not the cabin where I was held. I don't see the water behind the cabin. See? There are more trees surrounding it."

"I don't see anything but water, Erin," Leila said.

Erin narrowed her eyes and spotted a sign on the door, the number six. Suddenly the image started to move. Pauline must have risen to approach the cabin.

She observed Pauline getting closer to the cabin and swore. She blew out the candles and rose.

"What is it?" her mother asked.

"I think I'd better hurry and find that witch before she gets into trouble."

She entered the front room and was just about to turn off the lights when she heard a sound on the fire escape. A chill of awareness slipped through her. She glanced at her window and walked up to it to push back the curtains with a rising sense of unease.

"Good evening, Erin," Dane greeted.

She inhaled sharply and took a step back.

He smiled while looking her up and down, clearly noticing her disheveled appearance through the windowpane.

She brushed back her long hair, which was loose, wet and tangled. The brown trousers she had on were too long, and one of the rolled-up legs had come undone. She stood on shaky legs while he fixed his eyes on her face.

He gasped. "Are you on drugs?" His smile vanished and he clenched his fists in anger. "What the hell happened to you?"

"Oh, crap. Listen, I don't have time for this." She sighed.

"Don't make me repeat myself!" He shot her a steely glare.

She scowled at him through the window. "Why, what will you do?" A smile started in her mind and spread to her lips. "I'm not stupid enough to invite you in, so you can't touch me."

"Uh, Erin..." Altman began.

Dane bared his white teeth in what could have passed for a smile, but was more like a warning. Before she could blink, he appeared behind her. She felt the draft of the open window and glanced at it, puzzled that he'd managed to get in without breaking it—and without an invitation from her.

"A vampire doesn't need to be invited in," Altman explained.

She opened her mouth, but lost the ability to speak as the vampire put his arm around her waist and murmured in her ear.

"You are making me repeat myself." His voice had the dark seduction of black velvet. It caressed her skin and slid deep into her body, setting off electrical sparks.

"Answer me," he ordered, his lips almost touching her earlobe. His breath was warm, drawing her like a magnet.

Her body felt tight and unfamiliar. The effect of the drugs seemed to have escalated since her knees were unable to support her. Fortunately, he didn't seem to want to let her go.

"Huh? What?" she asked.

TOUCHED BY MADNESS

"What happened to you?" His nose touched her wet hair as he took a deep breath. "Did someone drug you without you knowing?"

She tried to move away, but he held her against the side of his body in an iron grasp.

"And whose trousers are these?" he asked. With what appeared to be deliberate slowness, he slid one of his hands down to her waist.

"Stop interrogating me," she protested. "And let me go. I'm really not in the mood for games."

He seemed reluctant, but released her. "Just tell me," he insisted, his voice tight.

"Okay," she snapped. "Someone I once knew managed to find me. We had a fight, and I won. Are you happy now?"

His eyes narrowed. "Who was he?"

"Who cares?" She started laughing hysterically. "He'll never bother me or anyone else ever again." Her laughter changed and became sobs.

He set his jaw as he inspected her. His hands clenched into fists, white knuckles standing out.

Annoyed at her weakness, she rubbed her cheeks and tried to regain her composure. She registered his presence and tried to act as if she hadn't just had a brief nervous breakdown. She had just killed someone. Surely, she was entitled to shed a tear or two.

She noticed his uncertainty when she had been crying. Now a shiver ran up her spine as she saw a fierce determination replace the doubt in his eyes. Somehow, she knew that the expression in his eyes meant trouble for her, and she felt threatened. "Get out," she snapped.

He moved automatically toward the door. His hand was on the doorknob before he appeared to realize what he was doing. Stunned, he turned to face her.

"Did you just try to put a thrall on me?"

Confused, she shook her head. "What? No. I just want you to go away!"

"Amazing," he muttered.

"Listen, I don't have time for this! I've got to go," she said as she picked up a pair of jeans that Pauline must have folded.

She kept an eye on Dane through the doorway while she changed in the bathroom. He seemed to be inspecting the apartment as he picked up some of the items she had used to locate Pauline.

"Where are you going at this late hour?" he asked with suspicion in his voice.

"That really is none of your business!" she said as she put on a dark coat and walked to the door. "Besides you shouldn't be acting like the injured party here. You're the one who lied to me."

He was quick to block her exit. "What the devil are you talking about?"

"I talked to Philippe Lepareur yesterday about what happened at the Devereaux Church twenty years ago. At least, I think it was yesterday. You can imagine how surprised I was when your name came up." She scowled at him.

He shrugged. "I was there, so what? It doesn't matter. I wasn't there when the ritual took place."

TOUCHED BY MADNESS

She ignored him and tried to pass him. He refused to budge. "If you don't tell me where you're going, I'm going with you."

"What?" Alarmed, she noticed a determined glint in his eyes. "Oh, no! No, this is a really bad idea."

He stared unswervingly at her until she eventually sighed with defeat. "Okay. I have a new roommate. When I didn't get home on time, she went out to find me. And now I want to let her know I'm fine."

"And you were late because you were in a fight, right?" He spoke carefully, but anger slipped into his voice.

She flashed him a scowl. "I can't deal with this right now. I told you why I needed to leave, so let me go." She felt relief when he finally moved aside. Unfortunately, as soon as she passed him to leave the studio apartment, his hand snaked out to catch her wrist. She sucked in a sharp breath and stiffened, but desire flared inside her.

You've gotta be kidding me, after the night I've had?

"I'm not satisfied with the explanation, so I'm joining you."

"No," she said. "Absolutely not. You cannot go with me."

He smirked.

She glared back at him, but he refused to release her.

She glanced at the time. She'd already taken too long to find Pauline. Resigned to her fate, she nodded.

"Fine, join me then, but don't you dare hinder me in any way."

"I wouldn't dare," he promised.

FOURTEEN

Pauline watched the lights inside the cabin go out, and the small wooden building was plunged into darkness. She hoped it meant that Selena and the others were going to bed, but she knew them too well. They were probably busy preparing a ritual with Erin as the sacrifice.

Poor Erin.

Pauline hoped that the security guard was still locked up inside the basement and that the ceremony hadn't started yet.

Now that the house was draped in darkness, she knew she needed to head toward to the cabin.

Before making her move, she swept her gaze over the area. She didn't detect any unexpected movement, but the swamp offered many places for concealment.

She watched lizards scurrying through the brush. Heavy raindrops hit the leaves, making branches sway. In spite of the canopy of trees, the rain had drenched her while she'd waited. Despite shivering with cold, she preferred remaining outside in the wet than the alternative.

"Better wet than dead," she murmured as she sneezed for the fourth time that night. The wet ground sucked at her when she dragged herself out of the mud. An uneasy sensation gripped her stomach as she approached the small building.

She slowed—not wanting to give away her exact location by stepping on squishy leaves or wet twigs.

The unpleasant feeling intensified. Not one to question her instincts, she closed her eyes to chant another incantation in order to blend in with the environment. Unfortunately, she feared that her witchcraft would be no match against Selena's magic.

With her heart pounding, she walked up to one of the windows at the side of the cabin. She quickly whispered a Hail Mary before risking a peek inside.

Her gaze was immediately drawn to a pale Aislin, who was busy drawing the magic circle with the ceremonial black-hilted knife.

Eartha stood beside Aislin, leafing through Selena's grimoire. They were both wearing long white gowns.

Pauline clamped her hand over her mouth to mute the scream that welled in her throat when she spotted Gregorio staring out of the window.

The vampire with the long brown hair made an impression. As always, Gregorio took up more space in the room than he should, as if he were weightier, both physically and mentally than he ought to be.

TOUCHED BY MADNESS

She was afraid that she had made a sound because the old master vampire seemed to be staring straight at her.

Even though Selena had managed to hide the burnt flesh, the man never stopped giving her goosebumps. Whenever she glanced into his brown eyes, she felt his emptiness.

She wanted to sigh with relief when he walked up to the sofa without warning anyone of her presence. She waited for him to sit down and close his eyes before she allowed herself to move away from the window, surrendering once more to the shadows.

She pressed her ear to the wood, straining to hear what she could. Only the hiss of rain and the buzz of crickets echoed through the night. In the distance, she heard footsteps. As she watched Hazel run toward the cabin, Pauline realized that there was a possibility that her witch colleagues weren't planning to perform a ritual on Erin after all.

She wondered if they would dare attack Gregorio's vampire while he was present in the room. He must have given his approval. Would she dare to be present when the attack happened? On the other hand, she might be able to take advantage of the situation. She was convinced Hazel would create quite a diversion, thus enabling her to sneak into the basement.

Hazel's panting told Pauline she was agitated. Her loud pounding on the door was another indication.

She waited for Hazel to enter before she made a move to follow her. She gave a start when a large black bird of prey landed on the terrace. Heart hammering, she returned to the shadows.

Merely a couple of seconds had elapsed when the bird shifted its form, and a tall gray-haired man materialized.

She recognized him from the vampire file Selena had set up. Fortunately, the vampire didn't wait to scan the surroundings before he silently opened the door of the cabin.

Pauline was lost in thought. *Should I go in after him?* He must have secretly followed Hazel for a purpose, and she doubted that his intentions were honorable.

In spite of Hazel's loud arrival, she doubted that it would be easy for her to sneak into the cabin undetected. The house was too small and too crowded not to get noticed. Perhaps she could think of an excuse for her tardiness. She told herself she could do it. She had to stop procrastinating.

When she briskly rapped on the door, there was no response at first, so she knocked again. It was a long moment before the door swung open.

Eartha stood in the doorway, wearing a scowl on her face. Upon finding Pauline, she opened her eyes wide in shock. "Where the hell have you been?"

"I-I—I'm sorry," Pauline stammered.

Eartha made a noise of annoyance. "It's not me you need to apologize to." She leaned over to whisper, "Where are the drugs? Hazel is here."

"Um, that's why I'm late. I got caught, but eventually I managed to escape," she hurried to explain.

Eartha's teeth gleamed as she flashed a wicked smile. "I can't wait for you to tell Selena."

She felt sick when it dawned on her that she must have jumped to the wrong conclusion. "So you never went to the hospital to look for me?" she asked hoarsely.

Eartha glared at her. "Now, why would we do that?"

Pauline cringed. If they had never gone out to search for her, they must not hold Erin hostage. She should have stayed safely at the studio apartment. She glanced at the front room, where she could hear Selena and Hazel arguing. There was no sign of the gray-haired vampire. She hoped he would stay gone. All thoughts of the mysterious vampire vanished when she caught Selena's eye. Her brain shut down.

Selena's dark expression caused an anxious knot in her stomach. She glanced at Aislin, who had entered the hallway, and then at Eartha, finding the same annoyance reflected in Eartha's eyes.

Hazel was watching the interaction between the four witches. "While you continue this little staring contest, I will have a chat with Gregorio," she said.

Selena scowled, but before she could utter a word, Gregorio walked up behind Hazel.

"I am curious to hear what she has to say. You four go on."

Selena narrowed her black eyes to slits when she looked at Pauline. If looks could kill, Pauline would have been cremated by now.

Eartha then walked into the kitchen with the others following her in silence. When they entered the room, Selena shut the door behind them.

With horror closing her throat, Pauline turned to face the powerful witch. What if they had gotten so angry with her that they were going to get rid of her instead of the red-haired vampire?

Pauline opened her mouth to speak, but stopped as Selena's hand rose, demanding silence.

"Hear me well," Selena spat out. "You were given a job to do, an easy job."

Pauline tried to defend herself, but decided to keep her mouth shut when she spotted Selena's fists clench.

"I know you want out," Selena continued.

Pauline's jaw dropped as she stared at the witch.

Selena laughed when she saw her shock. She nodded to Aislin. "Of course I know! And we will talk later about your plans."

"She didn't bring any drugs," Eartha said in an angry tone. "I still have some left, though. It should be enough for tonight."

Since Pauline was the one who always had to steal the drugs, she knew how much was left and doubted it could floor a vampire. She was also worried that Gregorio might object to them attacking Hazel, but did not want to draw any additional attention to herself. They seemed to be in a rather bloodthirsty mood, and if Hazel got away, they would probably turn on her instead.

Eartha went to get the tranquilizer gun while Selena described her strategy. It appeared that Gregorio had been made aware of her plans, and they would know he approved of the killing tonight if he uttered the words, "Then it's done."

Pauline thought it was weird that such a powerful creature could not deal with his vampire alone, but as usual, she didn't speak up.

After Eartha returned with the gun, she hid it behind her back, and they walked toward the front room.

Pauline cocked her head when she heard Hazel's whiny voice.

"Please, Gregorio," the vampire begged. "You must believe me. Karma knows you're alive. He'll tell." Hazel tried to touch his arm in order to convince him of her sincerity, but Gregorio's body went rigid as his face turned to steel.

"So our game is over?" He sounded very cold.

Hazel nodded. "Yes, they will find out about the missing vampires. We can't hide any longer."

He contemplated Pauline, and she knew he was about to say the words that would condemn Hazel.

"Then it's done," he stated, very matter-of-factly.

Pauline held in her breath as Eartha took aim, but was horrified to see that instead of pointing the tranquilizer gun at Hazel, Eartha directed it at her.

Before she could duck, the shot rang out. The dart hit her straight in her chest. A black web began to fall over her vision. She had a split second to think.

So that's why they have enough drugs for tonight's ritual. They only needed enough to knock out a human.

Then everything went kind of hazy.

Erin should have been relieved that Dane had not continued to interrogate her about Doctor Quirkhart throughout the car journey, but she probably would have preferred his probing questions to this brooding silence.

It took them less than fifteen minutes to arrive at the cabin. She ordered him not to park in front of the cabin, and he had acquiesced. But when she told him to stay in the car, he chose to ignore her.

"Listen, you can be intimidating. When my housemate sees you, she will probably hide so thoroughly that it will be daylight before we can find her." She paused for dramatic effect. "Oops, before *I* can find her because daylight means *poof* for you, right?" she taunted.

True to form, he did not take the bait.

That's the thing about Dane Lynch, she thought. *He rarely loses his cool. He's probably just as cool in the bedroom. Where the hell did that thought come from?*

TOUCHED BY MADNESS

They were walking up to cabin number six when his hand suddenly shot out, caught her arm and yanked her against a tree.

She had the most horrifying reaction, a shiver of anticipation that made her womb clench and set wings fluttering inside her stomach.

"Stay here," he commanded.

Before she could think of an adequate response, he moved away from the tree to face the cabin and the redheaded woman who had just left the building, shrieking loudly. The woman froze when she spotted Dane.

"Great, so Karma told you." The woman lifted her hands in the air, surrendering. "I give up! I want nothing more to do with those crazy bitches. I'd rather have you kill me now than be sacrificed by Gregorio and his witches."

Applause suddenly broke out behind the redhead.

They all turned around to look as a gray-haired man walked up to them.

"I haven't said a thing, Hazel. Although I do wonder how Dane finally managed to figure it all out."

Dane stared in complete disbelief. "Gregorio is in there?"

The woman didn't notice Dane's surprise and rattled on. "Yes. First, he made them get rid of Jerry and Rafferty, then Vincenzo, but that was a total disaster. I was convinced I would be the next vampire on their list, but thankfully they decided to go after one of their own instead."

A chill caught hold of Erin. She stepped away from the tree, scared but under control. She thought of the sacrifice the female vampire had mentioned and shuddered. She wished that no one would have to experience what she had gone through all those years ago, even if she couldn't remember any of it. The nightmares were bad enough.

"Is it Pauline?" she asked.

The woman shrugged and nodded. That was enough to galvanize her into action.

"Wait!" Dane yelled. When she continued to race toward the cabin, he went after her. She hadn't gotten far when he lunged for her legs and tackled her to the ground.

She came down hard, grunting, but immediately scrambled onto her back and started hitting his face with her fists.

Dane saw a painful burst of hot stars as a powerful blow connected with his eye. He managed to grab both her wrists and pinned them down over her head.

"Enough," he growled next to her ear. "Use your head. You need my help here." He stood and pulled her up with him. Without waiting for her consent, he dragged her to where the others stood.

Erin's face was red with anger. He ignored her and glared at Hazel instead.

"Hazel, I will not kill you now, because I have other priorities. If you want to go home and pack your things, be my guest. But, be sure that you're gone by the time I get back because if I ever see your traitorous face again, I will not only kill you—I will get out my blowtorch and torture you for such a long time, I will make Gregorio look like a softy."

Hazel didn't say a word. She turned on her heel and ran away before Dane changed his mind.

He stared at Karma. "I'm going to regret this, aren't I?"

Karma shrugged.

Dane foiled Erin's attempts to remove her hands from his by possessively tightening his grip on her.

"We have to go in and stop them," she cried.

He stared down at her without loosening his grip on her arm, and then he raised his eyebrows at Karma.

"What do you say, Karma? Are you feeling up for a fight?"

Karma grinned. "I thought you'd never ask!"

Pauline jolted awake to the sound of raised voices. Opening her eyes, she noticed she was tied down on the magic circle.

Aislin and Eartha were sitting on each side of her with their eyes shut while Selena had positioned herself at her feet with her eyes open wide.

Pauline moved her head to see if anyone was standing above her, but that position was empty. Gregorio stood by the window, staring down at her.

She recognized the ritual and knew they would soon bring out the knife. She squeaked as her eyes filled with tears, but she didn't move or dare to make any real sound. She was still terrified of making Selena angry, which of course was ridiculous since Selena was going to kill her anyway, angry or calm.

Old habits die hard.

Aislin gasped and opened her eyes, but her gaze seemed empty. "She's here," she mumbled in trance.

Eartha glared at Pauline. "Your replacement," Eartha explained gleefully.

Before Pauline could think about what that meant, Erin and the gray-haired man she had seen following Hazel entered the front room.

At the same time, she heard the window break. Reacting on pure instinct, she closed her eyes and tried to brace herself as her body was showered with glass. Fortunately, the vampire jumping through the window landed not on her, but on a furious Gregorio.

She reopened her eyes to see the two vampires fighting, their fangs aggressively sticking out.

Eartha screamed while Aislin let out a nervous laugh. Aislin turned her now lucid gaze on Eartha, and a silent understanding passed between them.

TOUCHED BY MADNESS

Within seconds, they had got to their feet and fled the scene.

Pauline glanced at Selena and noticed an angry tic working in her jaw. Pauline swallowed a nervous lump in her throat as she watched the witch take out the big ceremonial knife. Her heart skipped a beat in pure terror. She shook her head frantically.

"Drop it," she heard Erin growl. Selena seemed so startled by the inhuman sound of Erin's voice that she unconsciously let go of the knife.

Even though she now had no weapon to defend herself with, Selena refused to surrender. She lifted her hands as she called out.

"I invoke and conjure thee, Kali. Fortified with the power of the supreme Majesty, I command thee to kill these intruders! I—" Selena went still as Erin's fist connected with her cheekbone.

The blow was powerful enough to knock her off her feet, and into unconsciousness.

Pauline watched Selena slam into the nearby wall and slump down it into a heap on the floor. Erin didn't waste time checking whether the witch had really passed out, but concentrated instead on releasing Pauline.

The gray-haired vampire came to assist Erin.

Erin glanced at him. "We're fine, Karma. Shouldn't you help Dane?"

She pointed to the wrestling vampires. They had each succeeded in biting chunks of flesh out of each other's bodies and were continuing to inflict damage upon each other.

Dane grunted, but Gregorio was deadly quiet and all the more frightening for it. Both were aiming for the kill.

Karma tore open one of Pauline's bonds, before casting Erin an apologetic look. "In order to be the true master vampire of Hope Acres, he will have to do this himself."

Karma held out his hand to Pauline, who accepted it gracefully as she rose.

While Pauline was unable to take her eyes away from the unconscious witch, she noted that the other two were more interested in watching the fight.

Erin held her breath as frustration sliced through her. Dane had knocked the other vampire to the ground, where they now wrestled. She resented not being allowed to participate in the fight.

When Gregorio managed to bite open Dane's wrist, she flinched. He then pushed Dane off him and jumped to his feet, but Dane didn't wait around to be kicked while he was down and rolled into a crouch before also rising to his feet.

They broke apart and stood with their fangs bared. Blood dripped off their bodies and formed little puddles on the wooden floor around them.

Gregorio bent his head, gave a wild shrieking cry and ran full tilt at Dane. He hit Dane with the impact of a battering-ram. His bloody head struck the center of Dane's chest, sending him reeling against the thin wall behind him.

Erin swore. She automatically took a step forward. Distracted by Dane's crash into the wall, she had only Pauline's cry to warn her that something was wrong before she felt hands grabbing both her ankles, pulling her to the ground.

She scowled at the dark witch, who had awakened with a lust for vengeance. The woman used her nails to draw Erin's blood before Karma bent over, grasped the witch's black hair and dragged her out of the front room. Erin heard the woman's final scream, but could find no sympathy whatsoever for the evil witch.

Erin peered at Pauline who was still staring at the empty doorway, looking numb.

Before she could try to offer Pauline some solace, a cold hand took hold of her neck, squeezing it. Someone roughly lifted her up, an arm as strong as steel circled her waist.

As she clawed at the hands around her throat, she could see a furious Dane lifting himself off the floor. He glared at the person behind her with an expression of cold, intense anger. But there was something else, something she had never seen in him before, a flash of fear. Was he afraid for her?

"Hmm," she heard Gregorio's voice gloat in her ear. "I heard about this one." He licked Erin's throat.

Dane snarled and took a step in their direction.

Gregorio laughed. "That's far enough. You don't want me to hurt her now, do you?"

Dane froze.

"Why don't you look at me, little human? You're not afraid of me, are you?" Gregorio taunted.

Her heart sunk when she reluctantly turned to look at the creature behind her.

Gregorio clicked his tongue and cast a condescending look at Dane. "Did you know your lover locked me in a burning building?"

Instead of denying that Dane was her lover, she blurted out, "I'm sure you did something to deserve it."

She immediately regretted opening her mouth when Gregorio's eyes narrowed to slits. She held her breath, waiting for Gregorio to kill her.

Instead, he chuckled. "She's funny, such a pity to rid the world of one so interesting. Have you considered turning her?"

A chill stabbed through her body. Turn her into a vampire? The only reason she had come to Hope Acres was to become normal again. Like hell she was going to let that happen!

She looked around the room for help. Pauline was staring at them, too terrified to move while Dane's eyes shot daggers at Gregorio. He was in attack stance, but he made no move to help her. Did he want her to become a vampire?

It dawned on her that he was probably afraid she'd be hurt as if she was a fragile thing. She frowned. She wasn't some weakling. She didn't need anyone to rescue her! She had just eaten Doctor Quirky. What was one more victim?

She called upon her magic once more and let the energy brush over her skin while the world paused. Magic moved and settled around her.

"Or maybe you're not so human after all," Gregorio commented.

She could only think of breaking his grip, and she twisted, writhed, kicked and broke his knee.

He screamed into her ear, a sharp, high-pitched noise that deafened and hurt. Yet still, he refused to release her.

Then power took over and blocked out the pain as he wrung her neck.

She was too far gone to pinpoint exactly what kind of energy she was drawing from. Leopard, vampire, witch or warlock—she didn't know. It was just there.

"Release me." Her voice didn't sound like her own. Her power vibrated through it with strength and dark energy commanding her tone.

The ancient master vampire dropped his hands as if he had no will of his own. He shook his head as if trying to break her hold over him and clear it.

In the corner of her eye, she saw Dane moving forward, ready to pounce on Gregorio now he had released her.

She lifted her hand and fired a blast of magical energy at Dane with the word, "Stop!"

She turned to Gregorio feeling something dark and angry growing inside her. "He is mine!"

She lifted her hand to Gregorio's throat. He opened his mouth, his fangs glimmering.

"Don't move," she ordered, letting out a laugh when he froze with panic in his gaze.

She bared her leopard's teeth at Gregorio, leaning into him and taking a deep breath.

"Hmm, the smell of fear, what if I take a little bite of you instead, or will that make me a vampire?"

She licked his throat and giggled.

"Erin, what are you doing?" her mother asked anxiously. *"Stop it at once!"*

"No, let her have some fun," Gideon contradicted.

"Hmm, some fun. You know what would be fun?" she asked as she stroked Gregorio's arms. She paused with her hands on one of the wounds on his wrists. She poked her fingers deep inside, watching his eyes tear up with pain.

"Ooooooh, poor you. You're leaking. I'm sorry," she said while she pretended to sound apologetic. "You know what would make you feel better?" she added cheerfully. "Blood! You would like some blood, wouldn't you?"

He kept silent. "Why don't you have some?" she suggested as she took Gregorio's wounded arm and put his open wrist to his mouth.

"Suck it!" she commanded, and Gregorio drank his own blood as if he would die of thirst if he were to stop.

She heard a muffled sob followed by a choked scream behind her. She turned to see Pauline crying silently with her mouth covered to keep more sobs from escaping.

Erin's mind seemed to register a change. She saw the circle on the floor next to Pauline and frowned. The tableau triggered a memory. Instead of a dark-haired woman in her twenties, she saw a little girl with curly blond hair and golden eyes, staring up at her accusingly.

The vision troubled her to such an extent that it interfered with her magic. Fortunately, before Gregorio could retaliate, Dane flew at him.

Dane wrapped his arm around Gregorio's neck and tore off his head in animalistic rage. Looking as if he'd showered in the vampire's blood, which covered both his arms and chest, he dropped Gregorio's body parts on the floor and moved toward Erin.

"Are you okay? Did someone possess you?"

Before she could answer, a dozen vampires, male and female, came running in dressed like a gang of bikers in leather jackets. They quickly surveyed what was going on while they swarmed into the front room.

Karma walked in behind them. Two vampires examined what was left of Gregorio while two other vampires checked on Pauline. The rest walked up to Erin and Dane.

"A present from the council," Karma said. He turned to the group of vampires. "Two witches got away, but their leader won't be able to create problems anymore."

Erin and Dane both looked around in unison. Karma sighed. "Yes, too late, I know. But at least you have a large crowd who can testify that you killed the former master vampire of Hope Acres in a fair fight. From now on, the council will leave you alone, at least about this subject."

When Dane glared, Karma nodded. "I know, we're irritating. We always find ways to meddle. However, we're not all bad. You can leave if you want. We will take care of the mess."

Dane met Karma's eyes with respect for the first time, before nodding. Then he grabbed Erin and held her in a crushing embrace. He sensed her resistance even though her body was as limp as it could be. Her skin was cold, and her eyes were empty.

She feels like a corpse.

He was quick to suppress that unpleasant thought. She was safe. That was all that mattered. He let the reality of her and the smell of her scent push away the violence inside him. He had come so close to losing her.

Again.

And then the miracle happened.

He felt her rest her cheek against his shoulder while she wrapped her arms around his waist. He tightened his arms around her as a feeling of pure happiness exploded in his chest. He wanted to shout with joy and celebrate the moment, but he knew they weren't there yet. Their relationship was still uncertain. She had too many unresolved issues. Her behavior toward Gregorio had proved it.

She obviously had more of her father inside her than either of them had imagined, but they would deal with it, and with her powers.

He gently stroked her hair as he continued to breathe her in. Perhaps she saw it as merely seeking comfort. He preferred to believe that her body had finally made a commitment to him.

And he was going to hold her to it.

FIFTEEN

A knock on her door interrupted Erin's shower. She would have ignored it had it not been for Pauline.

She heard her housemate open the door of the apartment and froze in the act of rinsing the shampoo from her hair when she recognized the voice of her caller.

She swallowed a curse and turned off the faucet. She quickly grabbed a towel, in spite of the soap still in her hair. She should have known Dane was going to visit her.

She had actually expected him to drop by the previous night. When he hadn't, she had felt mixed emotions that she refused to analyze. Really, she should not be thinking about him at all.

If only Pauline hadn't opened the door.

She should have known better than to get a housemate, too.

It took her less than a minute to leave the bathroom. She put on her white cotton panties and the long T-shirt that she was using as a nightgown. Fortunately, it covered her up to her knees.

TOUCHED BY MADNESS

She entered a silent living area. Apparently, neither Pauline nor Dane was very adept at small talk. Pauline was busy cleaning, although her housemate was so thorough, Erin wondered if there was any dirt left for her to clean.

She could see the relief in Pauline's eyes when she appeared.

Pauline picked up her bag and coat. "I've got some shopping to do. I'll be back in a couple of hours."

Erin wanted to stop Pauline from leaving, but clenched her fists instead as she watched her leave the studio apartment.

"Not a very good chaperone," Dane joked. His wide mouth curled up with an expression that seemed half-smile, half-challenge.

Concerned, Erin wondered if she needed a chaperone, but was proud of her restraint when she managed to keep that question to herself.

She glanced down at her bare legs, feeling vulnerable, almost naked in comparison to Dane, who was respectably dressed in jeans and a t-shirt. The tight black shirt he wore stretched across his hard, well-defined muscles, drawing her gaze. His knowing eyes watched her as if he could see deep inside her—as if he sensed her interest.

"You can't be surprised to see me, Goldilocks," he continued when she didn't respond. "I told you that I would visit you as soon as I could. I wanted to see you yesterday. Unfortunately, I had visitors."

She knew he meant the council. She was grateful for their interference. She had needed that extra day to come to her senses.

She realized she had come very close to giving in when Dane had held her after Gregorio had died, and that would have been catastrophic.

She felt sick whenever she thought about her behavior two nights ago, the way she had toyed with Doctor Quirkhart before eating him, and the joy she had experienced when she had made Gregorio cry. She had become a monster. And if she wanted to act like a normal human being, she had to be around human beings, not vampires.

She peered up at Dane and saw him staring at her with intent.

She sighed. This was going to get ugly. "I er, I appreciate your help with Pauline the other night..." she trailed off.

He frowned and folded his arms across his chest.

"But I would like to put the whole thing behind me and not have anything to remind me of that night."

"Hmm, really?"

Was she imagining that sparkle in his eyes? Was he making fun of her?

She nodded. "I think it would be best if we stop uh, meeting one another."

The corner of his mouth lifted. "Don't you mean 'seeing'?"

She shrugged. It didn't matter how he wished to define things as long as she got rid of him.

"No."

She stared at him.

What is he, deaf? He's supposed to leave now.

He grinned when her mouth dropped open in disbelief.

"W-w-what?" she stammered as he approached her.

"I'm not going anywhere."

With him standing so close and the wall right behind her, she felt hemmed in, trapped. She found it difficult to breathe. The earthy, tantalizing scent of him filled her nostrils. Did he have to stand so close to her?

She shot him an annoyed look. "That's not really up to you. I'm telling you that I don't want to see you anymore. You just have to accept that."

He shook his head. "Well, I'm not going to. What are you going to do about it?"

She hesitated. "I could make you leave."

He smiled. "Ah yes, so you could, but do you want to? You seemed rather upset the last time you made someone *do* something against his will."

She averted her eyes. He was right.

"Besides..." he went on, "if everything works out well, you won't be able to make anyone do anything anymore after tomorrow, right?"

Shocked, she shot him a look of surprise.

"You're wondering how I know about tomorrow?" he asked. "Your new houseguest did a lot of shopping yesterday. It's quite obvious that on Halloween, you're going to try to undo what happened to you all those years ago, and I understand that."

"Do you?" she asked.

He laughed. "Of course! Well, maybe a part of me wants you to fail, but that's only a small part. It will make my job much easier if you succeed."

She wasn't sure that she understood him, but she knew she should remain quiet.

"I was kind of looking forward to a fight," he explained. "Making up is so much sweeter afterward."

She didn't appreciate his humor.

"Although I'm sure that you'll still be able to fight me a little if you manage to revert back to your old self. It's not like you were human to begin with."

Her head swung around fast, feeling the blood drain from her face. To hear her worst fear spoken out loud for the second time... Her stomach lurched.

She took a deep breath and tried to bolt, but he was ready, lunging and catching her arm. Unsuccessfully, she tried to escape his firm grip.

"You didn't think you were, did you?" he asked her. "I have told you this before. Your mother was a witch and your father was one of the most powerful voodoo priests in the U.S. You must have inherited a couple of their powers. In fact, I think you can put thralls on vampires because of your father's powers. I know he created several zombies. Maybe you have the power to control any undead creature."

"God, I hope not," she blurted out.

TOUCHED BY MADNESS

"I'm not that fond of that talent of yours either," he agreed. "It might attract the notice of people whose attention you don't want."

When she pointed at the hand on her arm, he smirked. "I don't mean me! In fact, I think you don't mind my attention that much— Don't lie," he said when he read the denial in her gaze. "Ever since I touched you, your skin has flushed, the pulse in your neck has accelerated and your nipples have hardened."

The smile he flashed her was pure sin. "How long did your housemate say she would be out?"

She felt her cheeks flame up as he let go of her wrist and placed his palm on her stomach.

She turned her head away with embarrassment, but the essence of him enveloped, tempted and warmed her on a basic primitive level. He did not carry any chemical traces of aftershave.

Nothing artificial, just pure man.

"No more lying and no more running, if you do run, I will punish you for it." This time a thin veneer of civilization cracked through. She could hear the edge to his voice and nervously moistened her lips.

Punishment?

"You're freaking me out here," she said.

He chuckled. "Yes, but I'm not really frightening you."

"You're not?"

"You're powerful enough to fight me if you really want to resist me."

"Maybe I'm tired of fighting you." She sighed.

"Maybe you're tired of fighting yourself," he challenged.

At that moment, her gaze met his, and she knew he was right. She had felt their connection right from the beginning. So what if he wasn't human, neither was she. If he was right, she probably never had been.

But I'm not going to make it easy for him, she thought noticing the devil's own gleam in his wicked blue eyes.

Without thinking, she moved in a blur of preternatural speed.

He leapt to one side to block her escape.

"Now, what did I tell you? Do you want me to be rough, then? Do you want me to tie you down, fuck you and force you to come?"

The harshness of his words sent a shiver of excitement through her body. The images he invoked in her mind from just a few words caused unexpected tremors of pleasure.

She raised an eyebrow, determined to appear cool. She failed miserably because the rest her body betrayed her emotions. Desire was gouging her belly like a hot sword at his provocative words. He was devouring her with his eyes.

She turned her head away, trying to clear her mind and resist his seduction. But then he breathed her name, so softly she thought she'd imagined it.

She moved back toward him in a moment of submission. He caught her off guard when he grabbed her upper arms and pushed her against the wall. She gasped as her back hit the hard surface, and before she realized what he was about to do, he held her head between his hands and leaned over her.

He slanted his mouth over hers and took her lips in a searing assault. It was not a gentle kiss. It was as if he wanted to own her, possess her and keep her forever. The kiss was urgent, demanding and absolute possession.

She felt as if he'd steal her soul with his kiss if he could. His lips felt as brutal and harsh as the man himself, and yet her heart raced, and her body ached for his touch.

She found herself eagerly returning the kiss. Heat rippled through her, loosening some muscles and tightening others, preparing her to be enslaved.

Her nostrils flared in annoyance at her weakness. Her mind was conflicted. Part of her wanted to surrender while another part thought she was an idiot for being a slave to her hormones.

For a moment, the second part ruled her actions. She shoved him away from her. Her stomach jumped with nerves while she stared at him, feeling on edge.

His furious blue eyes raked over her body, making her feel naked in her loose T-shirt.

Her hands fisted as a haze of hunger washed over her, blowing any sense she might have had out of her mind. He made her want to touch him. Her fingers itched to rip apart his T-shirt and expose the hard, broad contours of his chest.

The air was alive with sexual tension, like electricity crackling around them.

His hand reached out and roamed over her breastbone, his fingers following the dips and curves of her collarbone and trailing down the center of her body.

She tried not to react to the feel of his palm as it stroked her every nerve to full attention.

"Stop," she said, but it came out breathy as his other hand clamped around her hip and drew her back against his long, strong body.

She tried to focus, to break from the sexual spell that had swept her up, but it was impossible.

"I'll try not to hurt you. For once, let me be gentle. All I want is a taste," he murmured as his mouth lowered to drift in sensuous caresses against her neck. "I want to know if you taste as delicious and soft as you smell." His tongue flicked out against her skin before he kissed away the moisture.

Her heart was speeding up, racing until she swore she could feel it in her throat.

She turned her head. "No biting."

His smile bloomed while he tightened his grip on her, forcing her backward. He appeared triumphant. She knew he'd won. He had her now.

"W-w-wait th-the the others," she stammered. Her body shook with the ever-increasing tide of lust, but in spite of having her thoughts scrambled, she could still manage to think a little.

"They're not here," he said.

She frowned. It was true that they had been remarkably silent. "How do you know?"

TOUCHED BY MADNESS

"Do you want me to explain this now?" he asked wearing an incredulous expression.

"No," she agreed as his hands stroked away her concerns, roaming down her sides and brushing against her waist, her breasts... She stopped fighting her passion for him and gave in to the pleasure of his touch.

He stood behind her as he slid one of his hands up her leg. Then grasping the bottom of her T-shirt, he pushed it up to bare her thighs. His quick hard breathing warmed her neck as his hands slipped between her legs, pressing against her feminine cleft. The firm, knowing touch sent spirals of sensation through her body with near-violent desire.

"Dane..." she murmured.

"Be quiet."

A moan escaped her as he cupped her mound and let his fingers play along the cotton of her panties. He found the tight little bud of nerve endings and worked it gently with his fingers until she gasped his name. He slipped two fingers under the cotton barrier, then inside her and pressed upward.

The other hand eased up below her nightshirt until it cupped the swell of her breast.

Dane froze. Erin's skin was coarse there, where the sword must have entered her body.

She glanced back and their eyes met. It hit him with renewed force that he could have lost her all those years ago. He realized he could have lost her again during these last few days, and that thought was unbearable. He would not allow it. She had to understand that she could not leave him.

She frowned. "Dane?"

He pushed away his gloomy thoughts and focused on pleasing her, and on tying her to him, making sure that she would never want to leave him. He resumed moving his fingers inside her.

He let one fingertip graze a nipple, and she arched her back, inviting him to continue. He gripped the nipple sensually, tugging at it. His lips brushed the nape of her neck. She shuddered in his grip as he sensed tremors of need race beneath her skin.

Her trembling body was driving him crazy, and his cock pressed imperatively against his jeans. His breathing was harsh now, uneven, but he refused to allow the hunger to override his control.

He turned her around, lifted her onto the table and stepped between her thighs. While one hand continued to move subtly against her, he used the other to push up her T-shirt. He bent his head and chased a bead of perspiration that slipped down the valley between her breasts, catching it with his lips. The taste of her exploded against his tongue. A flavor that he knew he could easily become addicted to.

He nuzzled her neck, rubbing her blond hair, which was still moist from the shower, and deeply inhaled her scent. It intoxicated him. He was bombarded with her natural perfume, her arousal. He fought to control his desire for her while her body shuddered against him.

She moaned as his fingers continued to thrust between her legs, faster and faster.

"Come for me," he murmured in her ear as her body trembled in his hands. Her climax shook through her body, making her arch against him and claw at his chest. She cried out his name, clinging to him in urgent need.

She went limp in his arms when the shudders had subsided. He held her upright while he tugged her T-shirt up her body and over her head, drinking in every inch of her with his eyes. With a burning hunger fighting inside him to be sated, he scooped her up into his arms and carried her to the bed, gently laying her on it. His eyes were fixed on hers when he drew back.

He quickly removed his T-shirt and threw it onto the floor. He stared at her while his hands dropped to his hips with his eyes locking hers as he unbuttoned his jeans and tugged down the zipper.

He watched her body tremble on the bed and awareness of his intent appeared in her eyes. As if helplessly pinned to the bed by his stare, he heard her moan his name in a cry of desire, submission and need, all rolled into one.

He pushed the jeans over his hips with a deliberate slowness that caused her to squirm on the bed in delicious torture. Her bright eyes were fixed on him as he tugged down his briefs, and his swollen arousal sprang free.

Rising to her knees, she met him as he crawled across the bed toward her. She was wearing only her panties. Her skin was flushed, her golden eyes bright and eager.

He knelt in front of her, his hand reaching out to touch her shoulder and slowly moving up toward her neck. His fingers stroked the slim column of her neck, causing her body to shiver.

He fisted her blond curls and drew her closer while he lowered his head to take possession of her mouth. Her body eased into his, as though it realized what her mind didn't—that she belonged to him.

His kiss bruised her lips as his own volatile hunger rushed to the surface. She gasped for air when his lips left her mouth to nibble her ear. Without drawing blood, he softly bit her earlobe.

Her pulse beat right beneath his mouth. He felt her heat beckoning him, the scent of her, and the spice of her blood crying out to his.

In his mouth, his fangs fought for liberty. He battled the urge to bite and paused, his fangs poised over her exposed throat.

He needed to mark her so everyone could see his brand of ownership on her. More importantly, he wanted to mark her. The animal inside him was crying out for it. His teeth ground together as he closed his eyes, fighting against the demands of his body.

TOUCHED BY MADNESS

No biting... With a sharp sigh, he suppressed his hunger. Instead, he decided to focus his attention on other parts of her body. His arm circled her waist, locking her to him as his teeth skimmed down to one breast.

He felt the slow caress of her hands sliding up his chest. Her hesitant fingers stroked until they gripped his shoulders. He enjoyed the feel of her urging him on, clawing at him in passionate need while his tongue lingered on her nipple and stroked the hard peak.

He lifted her up against him and laid her on her back, kneeling over her. He placed his hands on her knees and moved them up her thighs.

"Spread your legs, Erin," he ordered. She seemed hesitant, so he forced her knees apart, giving him better access to her feminine heat.

He slid his fingers to the edge of her panties. She stiffened beneath him. Fearing that she would pull back, he grabbed her wrists and held them over her head with his right hand. With the other hand, he cupped her bottom and pinned her beneath him.

He could feel her heart racing, her hot breath against his neck. Her body was trembling, and there was a glint of excitement in her eyes.

Roughly, he ripped off her panties and pushed her thighs wider apart. He lifted her left knee as he positioned himself between her legs.

She sucked in a sharp breath and froze, her gaze locking with his as he leaned forward. His lips grazed hers before he began to enter her narrow opening. He stretched her and the muscles in her legs tightened. She let out a breathy gasp while he watched her body submit to his touch.

Her head fell back while her hips arched against him in rhythmic lust. With his fingers between their bodies, he rubbed against her clit to drive her over the edge.

As he moved, the tightness of her velvet sheath clenching him felt so addictive that he wanted to lose himself forever in her. He felt her quiver and heard her moan his name. He pounded into her. "Want more?" he fiercely rumbled while staring down at her face.

"Don't close your eyes." He gave a guttural growl. "Watch me," he said.

She opened her eyes and gazed at him as he continued to bury himself inside her deeper and harder. He wanted to drive so deeply inside her that no one would ever be able to separate them.

"You're mine," he bit out. "All mine."

His hands tightly gripped her hips as he continued to plunge into her, each stroke throwing them both closer to an orgasm.

When he sensed her going taut and starting to tremble into another climax, he finally released the chains of control that had bound him for what seemed like forever. He followed her over the edge and shouted out her name as he poured himself into her.

TOUCHED BY MADNESS

A couple of minutes passed before Erin stirred beside Dane, locked tightly in the vampire's arms, her cheek against his chest.

She drew back her head, scarcely able to weave her thoughts together. She recalled the determination on his face when he told her that she was his. And where were Altman, Leila and the others? How had he known that they were not there?

She gave a shake of her head and tried to escape his hold.

"Stop wriggling around, unless you want me to make love to you again?" he teased.

She stopped moving. "Make love?"

He grinned and stared at her with a gleaming gaze, a gaze too proud and possessive for her taste. "Of course, what I'm feeling could just be the product of truly amazing sex."

She wrinkled her nose at him. "I think you should go now. Pauline will soon return."

"I'm not letting you go, Erin."

She bared her teeth at him. "You can't keep me." She put her nails in his arms and pinched him.

He sighed but refused to relinquish his hold on her. "I'm aware that I'm still facing a battle with you, but you have no choice. You never really had a choice, not since I saw you that night at Star's party. Or maybe it happened twenty years ago when I first laid eyes on you. You belong to me."

She felt worn out, and decided to ignore him instead. He would be forced to leave anyway when her new housemate got back.

"Did you know that in some cultures when you save someone's life, you become responsible for it?"

He chuckled when she remained quiet. "I saved you. You probably don't believe me, but it's true. You were wounded very badly, so I fed you some of my blood to heal you."

She stiffened, and he kissed her neck before whispering, "Yes, you heard me. You drank my blood. So we're linked, you and I."

"W-we are?" she stammered.

"Well, not entirely. We need to have a full blood exchange for our connection to last, but some of the magic of that night has not gone away."

"Stop speaking in riddles," she ordered. "What magic?"

"The magic of my touch," he answered.

Erin frowned. "Your touch?"

"I helped to silence the voices in your head," he explained. "When I put my hands on you, they went away."

She pondered his words. It seemed very unlikely. She found it too convenient for him to claim such a thing. He wanted a relationship with her, and suddenly he appeared to have some kind of magic touch. "Is that why you said that the others weren't there?"

When he nodded, she continued, "Even if it's true, you didn't touch me all the time. Oh, God, they were probably there after all! I can't believe they didn't say anything!"

His hand stroked through her hair. "I can. You deserved some time on your own. I think they realized that."

She pictured Gideon and shook her head, but the voices weren't there to contradict him. It actually felt rather peaceful, lying in Dane's arms without having to worry about the others observing her. Or were they still present, but silenced?

She shivered. "Do you think they are still here?" she mumbled.

"Hmm, I hadn't thought about that. I hope not, but who knows? Maybe tomorrow, you'll be able to get rid of them."

She elbowed him in the stomach. "I'm not getting rid of them! I just want them to cross over and find some peace in their afterlife."

"And of course, you are going to try to get rid of your powers," Dane went on.

"We already talked about that. I don't really want to hear more about your theories."

"I will be there tomorrow. I will pick you up, and before you start to object, think about the fact that I was there twenty years ago. I can help you and your new witch friend relive the past."

She shivered.

"Ah, you're cold," he concluded before giving her a last hug. "I'm afraid I've got to go now." He left the bed and picked up his clothes.

She parted her lips when she experienced the full effect of his nudity. His well-muscled torso rippled with every move. Her gaze raked over him, lingering at a thick, silky trail of dark hair that began just above the navel on his ripped abs. She swallowed, watching him get dressed. He drew her as no other man ever had.

He glanced back over his shoulder as he opened the door. "Hopefully, we can spend tomorrow night celebrating after you have successfully completed the ritual. It's probably best if you get rid of your powers. You don't want the wrong people to find out what you can do," he said.

She stared at the door after it had shut behind him, filled with a sense of foreboding.

You don't want the wrong people to find out what you can do.

She thought about the camera at Doctor Quirkhart's cabin. It was too late.

They already know.

SIXTEEN

Despite there being only a crescent moon, the reflected light was bright enough to bathe the entire Devereaux Church in a silvery glow.

As Erin approached the building, she noticed the way the cold light made the church appear dark and empty. A chill crept up her spine while her heart hammered. Its beat felt loud enough to wake the dead, yet the night was oddly silent. Even the wind appeared to be holding its breath as she walked up the stairs.

Now an entirely new chapter of her life was about to unfold. Today, all that seemed familiar was about to disappear, and instead of cheering at the thought, she felt frightened. Irritation flared within her when she felt tears streaming down her cheeks.

She lifted her hand to open the door.

"Good luck," her mother said.

Erin froze. "Mom?"

"I just wanted to wish you good luck," her mother continued.

Erin turned away from the church and sat down on the steps outside. Her knees were too wobbly to stand straight.

"I thought you were angry with me. I thought all of you were."

"Why would we be angry with you?" Altman asked.

"B-be-because of last night," she stammered.

"Of course not, dear!" her mother protested. *"Well, maybe I would have preferred seeing you with someone... more human."*

Erin sighed. "I'm not human either."

"Being human is overrated," Leila muttered. *"Humans show a lot more cruelty to their own species than any other animal out there."*

"So you're not angry?" Erin repeated. "I was worried, because you didn't say anything."

"We were quiet because we thought you deserved some time alone," Altman explained. *"Even Gideon agreed."*

"But if it all works out, after tonight I won't be able to hear any of you ever again." She was unable to suppress a sob.

"Isn't that the whole point? What the hell is wrong with her?" Gideon complained.

"It would be a good thing," her mother said gently.

"But where will you go?" Erin asked. "What if it's somewhere bad?"

"It is what it is. There are no certainties in life, dear, except death. You have to let us go. We have to let you go," her mother stated.

"Are you sure you want Pauline to do the ritual? She wasn't that great earlier," Erin mumbled.

"Stop trying to find excuses," Altman ordered.

"Yes, stop whining," Gideon added. *"I can't wait to cross over and be free of you. Not even hell could be this awful!"*

"Thanks, Gideon." She laughed as she wiped the tears from her face. "Thank you all."

Everyone said his or her goodbyes, and with a sense of sadness, she finally entered the building where Pauline was waiting for her. She paused in the corridor. She had been here before. She tried to ignore the sense of foreboding that seeped into her bones. A flash of the corridor as it had been that night twenty years ago crossed her mind, and suddenly she was there. The corridor was brighter. She stared up at the moon as she was led to some thick wooden doors.

She was holding someone's hand, a man's hand. She raised her eyes to stare at a dark-skinned man with golden eyes.

"Hurry up, ma petite. We're all waiting for you," he said.

"Daddy," she whispered.

The full implication slammed into her, bringing her back to the present, stealing her breath and replacing it with a pain so intense that she nearly doubled over.

Thick horror slid through her, and nausea filled her. Hands shaking, breath short, she gaped at the doors she had to walk through. She couldn't move.

"So, there you are," a familiar voice said behind her. "You are really bad at following orders. We'll have to do something about that."

Trying to quell the dread roiling in her stomach, she turned her head to face Dane. His expression was tight-lipped, and there was a muscle ticking along his jaw.

How dare she ignore my command to wait for me before going inside the church? Dane thought furiously.

He glared at Erin.

Is she ever going to do as I ask?

Not used to having his requests ignored, he clenched his hand into a fist. It took a moment for him to notice the coldness that had entered into her eyes, a chill he had never seen before.

He frowned. "Erin?"

She had turned deathly white, and a strangled sound escaped her throat.

His anger instantly evaporated, and he pulled her close, pressing her head to his shoulder.

"Are you all right?" There was concern in his voice. He gazed down at her and put his hand underneath her chin to make her look up. Her eyes brimmed with tears.

He lifted her in his arms and turned around to leave the building.

"No!" she protested.

"I'm taking you home. You're in no condition to perform any rituals."

She started struggling.

"What's going on?" a voice behind them asked.

He turned to face the witch. She was glancing up at them, her eyes bright with excitement.

"Nothing," Erin said as she liberated herself from his grip. "Let's go."

He followed them while shaking his head as they left the corridor to enter the main chapel of the church.

The smell of rosemary and sandalwood incense hit Erin's nostrils as soon as they entered the room. She also smelled other scents, but she couldn't recognize them.

Pauline must have pushed all the benches against the wall to clear the area. On the floor, she had drawn a pentagram with white chalk. Five candles in different colors were strategically placed around the drawing. Next to the green candle, Pauline had put down a small bowl containing a lock of Erin's blond hair that she had cut earlier that day.

Erin supposed that the candle represented her. A little shiver went down her back. Next to the bowl, there was a small pile of items they were going to need during the ritual. A needle glistened on top of the pile.

"You didn't do it right," Dane said. "You should have drawn a pentagram with blood."

"Oh. Well sometimes with magic, you just have to improvise," Pauline retorted.

"The pentagram is also pointing in the wrong direction," he continued. "It should point toward the exit of the church."

Pauline's face was a mask of pleasure. It was obvious to Erin that her new friend refused to let Dane spoil her mood.

"It's a good thing that I used chalk, then. Blood is so much harder to erase," she joked.

As Pauline got on her knees to change the pentagram, Erin continued to assess her surroundings.

The building was shaped like a cross with a dome to draw attention to the heavens. She thought about the way the building was supposed to represent bringing light to the world, and it made her shake her head.

In the center, a statue stared down at her, depicting the crucifixion of Jesus. She swallowed nervously.

"I hope you don't need more time," Pauline said, her voice high with nervous excitement. Ever since Selena had died, it was as if the witch had undergone a complete transformation.

Erin could understand that Pauline was thrilled about tonight. She could finally use magic without having to kill any living thing.

Unless the spell backfires...

Erin tried to smile. "No, I'm ready."

She felt relieved that she was no longer suffering from flashbacks, but her body seemed to remember the location. She had already been to the toilet three times that night, but her nerves made her feel as if she needed to go a fourth time.

She couldn't stop shaking. She watched Dane telling Pauline what to do and smiled because he always had to boss everyone around.

"Shall we?" Pauline grinned as she sat down in the middle of the pentagram.

She put the bowl and the other magic items on her lap. Inside the bowl, a piece of charcoal had been lit together with myrrh, sandalwood and rosemary incense.

Erin laughed edgily when Pauline added additional items to the mixture; pepper, rose petals and lavender flowers. In order to be safe, the witch was apparently tossing in every healing herb in existence.

Pauline pointed at the green candle. She held out her hand, palm up. For once, her hands were bare. Apparently, for magic's sake, the witch was willing to overlook her mysophobia.

Erin glanced at Dane who was leaning against the wall. Light illuminated only one side of him, leaving the other concealed in a dark shadow. He nodded at her with an intense stare.

She thought of a little prayer to fortify herself, and then placed her hand in Pauline's. Pauline closed her eyes in concentration and wrapped her fingers around hers. She then lifted her other hand, holding the needle, and pricked Erin's right index finger. Meanwhile, Erin removed a piece of paper from her pocket to read the incantation she was going to chant with Pauline.

Her new houseguest seemed so well prepared that she must have learnt the words by heart. She frowned when Pauline started to forcibly squeeze her finger.

"What the hell...?" Erin complained, pulling her hand free from Pauline's grip.

"The wound is already closed. I need three drops of blood. You do it, then!" Pauline snapped.

Without any hesitation, Erin grabbed the needle and stuck it into her finger. Before her body could heal itself, she pinched out several drops of blood into the smoldering incense.

"Stop! It's too much!" Pauline yelled as she jerked the bowl away.

Erin shrugged. Wasn't it Pauline who had said something about improvising?

"Okay..." Pauline mumbled as she closed her eyes. "Stay focused. Relax." She started doing breathing exercises.

Erin glanced at the young woman in front of her, slightly worried that they might have a falling-out soon.

Pauline opened her eyes again, appearing calm. She nodded at her.

Erin tried to empty her own mind, and lifted her left hand once more to hold Pauline's hand. Soon a surge of electricity took her by surprise as it leapt from their skins and spread up Erin's arms like wildfire.

TOUCHED BY MADNESS

She found it hard to breathe as the wash of power filled her and made the hairs on her arms stand on end while her pulse raced as if the essence was somehow entwining around them. She gasped as it burned across her senses, unlike anything she'd ever felt before. The energy seemed dark and dangerous, and it sent chills racing over her flesh.

She watched as the lock of her hair was dropped into the burning incense and waited for Pauline to open her mouth before she too began to read the incantation out loud:

"With blood, candle and herb times three,
No longer shall this binding be,
The ritual performed in this building,
Will no longer create a merging,
The link between witch, leopard, warlock and vampire,
Will from this moment on be broken, as is my desire,
Those who died here will now find peace,
From this world they will be released,
As they leave, they will no longer condemn,
Me to live with powers that once belonged to them,
Free to live and free to soar,
Let me leave the church once more.
As I burn this hair, a part of me,
Let my body and soul be free!
As is my will, so mote it be!"

Erin screamed as light exploded within her. It was a pain so searing it tasted of the blood that ran through her veins. She felt herself slip away, her heart and mind consumed by the light that slowly dimmed. Her lungs fought for air until her chest burned and darkness swallowed up everything.

Cautiously, Dane approached Erin. She was breathing evenly now, like the witch who also seemed to be unconscious.

Erin appeared so thin and lost. He noticed the paleness of her skin as he watched the movement under her closed eyelids. A lump formed in his throat when he bent down and brushed a lock of hair behind her ear. The memories of twenty years ago came flooding back while he stroked her curls. She had looked fragile then too. He remembered her drinking from him. He remembered the interruption.

A forbidden thought emerged.

No policemen are going to barge into the room this time.

He contemplated her once more. Her head was thrown backward, leaving her neck unprotected—leaving her unprotected.

He recalled all the times she had been in danger without him to help her because he hadn't known. He could make sure that from now on he would always know if someone threatened her. He could save her from herself.

A grim smile touched the slightly cruel edges of his mouth. His lips thinned back exposing his fangs. He swept aside her hair, so that his mouth could blaze a trail of fire along her neck, lingering for a moment to swirl his tongue over the temptation of her pulse.

He took a deep breath and nearly moaned with pleasure. She smelled heavenly. If only he could leave a mark, a brand of ownership for all to see.

He realized that she would probably not appreciate him taking advantage of her while she had passed out, even if he was doing it for her own protection. His gaze moved to her mouth, which was slightly open.

Unable to stop himself, his tongue caressed her bottom lip, followed by the scraping of his teeth. Her eyes remained shut. He opened his mind and focused on hers.

An image of darkness arose. Relieved that she was unaware of his actions, he let his teeth clamp down, tight.

He closed his eyes in ecstasy when ambrosia flowed into his mouth. His lips were locked on the cut, eagerly sucking it. Heedless of his surroundings, he slid his hand under the thin material of her shirt to cup her breast in his palm. When he felt her nipple harden, a part of him responded similarly.

His hand glided down to the zipper of her jeans, when awareness hit. She wasn't responding.

He removed his hand from her waist and stared down at her. Crimson blood stained her lips, and her breathing had become shallow.

He licked her blood from his mouth, suppressing the urge for more. He used his fangs to cut open his tongue before bending down and urgently kissing her, ruthlessly feeding her his blood. His hand stroked her throat until she began to convulsively swallow.

When he felt he had given her enough for them to form a proper bond, he reluctantly broke off the kiss. Again, blood covered her bottom lip, only this time it was his.

She was still knocked out, but her breathing had returned to normal, and the color in her cheeks gave her a healthy glow. She was going to be fine. And now that the exchange had been made, they would be fine too. He cradled her in his arms and waited.

Erin slowly came around feeling disoriented. She had a salty, sweet metallic taste in her mouth, and her body felt heavy with jackhammers drilling through her temples.

She grunted as she burrowed into the warmth surrounding her before realizing it was Dane rocking her in his arms.

Her bottom lip stung, and she frowned as her tongue slid over the open wound. She concluded that she must have bitten her lip as the blast of magic had hit them. In spite of her exhaustion, she struggled to open her eyes. She needed to know what had happened and if Pauline was unharmed.

She felt Dane nuzzling the top of her head, and she was tempted to snuggle deeper into his arms. She was puzzled at how safe he made her feel. She shook herself mentally, forcing her eyes to open.

She had to wait for her stomach to settle before she could sit up. The room tilted as she reached an upright position.

"Steady," she heard him mumble.

She shivered as his breath touched her neck, and turned her head to face him. He was studying her, his face calm and unreadable. His usually pale complexion had faded to chalk white, and his blue eyes were dark. He seemed so worried that she experienced a surge of unaccustomed compassion.

She raised her hand to push a lock of hair back from his forehead and froze when she saw him flinch.

"Dane?" Her voice was drowsy.

He grabbed her hand and put it against his chest as he curled his body around hers.

"You shouldn't move, Goldilocks," he muttered as he brushed a kiss across her eyes. "Are you all right?"

"Never better." Her laugh sounded ragged even to her. She gazed at Pauline. She appeared to be sleeping peacefully on the cold hard floor of the church.

Too peacefully?

Worried, she tried to reach Pauline. A rush of nausea flowed over her like a wave. She collapsed on the stone floor, and without any warning, started vomiting blood.

Dane's hand held her hair back, and his other arm supported her waist. She threw up until she was empty.

He waited for her to lift her head before drawing her into his arms again.

"No, I want to see Pauline."

He refused to move. "You need to get well first."

"If you don't let me go, I will make you," she bit out.

He pierced his eyes at her. "Erin, be very careful what you say."

Defiantly, she lifted her chin. "I'm not afraid of you!"

"You should be. You're in no condition to fight me," he growled.

She merely lifted her eyebrows in silence, refusing to let him intimidate her. The silence hung in the air like a heavy fog, and she began feeling uncomfortable. She looked away, and her gaze fell on the still-unconscious Pauline.

He sighed, appearing deep in thought before he finally released her. She walked up to her sleeping friend on wobbly legs and gently touched her shoulder.

"Pauline? Are you all right?"

The black-haired woman moaned and blinked up at her. She frowned when she saw the bloodstain on Erin's shirt. "Shouldn't I ask you that?"

TOUCHED BY MADNESS

Erin's face flushed with an edge of embarrassment. "I just threw up a little."

"Oh, I'm sorry," Pauline said. "Well, did it work?"

Erin was confused for a second, then she remembered what they had been trying to achieve. She grinned sheepishly. "I don't know."

Pauline grunted as she got up. "Well, find out. I'd rather not do this ritual again."

She cringed when she realized that Pauline and Dane were staring at her, their eyes filled with curiosity.

She turned her back to them and walked to a secluded area of the church. She leaned against the wall, her legs weak. The spell seemed to have drained her.

She closed her eyes and tried to repress the tiredness. Ignoring it, she whispered, "Mom?"

No reply.

"Altman?" she tried again.

Silence answered her.

The ritual must have worked. She had expected to feel elation, but the sadness she had experienced earlier that evening was still there. Her mother had finally moved on. She wouldn't be there to comfort her anymore. Nor would Erin be able to gain wisdom from Altman, now that he had passed on.

She suppressed a sob and looked down at her hands, her human hands. She moved her fingers and watched them, her lips curling at one corner. Hairless. No more claws. No longer did she have to worry about leopard hormones raging through her body. No longer did she have to tolerate snide remarks from Gideon or Leila's whining. No longer would she end up eating her enemies. She was finally in charge of her body and could sleep without brooding over ghosts taking over her unconscious body.

She smiled and turned to face Pauline and Dane. "It worked!"

Pauline grinned and ran toward her. "Oh, that is so great! I would hug you if it weren't for my OCD. I'm just so happy that I am finally using my magic for something good," the witch continued. "Let's go home and open a bottle of wine to celebrate."

Erin nodded. "Go home and open a bottle. I'll join you later."

Pauline glanced at her, and then at Dane who had walked up to stand beside her.

Erin felt his fingers wrap around her wrist. "Oh okay," Pauline said with reluctance before walking to the pentagram to pick up a candle.

Erin shook her head. "Never mind that. I'll clean up the mess and take everything with me."

"Okay," Pauline repeated. Slowly, she walked toward the exit. She turned to face Erin one last time. "Are you sure?" she asked, pointing at Dane.

"Yes, go on," Erin insisted.

After Pauline had left the room, Dane and Erin both stood in silence as they waited for the sound of Pauline's footsteps to disappear.

Erin tried to escape his grip, but he pulled her closer instead. She swallowed and hoped she could pretend indifference. A tight smile curled her lips as she turned to glance at the vampire.

"I hope you're not going to read anything into this. I only wanted to tell you that I meant what I said earlier." She pointed at his hand on her wrist. "Do you mind?"

He slowly shook his head, locking onto her with his dark blue eyes. He leaned into her. "Are you sure your powers are gone?"

Puzzled that he wasn't claiming ownership again, she frowned. "Of course. The voices are gone, and so are my powers."

He didn't say anything.

The slight trembling of her hands betrayed her nervousness. "Why are you asking me this?"

He lowered his nose to her, the tip just barely grazing her skin. With a pounding heart, she watched as he took a deep breath, drawing her scent into him.

"I can still smell the leopard."

Her lips parted in shock. She peered down at her hands once more and thought about shifting.

Nothing happened.

"You're probably too tired because of the ritual," he said. "Maybe you should try something easier, like listening. Can you hear anything outside of this building?"

She forced herself to be calm and inhaled sharply. She closed her eyes and concentrated on sound. At first, she could hear only the thumping of her heart and her own heavy breathing, nothing unusual.

Relieved, she was about to open her eyes when she sensed the presence of rodents inside the church, unmoving with only their whiskers twitching.

She froze.

Outside she could detect the beating wings of a bird. There was a slight breeze coming up. Leaves started rustling in the faint wind and water bubbled somewhere close by. A couple in a house across the street appeared to be having a whispered quarrel. She shouldn't have been able to hear all that through the thick walls of the church.

She curled her fingers into a tight fist. Her senses were still heightened. "It didn't work," she whispered.

She felt her heart drop in disappointment. She allowed him to hold her, needing the support. He rubbed her back while he embraced her. She found his touch comforting.

"It's not so bad, is it?" he asked. "The voices are gone, at least."

"Yes," she agreed. "But why didn't it work completely? Did I put too much blood in the bowl? Was the spell wrong?"

"Who knows," he said as he continued rocking her against him.

"What if..." She fell silent.

"What?" he prodded.

"What if it didn't work because we were missing some people?" she muttered against his chest.

TOUCHED BY MADNESS

He stopped moving, gripped her shoulders and pushed her back a few inches so he could glare into her eyes.

"I will only say this once." He threw her a hard, heated look, his lips curling into a sneer. "You weren't missing anyone. I don't ever want to hear you say that you were."

She took a step back when he released her. "You're not my master!" she shot back, furious with him.

"I'm really tired of having to repeat myself, Erin," he complained. "But this is really important."

She clenched her teeth in frustration. Realizing she had no choice but to listen to him, she gave a sigh of resignation and crossed her arms across her chest, which had the unwanted effect of attracting his gaze to her breasts.

When his eyes raked her, she quickly dropped her arms to her sides.

"I know who you think is missing and I want you to understand that it's a blessing he's not here. You don't want to search for him because we're talking about going from the frying pan into the fire here. Listen, you've lived with these powers for twenty years. They don't make you a monster. Pauline is a witch, and she's not a monster, right?" he cajoled.

Her nod was hesitant.

"And how about me? I'm a vampire, but I'm not a monster," he assured her, the corners of his lips twisting up into a wry smile.

She drew a shaky breath. "I'm not so sure about that."

"You're only saying that because you're afraid of your own reaction to me." He sounded convinced. He raised his hand to stop her from speaking when she opened her mouth.

She took a step back. The sensual promise in his gaze made her wary.

"Please go. This argument is pointless," she said, even though she could hear the breathlessness and longing in her voice.

He hesitated. "Very well, I will leave for now." He walked to the doorway and turned to look at her one last time. There was a challenge in his gaze. "But you should not underestimate my determination. I'll see you soon."

She waited for the vampire to leave the church before she let herself fall to the ground, her knees too wobbly to remain standing.

"Mom?" she cried. "I could really use your help here..." She smiled with self-mockery. "Great, now that I want to hear voices, you're gone. So now, who can I talk to? I'll be like one of those old ladies, talking to themselves. I should call the loony bin straight away. Although, they may not want me, since I ate my last shrink."

"I'm still here, Erin." Her mother's soft admission was a welcome sound.

"Mom?" she whispered. "Is that really you or am I imagining things?"

"It didn't work," her mother continued. "I'm so sorry."

"Well, I'm not." She drew a breath of relief. "But maybe I should feel sorry. You probably all wanted to leave."

"I'm not going anywhere," Gideon stated. *"And apparently, you and that witch of yours can't make me."*

She laughed. "I really am losing my mind. I'm even relieved to hear Gideon."

"You don't know what you've got till it's gone," Leila sang teasingly.

"I guess I got used to having you with me. When I thought you were gone, I missed you," Erin realized. "But why were you silent before?"

"We thought that was what you wanted," Altman explained. *"We didn't want to disappoint you, so we decided that if the ritual didn't work we would break the news gently. Ann only spoke now because she heard you calling out for her."*

"And to be honest," Leila said. *"At first, I thought you had succeeded, because I was away for a little while."*

"So was I," Gideon added.

"I came back when you approached Pauline," Altman told Erin.

"Came back from the dark place?" Erin mumbled.

"Don't worry about it," Altman told her. *"I think you should still try to get rid of us. And perhaps you should consider getting rid of your new vampire boyfriend too."*

"Just because we slept together once doesn't make him my boyfriend," she protested. "Besides, you were a vampire."

"But I want what's best for you, Erin, a normal life, maybe even a family. I don't want to open old wounds, but you could still have children. Maybe that's why a vampire seems safe," Altman said. *"But vampires aren't safe, and Dane Lynch can be ruthless. You'd probably be better off somewhere else."*

She sighed. "I don't have anywhere else to go, and I have Frank here. Frank's nice. And Pauline seems quite nice too, even if she is a bit of a neat freak. I like having a friend who is into witchcraft. And I have a job I can't leave." She got up and looked down at the pentagram.

"I could probably stay hidden somewhere. I'm just tired of having to hide myself. I don't want to do that anymore."

She blew out a candle, grabbed a bag and put the candle away. "You know, maybe Dane's right. Pauline's not a monster, and even though Dane gets on my nerves, he was helping me earlier. I should stop whining and accept myself as I am." She chuckled. "Even if I am a freak."

"You're not a freak, Erin," Ann protested.

"You're right, mom," she continued, putting away the items they had used for the ritual. "No more whining. I'm going to stay positive from now on, I mean it."

She wet a towel and used it to remove the chalk from the floor, before cleaning up the blood she had thrown up. "So no more worrying. I'm not going to worry about the camera taping me as I ate Doctor Quirky, no more worrying about getting rid of my powers, at least not if that means I would have to find and confront my psycho father. Nor am I going to waste time thinking about a vampire I might never get rid of."

She got up and placed the benches in the center of the church, facing the cross. She walked up to the exit and cast a final glance at the room. "You know what? I feel free now. Leila was right. It's good that you were silent for a little while because now I know I kind of like having you in my life. Well, usually." She grinned before pivoting on her heel and striding from the room.

She left the church. When she was outside, she stood still and glanced around.

Dane was standing across the street, waiting. He nodded to her. Resigned, she waved back at him. She blinked, and suddenly he was gone. A familiar, large bald eagle stood in his place. The eagle continued to stare at her, and she frowned. The bird spread its wings and flew toward a lamppost, landing on top of the streetlight.

She walked down the street, and the bird flew above her, watching over her.

She smiled and shook her head.

She arrived at her flat and saw that Dane was waiting for her to enter the building.

What a gentleman!

She waved at him once more before going in. She shut the door behind her and peeped one last time through the window.

He was still there.

She was never going to get rid of him.

She closed her eyes and leaned against the door, thinking about Dane and her complicated feelings for him.

She looked deep inside herself and sudden realization hit—he already lived there. Maybe it was just the leopard hormones, but the feeling was strong enough to convince her. She did carry him deep inside her.

And in that instant, she realized it felt quite nice.

THE END

AUTHOR

As a child, Nicole always wanted to be an actress. However, her only shot at becoming the next Meryl Streep was during her one-second appearance in Paul Verhoeven's film 'Black Book' where her shirt got ripped off her body. After that, she decided to focus on her writing career instead.

When she's not writing, she spends her time as crazy cat lady, playing with her cats Buffy and Garfield. In addition, Nicole's hobbies include trying to chase tornadoes (although she still hasn't seen any), fantasizing about villains (isn't Lex Luthor far more interesting than Clark Kent?), and most of all reading stories somebody else wrote.